Death Knells and Wedding Bells

Also available by Eva Gates

The Lighthouse Library Mysteries

Death by Beach Read
Deadly Ever After
A Death Long Overdue
Read and Buried
Something Read Something Dead
The Spook in the Stacks
Reading Up A Storm
Booked for Trouble
By Book or By Crook

Writing as Vicki Delany

The Sherlock Holmes Bookshop Mysteries

The Sign of Four Spirits
The Game Is a Footnote
A Three Book Problem
A Curious Incident
There's a Murder Afoot
A Scandal in Scarlet
The Cat of Baskervilles
Body on Baker Street
Elementary, She Read

The Year-Round Christmas Mysteries

Have Yourself a Deadly Little Christmas
Dying in a Winter Wonderland
Silent Night, Deadly Night
Hark the Herald Angels Slay
We Wish You a Murderous Christmas
Rest Ye Murdered Gentlemen

The Ashley Grant Mysteries

Coral Reef Views
Blue Water Hues
White Sand Blues

The Constable Molly Smith Mysteries

Unreasonable Doubt
Under Cold Stone
A Cold White Sun
Among the Departed
Negative Image
Winter of Secrets
Valley of the Lost
In the Shadow of the Glacier

The Klondike Gold Rush Mysteries

Gold Web
Gold Mountain
Gold Fever
Gold Digger

The Ray Robertson Mysteries

Blood and Belonging
Haitian Graves
Juba Good

The Tea by the Sea Mysteries

Steeped in Malice
Murder Spills the Tea
Murder in a Teacup
Tea & Treachery

The Catskill Summer Resort Mysteries

Deadly Director's Cut
Deadly Summer Nights

Also Available by Vicki Delany

More than Sorrow
Murder at Lost Dog Lake
Burden of Memory
Scare the Light Away
Whiteout

Death Knells and Wedding Bells

A LIGHTHOUSE LIBRARY MYSTERY

Eva Gates

NEW YORK

This is a work of fiction. All of the names, characters, organizations, places and events portrayed in this novel are either products of the author's imagination or are used fictitiously. Any resemblance to real or actual events, locales, or persons, living or dead, is entirely coincidental.

Published in the United States by Crooked Lane Books, an imprint of The Quick Brown Fox & Company LLC.

Crooked Lane Books and its logo are trademarks of The Quick Brown Fox & Company LLC.

Library of Congress Catalog-in-Publication data available upon request.

ISBN (hardcover): 978-1-63910-345-4
ISBN (paperback): 978-1-63910-727-8
ISBN (ebook): 978-1-63910-346-1

Cover design by Joe Burleson

Printed in the United States.

www.crookedlanebooks.com

Crooked Lane Books
34 West 27th St., 10th Floor
New York, NY 10001

First Edition: June 2023
Trade Paperback Edition: April 2024

10 9 8 7 6 5 4 3 2 1

To the Hall sisters, Gail and Joan:
Always an inspiration

Chapter One

"I can't remember when, if ever, my feet hurt this much," my husband said to me.

I leaned my head on his shoulder and attempted to smother a burp.

Connor ran his fingers lightly across my cheek. "I'm about ready to go. What do you think?"

"If we slip away unannounced, my mom will kill me."

"I agree that your mother is somewhat of a control freak, Lucy, but you have to admit, all that control gave us a mighty nice wedding."

I wrapped my arms tighter around his waist. "You're right. She deserves to have a kiss and a thank-you."

From our vantage point at the head table, Connor and I looked across the dance floor. It was nearing the end of the evening. The vows had been made, the official photographs taken, the canapes served, the speeches made, the toasts drunk, the meal consumed. I'd danced with a surprisingly shy Connor and then with my beaming dad. Earlier, we'd cut the cake, a gorgeous three-tiered concoction of chocolate, vanilla, and lemon artfully decorated with stark-white buttercream and adorned with floating pale-blue and violet sugar flowers, and now it was almost time for the dessert buffet to be brought out. I was so full of champagne and cake, the thought of more food made my stomach roll over.

Come to think of it, I hadn't had all that much champagne, and I'd barely touched any of my meal. All those nerves that had been churning through my stomach for days were still having their effect. The entire day had gone off perfectly, and I felt a warm happy glow as I snuggled with Connor—my husband—and we watched our friends and family partying and celebrating our union.

"You don't want to wait for the dessert buffet?" I asked Connor.

"For the first, and I hope last, time in my life, I'm okay with passing on the free desserts," he said.

My mom sailed by, absolutely resplendent in a sea-green gown and diamonds, in the arms of my uncle Amos. Mom laughed at something her brother-in-law-said, and he smiled at her. My dad was dancing with Mom's sister, Ellen, and they actually looked happy together. They'd never liked each other much, but there's something about the magic of a wedding that brings families together.

Sometimes. At the thought, I couldn't help glancing toward my sister-in-law Kristen, sitting in a far corner by the kitchen. Mom had prepared the seating plan, and she'd made some last-minute adjustments to ensure Kristen was put as far away as possible from the center of the room without actually being in the kitchen chopping vegetables. When the wedding invitations had gone out, one had been addressed to Kristen and Kevin Richardson and family. In the months since, Kristen had left Kevin (or Kevin had left Kristen; reports differed), but as far as Kristen was concerned, she'd been invited and she was going to attend. So there! That might have been okay, except she'd brought her new boyfriend and had no hesitation in showing him off to her estranged husband and his parents. Fortunately, she'd had enough sense to leave their two children in Boston with her own parents rather than drag them into a family squabble.

"Do you think Kristen's partner's a hired escort?" I whispered to Connor. The man, whose name had flown past me in the flurry of introductions, appeared to be in his late forties. He still clung to traces of what had once been a boyish handsomeness, though his belly was filling out, his cheekbones were not as pronounced as they probably had once been, and the skin on his face was sagging into the start of jowls. His dark-brown hair was thinning on top, and his suit showed signs of a lot of wear.

"Who's Kristen again?" Connor asked.

"Table next to the kitchen. Red dress. The one trying so hard to pretend she's not watching my eldest brother, she might as well have binoculars fixed to her face."

"Why do you think he's an escort?"

"No reason, really, except that she's so over-the-top in showing off what a good time she's having in his company. As for him, he looks totally bored, and he's doing some serious damage to the bar stocks. Oh, look, the boyfriend's getting up. Yup, off to the bar one more time. Mom's noticed. She's saying something to Uncle Amos, and they're leaving the floor."

"Let your mom handle it," Connor said.

"She's not going to make it to him in time to intercept him. Aunt Joyce is beckoning to her."

"That's quite the set of jewelry your aunt's got on her. Even more impressive than your mom's."

"Those are my paternal grandmother's diamonds. When she died, they went to her only daughter, as they should have. Aunt Joyce married three times, but she never had any children. I don't know what will happen to the diamonds after her."

"You're the only granddaughter," Connor said.

I studied the sparkling two-caret stone on the third finger of my left hand, the one now joined by a simple engraved gold band. "I've got all the diamonds I need, thank you. I don't think I've seen Dad's sister more than a handful of times in all my life. I only invited her because Mom said I had to for the sake of family togetherness. I'm surprised she even came." In my mom's eyes family togetherness only went so far—Aunt Joyce and her plus-one had been given the same table near the kitchen as Kristen and her friend.

Whenever my father talked about his older sister, which wasn't often, he said she was a "free spirt." She'd spent part of her youth as the lead singer of a moderately successful rock and roll band. When the band folded, she'd tried her hand at acting; the highlight of that career had been advertising dishwashing detergent. Now she was in her early sixties, and she spent most of her days ensconced in in her apartment overlooking Central Park, being a "patron of the arts." Whatever that means. Her outfit tonight might have been an imitation of a rainbow. The long, wide skirt consisted of a silk underskirt topped by a tulle arrangement in shades of yellow, orange, red, and purple, all of which swirled together when she walked or danced. Above all that color, a high-necked black satin blouse formed the perfect backdrop for the diamond necklace and the matching earrings.

Connor hugged me closer. "It's like being at a movie, standing up here. Watching all the drama play out."

"Of which, fortunately, there's been very little."

My cousin Josie and her husband Jake danced past, and Josie gave me a thumbs-up. I wiggled my fingers in return.

"Speaking of Aunt Joyce," Connor said, "the guy with her doesn't appear to be having a good time, and he's also a regular visitor to the bar. Is he her husband? I missed the relationship last night amongst all the introductions."

My parents had hosted the Friday evening rehearsal dinner at Jake's Seafood Bar, my cousin-in-law's restaurant. "They're not married, but I have no idea how casual the relationship is, or not."

"I don't think he's smiled all night," Connor said. "He looks positively glum, and he's another one whose alcohol consumption your mother's keeping a sharp eye on. Do you think he and your aunt had a fight?"

"That's possible. She doesn't look all that happy either. I didn't talk to him much at dinner last night, but when I did, he was perfectly friendly, and I rather liked him. He told me he'd been an actor at one point but was now retired." He was around the same age as Aunt Joyce, with a head of thick silver hair swept back from a high forehead and strong cheekbones in a lightly tanned face, as though he'd spent the winter on a private Caribbean island or the Côte D'Azur. He wore a perfectly tailored suit accented by an ocean-blue tie the exact color of his eyes.

My mother had stopped at Aunt Joyce and her companion's table. Seeing her approach, Kristen had swiftly risen and scurried away. Mom's perfectly sculpted face settled into hard lines as she talked to Aunt Joyce and Joyce's companion. The man ignored her and stared off into the distance. Men of that age didn't often ignore Suzanne Wyatt Richardson. My mother had been an exceptional beauty in her youth, judging by the photographs I'd seen, and that beauty had transferred smoothly into classical elegance in her late middle age. Mom turned abruptly and walked away from Aunt Joyce and her friend, her back straight and her steps firm.

Connor's dad got up from his chair and gave her a small bow, asking her for a dance. All the anger faded from Mom's face in a flash, and she honored him with a radiant smile and the extension of her hand. Meanwhile, Aunt Joyce snarled at her friend. I couldn't hear what she said, but her tone indicated she was not pleased. She pushed her chair back, got up, and stalked away. He reached for the glass next to him and took a long drink.

"Lucy, Connor. Thank you for a lovely evening." The Harper siblings, Joanna and Ralph, and their friend Tim Snyder stood in front of us.

"Are you leaving already?" Connor said. "The night is still young, and the dessert buffet's on the way. Catered by none other than Josie and her staff themselves."

Ralph's eyes gleamed with interest, but his sister said, "It's late. I've had a wonderful time, but . . ."

"But, although the night might be young, some of us aren't," Mr. Snyder finished.

It was far more than a matter of age. Joanne was a recluse. She'd barely left her own property, except for solitary nighttime walks, in forty years. She'd recently become friends with Mr. Snyder, retired high school teacher and regular library visitor, and he'd been edging her, ever so slowly, out of her shell. Her dress tonight was new, and although it was plain, it was a lovely soft blue with a matching jacket, and it fitted her thin frame well. Her cheeks were flushed and her eyes shining, and I was so very happy she'd come.

"Will I see you at book club next week?" I asked.

"No," Joanne said, in a voice that still showed signs of not being used very much. "I'm not comfortable with the works of Mr. Poe."

"He's not to everyone's taste," I agreed. "You're so well read, Jo; why don't you send me some suggestions for books you've enjoyed? We'd be happy to consider them."

"I will. I'd like that." She ducked her head and slipped away, her arm linked through Mr. Snyder's. Ralph gave me a nod of approval before following them. He was pleased that his sister was finding some happiness in her life at last.

"Mrs. McNeil. May I have the honor of the next dance?" Our friend Theodore Kowalski took the Harper siblings' place. He bowed deeply.

"I'd be delighted." I accepted his hand, and he led me onto the dance floor as the band struck up a new tune.

Almost everyone was on their feet now. The band was a local one, popular at weddings and outdoor summer concerts. Earlier they'd played great sixties to eighties dance music, and they were now striking up softer stuff to introduce the end of the evening. It made my heart glow to see our friends and family celebrating Connor and me and sharing in our joy.

Theodore was, to put it mildly, a dreadful dancer. Like Connor, I worried that I'd have to spend my first full married day with my feet soaking in a basin of hot water. Every time Theodore apologized for bumping into me or trampling my toes, I smiled and said, "Not a problem. Isn't this fun?"

"It is, Lucy, it is. I am so happy for you both. Oh, sorry, Mr. McNeil, I went the wrong way."

"Not a problem, Teddy." Connor's dad laughed. "I never mind bumping into my new daughter and her friends."

Marie, Connor's mother, gave me a warm smile as they danced away.

Theodore tightened his grip on my back as though I'd spring out of control without the benefit of his manly strength. "I wonder if Lorraine's feeling under the weather this evening."

"Lorraine? You mean the fiddle player? Do you know her?"

"I've known her most of my life. Her mother's a close friend of my mom. Lorraine's one of the founders of this band. A highly talented musician. She's a high school teacher in her real life, but she's devoted to the band. Something's off with her tonight, but she's making the effort like the trooper she is."

He spun me around, and I could see what he was talking about. Connor and I had met with Lorraine and one of her bandmates to organize the music for this evening, and I'd been impressed with her bouncy personality and sheer enthusiasm for her music. Tonight her face was pale, her eyes dark, and her smile forced as she stared out over the dance floor. She struck a wrong note, and the singer glanced at her in alarm. Lorraine didn't seem to notice.

"Now that I have you in private," Theodore said, "I have a confession to make."

"A confession? Of what sort?"

"Of a literary sort. I fear I overextended myself by suggesting we read *The Count of Monte Cristo* for next week's book club meeting."

"Told ya so. No one else has taken it out."

At the Bodie Island Lighthouse Library Classic Novel Reading Club, the members choose what to read. Theodore had eagerly proposed *The Count of Monte Cristo* by Alexandre Dumas. A handful of attendees put up their hands to agree, but when I mentioned that it clocked in at a hefty 1,200 pages, every hand went down, except Theodore's. Instead, the group chose a selection of the best-known stories by Edgar Allan Poe, and Theodore announced he'd read the Dumas classic as a companion piece to Poe's tales of revenge.

The song ended, and I kissed Theodore lightly on the cheek. He peered at me through lenses made of clear glass. Although he didn't smoke, he smelled, as he always did, of aged tobacco, tinged with a hint of moth balls. His suit was about twenty years out of date, and I suspected he'd last worn it to his high school graduation. Theodore liked to play the part of a British literary scholar, even though in reality he was a Nags Head native who dealt in rare books and other collectibles.

"Thank you for the dance," I said to him. "If you'll excuse me, I have to visit the ladies' room." He gave me a deep bow that wouldn't have been out of place in Dumas's classic novel.

It took me a long time to cross the ballroom, as everyone wanted to stop me and give me hugs and their best wishes.

"You should have told her to leave, Lucy." My youngest sister-in-law, Barbara, intercepted me.

"Asked who to leave?" I said innocently.

"Kristen, of course. She's not part of this family anymore."

"Kristen and Kevin have two children, who are my parents' grandchildren and your nieces. She's part of the family whether she wants to be or not. Or whether Kevin wants her to be or not."

Barbara snorted. Alcohol fumes hit me in the face. Then she gave me a big wink. "Be that as it may, I can't fault her for her taste in men. That hottie she's with could stand to lose a few pounds, but he still makes Kevin look like Santa Claus the morning after the elves' Christmas party. You've done okay for yourself too, Lucy." Another wink. "I wouldn't kick your Connor out of bed for eating crackers."

I choked.

Barbara glanced toward the Richardson siblings' table. All three of my older brothers had come to the wedding. Kevin, Lloyd, and Luke, Barbara's husband, had loosened ties and removed jackets and were sharing family stories over bottles of beer and shots of whiskey. "You have to admit, honey, the Richardson men aren't anything to brag about. Good thing they come with plenty of . . ." She rubbed her thumb and first two fingers together in the universal sign for money and roared with laughter.

"Uh . . . okay," I said. She gave me another broad wink and headed back to her table.

"Need some crowd control here?" a voice said behind me. I turned to see my friends Butch Greenblatt and Stephanie Stanton watching Barbara stagger away, none too steady on her stiletto heels.

"Families. Nothing like a wedding to get the tongues loosening. Don't worry about her. They're about to bring out the dessert buffet, and that'll get everyone sobered up fast."

Butch grinned at the promise of the treats and rubbed his big hands together. "Jake tells me Josie's pulled out all the stops on this."

My cousin Josie, who's married to Butch's brother, Jake, is a professional baker and owns her own place. She'd insisted on making my cake herself, and she and her staff were providing the midnight spread. Her wedding gift to us, she'd said.

"While we're waiting," Butch said, "I haven't had the honor of a turn around the floor with the bride yet."

"I'm actually in kinda a rush to get to the ladies' room. Later?"

Steph linked her arm through mine. "Let's go. That just happens to be my destination too."

She and I continued making our way across the room. The reception was being held at the Ocean Side Hotel, one of the nicest places in Nags Head. Connor and I had wanted a small, quiet wedding. *Good luck with that.* Between Connor's lifetime of Outer Banks friends and the longtime friends of his family as well as the friends he'd collected in his roles as mayor of our town and as a popular dentist, on top of my coworkers at the Bodie Island Lighthouse Library, numerous library friends, my brothers and their families, and my friends from Boston, small wasn't in the cards.

It was my wedding, but my mom had insisted that tonight I was not the hostess. I was the guest of honor. She'd taken all the hostess duties upon herself. And done a very fine job. Connor and I'd insisted on paying for our wedding ourselves, and Mom had, wisely, pared down her expectations fractionally. Mom and Dad lived in Boston, and Mom had wanted the wedding there so she could turn it into one of the highlights of the season at their country club. I'd squelched that idea from the get-go, and she'd graciously given in. My life was in Nags Head now. Connor's always had been.

Josie and Jake approached us as Steph and I were about to leave the ballroom on our way to the hallway leading to the restrooms and the private areas of the hotel. "We hate to leave early, sweetie," my cousin said, "but—"

I wrapped her in a ferocious hug. "But morning comes mighty early when you have a baby. I'm just glad you two were able to come, particularly after all the work you put in preparing the midnight buffet. I hope you didn't spend the entire night worrying."

"Josie might have sent a couple of under-the-table texts to Mom," Jake said. They'd left their three-month-old daughter, Ellie, in the care of Jake's parents. Josie had been my maid of honor. We'd had an extra-long break between the ceremony and the official photographs and the start of the reception to give her time to slip away to attend to the baby.

"I'll admit to some worry," Josie said, "plus the fact that I need to get out of here, as my boobs are about to explode."

I did explode. With laughter. Jake joined in the group hug, and Steph followed. Jake and Josie said good-night one more time and headed for the cloakroom.

"How are you feeling?" Steph asked, when she and I were standing in front of the restroom mirrors.

"Slightly queasy," I said. "Too much excitement on top of so much anticipation."

"No one would know. You look positively radiant, Lucy. That dress is beyond marvelous."

I studied myself in the mirror. After much searching, I'd chosen a sleeveless dress with a lace-trimmed V neckline and a beaded bodice cinched by a thin rhinestone-encrusted belt. The skirt clung to my hips and then flared slowly out at the knees to cascade behind me in a waterfall of white satin. The smooth lines of the dress and the high heels I'd worn for the church service and the photographs managed to make me look taller than my five foot three. Although, standing next to Connor and his parents and Butch and Jake, the groomsmen, I was still—by far—the shortest person in the pictures. Steph is even shorter than I am, and my mom and her sister, Ellen, are my height, so the people in the pictures of the brides' side are better balanced, although Josie takes after her tall, thin dad, Amos, who's close to Connor's height.

The hairdresser had allowed my normally out-of-control dark curls to remain largely out of control and had simply scooped them loosely behind my head and tucked them into a satin band sprinkled with sparkling white rhinestones at the nape of my neck. For the ceremony and photos, I'd carried a small bouquet of peach and white roses.

"Are you still planning on postponing the honeymoon?" Steph asked.

I dropped onto one of the blue velvet stools in front of the mirror. "I'll have tomorrow to rest up and bid farewell to my family and be back to work Monday morning. We're going to Europe next month."

"So exciting. A honeymoon in Paris." Steph sighed dreamily.

"Anything happening in your life you'd like to tell me about?" I asked.

She gave my reflection a crooked grin. "No. And that's fine. I love Butch beyond measure, but sometimes . . ."

"I know. You'll work it out."

Steph was a defense lawyer, the law partner of my uncle Amos. She was passionate about justice and determined to always do her best for her clients. Butch was a police officer, dedicated to the law. Law and justice, in Steph's mind, didn't always go together, and the couple regularly clashed in matters of opinion.

She gave my shoulder a light squeeze and left.

I studied myself in the mirror. I cocked my head to one side. "Good evening, Mrs. McNeil. How are you today, Lucy McNeil?"

"Talking to yourself already?" The door swung open, and Louise Jane McKaughnan came in. I blushed.

"This hotel's nice on the surface," Louise Jane said, "but the renovations were done on the cheap. The walls are like tissue paper." Louise Jane wore a high-necked cream blouse under a pinstriped pantsuit in shades of plum that looked great on her tall, lanky frame. Her feet were in black ballet flats, and she'd honored the occasion with a touch of pink lipstick. Louise Jane and I had had our differences in the past, but I'd been happy to invite her to my wedding.

"Bertie says you're coming to work Monday morning. Is that right? No honeymoon?" Bertie James was the library director. In honor of my wedding, she'd closed the library at noon today so everyone could attend the church service.

"Delayed honeymoon," I said. "We'd set the date for the wedding and started making all the arrangements, and then a big mayor's conference came up that Connor wants to attend. We were able to reschedule the trip without penalty. I hope you're having a good time."

"I haven't danced so much since I was in high school. Come to think of it, I didn't dance at all when I was in high school. I never was interested in the silly, childish frivolities my classmates were. The band's taking a break, so I came in here to catch my breath." She studied my face in the mirror.

I twisted on the stool. "What?"

She bent down and gave me a hug that had the breath shooting out of me. "I wish you well, Lucy. Now and always."

She went into a stall, leaving me stunned. I gave my head a shake and stood up. My wedding had been everything I'd ever dreamed of, but it was time for us to go.

I went into the hallway and took a moment to gather my breath. I'd love to slip quietly away into the night, me and my husband, but I didn't see how we could manage to do that.

The corridor takes a bend after the restrooms, leading to the business offices. A loud voice, the words slurred with too much drink, came from around the corner. "As I remember it, you ran out without saying good-bye. Stuck me with the rent."

Someone replied, but their voice was too low for me to make out the words.

"You look like you're doing okay for yourself. Bit rumpled, but some things never change, do they? I never quite hit the career heights I'd intended when we were young and foolish, but can't help that now. These days I'm dependent on the kindness not of strangers but of friends. Like the suit? My lady friend picked up the bill for it."

The voice responded.

"We all make mistakes. Maybe I've made more than my share, but that's water under the bridge now, isn't it? This isn't the time or the place to talk over old times, and I've decided to leave tomorrow. Going to cut my visit short. Maybe we can catch up another time. I'll be in touch. You still owe me for that rent. Plus interest."

A man walked around the corner. The speaker had been Wayne, my aunt Joyce's plus-one. His eyes were far away, his expression sad. He saw me, almost visibly shook the melancholy off, and forced his face into a smile. "Nice wedding," he said as he passed. "Thank you for including me." A wave of tobacco smoke followed him like a noxious cloud.

I hesitated, wondering if I should check and see if the person who'd been with him was okay.

A group of women poured out of the ballroom, heading for the restroom, laughing and gasping for breath.

"The midnight desserts are coming out," Marie said. "I swore I wouldn't overdo it tonight, but—"

"But," Denise, who worked at the library with me, said, "it would be rude not to try a bit of everything."

"Exactly." Marie gave me a wink, and the women went into the restroom.

"There you are." I winced at the sound of a sharp voice with a deep southern accent, accompanied by the *tap, tap* of a cane coming down the hallway. "I've been hoping to get a chance to have a nice chat all night." It was Gloria O'Malley, Amos's mother. Gloria is not related to me, but she'd announced that I was an honorary granddaughter of hers—and, as my honorary grandmother, she expected an invitation to my wedding.

Realizing I had little choice in the matter, I'd given in. Under the condition, I said to Aunt Ellen, that Gloria had no input into wedding plans. Unlike the way the matriarch had pretty much taken over Josie's wedding, to the point that Josie made noises about eloping.

"What I want to know," Gloria said, "is when you and your new husband are coming to visit me in New Orleans."

"We'd love to," I said, "but we have our honeymoon coming up, and vacation time is—"

"New Orleans is the perfect honeymoon spot. I'm surprised you're looking elsewhere. Ellen told me you're going to London. Why on earth would anyone go to London? I said to her. It rains all the time."

"Not London but Paris."

Her rings flashed as she dismissed the difference with an imperious wave of her hand. Gloria looked exactly like what she wanted everyone to think she was: a grand southern matron of the old school. She wore a floor-length yellow gown with a rhinestone-studded jacket, a yellow fascinator with sweeping gray feathers that wouldn't have looked out of place at a royal wedding, and enough heavy jewelry that it would have needed the escort of a security guard if it had been real.

I forgot about the men and the argument I'd overheard as I swallowed my panic at the prospect of a honeymoon in New Orleans, supervised by Gloria O'Malley.

"No time to chat," I said. "Connor's waiting for me." I fled to locate my husband and make our escape.

Chapter Two

"Good morning, Mrs. McNeil." Soft fingers caressed my cheek. I sighed with contentment and snuggled deeper under the blankets.

"Would that be the new Mr. Lucy McNeil née Richardson addressing me?" I mumbled into my pillow.

"It would, and Mr. Lucy McNeil's telling you it's time for you to get up."

"Meow."

I opened my eyes. Connor sat on the edge of the bed, extending a mug toward me. Charles sat on the dresser, watching me. It was Charles who'd said meow.

"How are you feeling?" Connor asked me.

"Better than I probably should."

He chuckled. "Me too."

"Do we have to go?"

"Yes, we do."

My parents, who had not been allowed to pay for (or control) our wedding, had thrown the rehearsal dinner Friday night at Jake's restaurant. Connor's parents were putting on the post-wedding breakfast. Sunday brunch at the Ocean Side Hotel had seemed like a good idea when it was proposed.

It didn't seem like a good idea now. I reluctantly sat up and arranged the pillows behind me.

"It's nine." Connor handed me the mug of piping-hot coffee, and I took a sip. "We're due at the hotel at ten, so you have an hour to get yourself ready. Would you like me to start you a bath?"

"Is that going to be the pattern of our married life? Coffee in bed followed by a hot bath?"

"No," he said, leaving the room.

Charles landed next to me. I gave his head a rub with my free hand. "Sorry you had to miss it, buddy. It was a great wedding. You would have hated it." Charles shrugged. Parties were not his favorite thing. When we had parties at the Lighthouse Library, where he served as the official library cat, he was usually confined to the utility closet.

I sipped my coffee and thought about last night. It had been marvelous. Truly the wedding of my dreams.

On the bedside table, my phone rang. I hesitated to pick it up, but the display showed that the caller was Bertie James, my boss at the library. In case she had a request for a scheduling change, I needed to answer. And so I did. "Good morning, Bertie."

"Lucy. This might sound like a silly question, but did you happen to notice what time Eddie left last night?"

"Eddie? Yes, I did. I mean, I thought I did. You left together, didn't you?" My eagle-eyed mother had spotted Connor and me stealthily making our way to the rear door and had sent my brother Kevin to intercept us. We were ordered to return to the head table and have one last toast.

Connor had turned to me, lifted his glass, and said simply, "To the woman I have loved since I was fifteen years old."

I burst into tears, and we laughed together and hugged.

I have to admit: Mother always knows best. It was the perfect send-off.

"As much as I'd love to stay for Josie's desserts," Bertie said to us as the charge for the buffet began, "we should be going. Eddie's not feeling too well."

I glanced over at her friend and saw what she meant. He was looking rather pale.

"Neither of us are as young nor as spry as we once were," Bertie said. "We'll leave the dancing until dawn to the young people. I'll see you on Monday, Lucy. If you want to come to work late, I'm sure no one will be overly bothered. Not me, at any rate."

"Thank you," I said.

Eddie had thanked us for the evening, but his voice was strained and his smile didn't reach his eyes.

"He did leave with me, right after we said good-night to you and Connor," Bertie said now. "He's staying at my house, and we caught a cab here. As we were about to get out of the cab, he remembered he'd left his tie on his chair and wanted to go back and get it. I told him the hotel would put it in lost and found and he could get it in the morning, but he insisted it had some sentimental value to him and he wanted to be sure it didn't get lost. Even at the time, I thought that was odd. I've never known Eddie to care one whit about his possessions, but off he went. I made tea and sat up for a while waiting. When he didn't come back, I assumed he'd been talked into having another drink. I have to say I was mildly annoyed at that. I wanted to stay at the party longer, but he said he needed to get away because he wasn't feeling well. I went to bed, and . . . I just woke up and he's not here."

"I can't say, Bertie. I didn't see him again, but Connor and I left shortly after you two did. Is it possible he got up early and went for a walk or something?"

"His bed's not slept in, and there's no sign of him making his habitual morning coffee before going out. Eddie's a coffee fiend. He never goes anywhere without first having his morning dose of caffeine."

"He didn't . . . maybe decide to go home early?" Eddie lived in Elizabeth City.

"His suitcase and things are still here, Lucy. Everything except the suit he wore last night. I'm sorry to bother you, this morning of all mornings. I'm sure he'll turn up. You know Eddie." She let out a strangled laugh as she hung up.

Connor came into the bedroom surrounded by a cloud of steam from the bathroom. "Something wrong?"

"I don't know. Bertie seems to have misplaced Eddie."

"Misplaced? Didn't you once tell me he's the perfect model of the stereotypical absent-minded professor?"

"He is that. Still, it seems odd." Professor Edward McClanahan was a professor of Ancient Greek and Latin at Blacklock College in Elizabeth City. He and Bertie had been an item in their own college days and had only reconnected recently. As she'd related the story to me, it was his sheer absent-mindedness and his tendency not to notice his surroundings or the emotions of other people (if they weren't speaking Latin, at any rate) that caused them to eventually go their separate ways in life.

"He probably had a couple of drinks too many at the party and someone took pity on him and took him home for the night," Connor said. "Your bath's ready, m'lady."

* * *

I've been told that in days past, a bride had a "going away" outfit, which she changed into at the reception to wear for immediately departing on her honeymoon. Connor and I had simply gone home to our cat after our reception, so I hadn't bothered to buy such a garment.

I studied the contents of my closet now, wondering if that had been a mistake. My clothes ranged from what I wore to do housework to beach-suitable to librarian attire to frilly dresses and skirts for nights out with Connor or my girlfriends. Nothing really said "wedding brunch." Certainly nothing my mother would approve of.

Why, I thought to myself, was I worried about my mother's approval? Force of habit.

"It's almost ten, Lucy," Connor called.

"We can be late this one time," I said. But I can never be late. Force of habit, once again. I had to make a decision. Now.

I took my one perfect little black dress out of the closet. If I dressed it up with a red scarf, red shoes, and my ruby earrings, it shouldn't look too somber. I threw the dress on the bed and rummaged in the closet for my red pumps. When I turned around, Charles had plopped his sizable bulk directly on top of the dress.

"Get off that!"

He hissed at me and, claws fully extended, scratched the fabric of the skirt.

I reached for him, intending to tell him to go bother someone else. He focused his intense blue eyes on mine and scratched at the dress again.

I hesitated. Charles, I remembered, was not only an exceptional judge of character; he had excellent dress sense.

I put my hands on my hips and eyed him. "Not suitable, you think?"

He yawned.

A quick glance out the window showed me that the sun had risen over the ocean in a sky of clear blue. "What's the temperature going to be today?" I yelled.

"High sixties," Connor replied. "No rain expected."

As we'd be indoors most of the time, a light summer dress should do. Charles was right, as he usually was. I needed to look bright and sunny and cheerful the morning after my wedding, not as though I were going to a business meeting or were the guest of honor at my own funeral. I grabbed a calf-length dress in colorful swirls of yellow, green, and red and held it up in front of me. “Do you approve?” I asked Charles. He rubbed his whiskers in acknowledgment.

When I came out, Connor gave me an approving look. “That dress is perfect for the occasion.” He ruffled my curls, which this morning once again resembled a mop that had been put away wet. “I don’t know why it took you so long to decide what to wear.”

“You look pretty perfect yourself,” I said. And he did, in a pair of black jeans with a wide belt and a pale-blue shirt worn under a navy-blue sports coat. He hadn’t shaved this morning, and the dark stubble on his strong jaw looked positively enticing. I gave him a wicked grin. “Maybe we can skip the brunch.”

“And leave me to deal with your mother’s wrath? I think not.”

We got Connor’s car and headed for the Ocean Side Hotel. It was late spring, and Nags Head was starting to come awake after the long, cold winter. A handful of out-of-state license plates were visible, a few cars piled high with beach balls and folding chairs and picnic coolers. People were walking on the beach, and fishing poles arched into the water. Some brave souls were lying in the sun or even wading in the surf.

Connor parked the car, and we walked into the hotel together, holding hands. I felt terribly self-conscious.

“Mr. and Mrs. McNeil, good morning,” the concierge called. I half turned, expecting to see Fred and Marie behind us. Then I realized he meant Connor and me, and I blushed. “Your party is in the Roanoke room, off the main dining room.”

“Thanks,” Connor said.

The clink of cutlery and china and the sound of conversation and laughter followed us through the dining room, along with the scent of coffee and bacon and other delicious things, as we made our way to the small private room where a table had been set for thirteen. Only two places were unoccupied. My mother saw us first and said, "Here they are now."

Uncle Amos was the first to stand, and then the rest of the guests joined him. They broke into a round of applause. Champagne flutes and coffee cups were lifted. I felt myself blushing again. Before Connor and I could find our seats, everyone gathered around us for hugs and handshakes. Josie held out Ellie's pudgy little hand, and I shook it. Deep-brown eyes stared suspiciously at me. A hair band with a bright-yellow bow attached had been slipped over her bald head.

Aunt Ellen took the baby as I settled into the chair my dad held for me.

"I can't stay long," Josie said. "Tourist season's starting up and we're getting busy, but I wanted to say good-morning."

"Good morning," I said to her. "I appreciate you coming. I know how dreadfully busy you and Jake are."

"Josie's already been to the bakery." Aunt Ellen lifted Ellie onto her shoulder and patted the little back. "To get the day's baking started."

"Business is business," Josie said. "People have to eat, and that means someone has to make the bread."

"Sleep is good too," I replied. Even before they had a baby, I'd wondered how Josie and Jake managed. Josie started work in the kitchen at her place, Josie's Cozy Bakery, at four AM, and Jake was the head chef at Jake's Seafood Bar, where he often worked past midnight. Their schedules were just about exactly opposite, and Josie's idea of a fun date night had been doing dinner prep at the restaurant. In a way, the opposing schedules helped with Ellie. Josie handled the baby's evening shift, and Jake the mornings. Jake's mother took the baby most afternoons, and Aunt Ellen filled in on occasion. I'd even taken a shift myself when

Josie's carefully constructed schedule encountered a hiccup on one of my days off work at the library.

"Motherhood must come first," Gloria pronounced.

"Gotta earn a living, Grandma." Josie kept her tone light, but I knew her well enough to hear the bite of annoyance she tried to smother. This was obviously an old argument. And one that would never be settled.

"Madam?" The waiter held the bottle of champagne up in question. I nodded, and he filled my glass.

My dad coughed and rose to his feet. He lifted his own glass, orange juice for him, and proposed a toast. Everyone joined in. Connor found my hand and gave it a squeeze under the table.

"Did you stay until the bitter end last night?" I asked when the toast was finished. "What time was the bitter end, anyway?"

"Your father stayed," Mom said. "I collapsed around twelve thirty, not long after you two left." She turned to Josie. "I have to say, dear, those pecan squares might have been the best I have ever had."

"Thanks," Josie said. I didn't spoil the moment by mentioning that my mom had probably never had a pecan square, or any other type of pastry, in all her life.

"The band finished at one," Dad said. "I stayed a while to help the boys finish the night." By *boys*, he meant his sons. Of whom only Kevin and Luke had joined us for brunch, along with Luke's wife, Barbara.

Mom noticed me noticing the absences and said, "Lloyd's feeling a touch under the weather this morning."

Barbara laughed. "Is that what he calls it?" Mom gave her a sharp look and continued, "MaryBeth will order them something light from room service."

"Where's your handsome man this morning, Aunt Joyce?" Barbara asked sweetly. "Also sleeping it off?"

"I . . . uh . . . believe he went for a walk along the beach." Aunt Joyce's voice was uncharacteristically hesitant.

"You don't know?" Barbara jerked as Luke dug his elbow into her ribs. "What? I'm just being friendly like."

"Wayne is a keen swimmer." Aunt Joyce studied the patterns in the champagne flute in her hand. "And an early riser."

People shifted uncomfortably and avoided each other's eyes. *Another missing man, as well as Eddie?*

I was about to ask if Wayne had struck up a friendship with Eddie McClanahan, but the waiter arrived, notepad and pen at the ready, and began taking orders.

I was, truth be told, starving. My nerves had been so bad yesterday I hadn't had much to eat all day. I ordered the smoked salmon eggs benedict, with a side order of extra hash browns, and whole wheat toast. I tried not to feel guilty as Mom asked for the fruit platter and a small bowl of yogurt.

"Where's Kristen?" I asked. "Also wanting a quiet morning?"

"Kristen," Mom said, "was informed that the presence of her . . . gentleman companion was not required today."

"I bet that went over well."

"As well as could be expected. She said she wouldn't come if he wasn't invited, and I told her that was fine with me."

"I'm sorry, Suzanne," Marie said. "When I mentioned it to her, I didn't realize—"

"No reason you should. We don't wash our dirty linen in public."

"Much," Barbara muttered, and next to her Luke smothered a laugh.

Kevin had declined champagne in favor of a glass of tomato juice. Judging by the shade of the drink, I assumed the glass also contained something more substantial than juice. "Guy's a gold digger."

"Do you know that for a fact?" Dad said.

"What else would he be interested in? A guy like that isn't after Kristen for her looks or for—"

"Careful, son," Dad said. "She is the mother of your children."

Kevin finished his drink in one go.

"What sort of money does Kristen have to attract a gold digger?" Mom said. "Or should I say, what does she expect to have? What are you two not telling me?"

"She's after every penny she can get, Mom." My brother snapped his fingers to attract the waiter. "I'll fight her to the bitter end."

"Don't be a fool. If that happens, it's almost guaranteed that the end will be extremely bitter," Mom said. "Are you sure that's what you want, Kevin? Millar, dare I hope you're not encouraging our son in this?"

Connor squeezed my hand under the table. Marie and Fred McNeil exchanged embarrassed looks.

Aunt Joyce lifted her head. "As I recall, you handled my first divorce, Millar. I didn't come out of it as well as I might have expected. It was then I learned about disregarding thoughts of forever after and having a good prenup."

"As you well know, Joyce," Dad said, "that was not me but my partner, and he—"

"I hope you have a good prenup, Lucy," Aunt Joyce said.

"I don't think—" my mom began, but I interrupted.

"As I have no money but what I earn myself, that's not a problem." My father's family is what some might call rich, and he himself does very well as the head partner at Richardson Lewiston, the law firm established by his own father. My parents paid for my education and helped me get settled in an apartment when I first started working, but otherwise, I received no financial support from them. I didn't have a trust fund, and I assumed my brothers didn't either. Maybe that assumption was incorrect, but then again people could, and often did, fight over insubstantial amounts of money. Kevin was a realtor in Boston, and Kristen was the receptionist and office manager there. If he wanted to cut her out, and if she could prove she'd helped him establish his company, yes the divorce could be bitter.

"This is not a conversation for the here and now," my dad said.

"In my day," Gloria said, "a married couple kept their dirty laundry to themselves and put the welfare of their children first. None of this divorce nonsense you young people are so fond of."

Josie laughed. "Didn't you tell me, Dad, that one of your great-grandmothers outlived four husbands? Three of whom died under what was considered at the time to be mysterious circumstances?"

"Josie's got you there, Mother," Uncle Amos said. "Sometimes divorce isn't the worst option available."

Gloria drank her mimosa and ignored him.

Aunt Ellen lifted her eyebrows in my direction. Ellie had fallen asleep on her shoulder, and Ellen had eaten one-handed while Josie, thankful for the break, wolfed down her bacon and eggs.

"As for our family," Marie said, "Fred and I plan on spending every cent before going to our reward, leaving nothing for Connor to inherit."

"Except for Dad's toolbox, I hope," Connor said. "I'm counting on getting that." Fred had made his living as a carpenter; he and Connor had labored for months knocking our new, old house, which had been unoccupied for fifteen years, into good enough shape to live in.

"When are you going home, Suzanne?" Marie changed the subject smoothly. "Fred and I would like to have you and Millar over for lunch one day before you leave. Just the four of us, so we can talk about our children when they're not listening."

The tension around the table broke, and my dad laughed. Mom said, "That would be lovely. We're leaving Tuesday, but we have no plans for tomorrow."

"Great," Marie said. "How about one o'clock? I'll text you our address."

The conversation moved on to other things.

Eventually, plates were cleared, refills of coffee refused, more toasts to Connor and me extended. Josie had taken the baby from her mother, wrapped Ellie snuggly in her carrier, and said her good-byes.

The waiter stopped by to ask if anyone wanted anything more. Kevin lifted his tomato "juice" glass and said, "I'll have another one of these."

"Perhaps not, dear," Mom said smoothly. "It's a lovely day, and I'm looking forward to a walk on the beach. You may escort me."

"Dad can go with you," Kevin said.

"Your father has business calls to make."

"I do?" Dad said. "I mean, right, I have business calls to make. Sorry, honey, but they can't wait."

"I'll take you, Mom," Luke said.

Mom's smile was radiant as she folded her napkin, put it next to her place, and indicated to the waiter that he was dismissed. "How lovely, a walk with two of my favorite sons. And perhaps my favorite son-in-law would like to join us?"

Connor threw me a pleading look.

"Not for us, thanks," I said. "We have to get home. I have to . . . uh . . . write thank-you letters to people who sent gifts but weren't able to come to the wedding."

Mom stood up. "I'll change my shoes and meet you boys in the lobby in ten minutes. Perhaps Lloyd has recovered enough of his strength to accompany us."

"Unlikely," Dad said with a snort of disapproval.

"Thank you for the brunch, Fred and Marie," Uncle Amos said. "Most enjoyable."

"Our pleasure," Connor's mom replied.

"I'd like to go to the ladies' room before we leave," I said to Connor.

"I'll meet you in the lobby."

"As we always have to go in packs, or so men believe," Aunt Joyce said, "I'll accompany you, dear. Noticeably, I was not invited on this beach stroll."

"If you want to come, Joyce," Mom said.

"I do not. Simply making a point. I have better things to do with my day." She slipped her arm through mine. "It was a lovely wedding, dear. I like your young man very much. Never mind all that talk about prenups, although it doesn't hurt a woman to make sure she's taken care of. I like to remind your father that he wasn't always the legal éminence grise he considers himself to be. His partner did a horrific job handling my first divorce, but Millar wasn't much help. My father, your grandfather, couldn't be bothered to involve himself in something as sordid as a divorce case, even though it was his own daughter's happiness on the line. Happiness, I like to think, I managed to obtain for myself eventually. As will you, dear."

We walked through the dining room, heading for the restrooms.

"How long have you known Wayne?" I was uncomfortable with Aunt Joyce's criticism of my father and grandfather and wanted to change the subject. I could think of nothing better to ask on the spur of the moment.

"Two weeks," she said. "I have to confess, if only to you, dear, that I'm already getting tired of him. He was in a nasty mood yesterday, and I don't need to put up with that sort of nonsense. We had planned to stay on for a few days, enjoy a little vacation in your charming town, but last night he suddenly announced, for no reason I could see, that he wanted to go home. I told him he could find his own way back to New York."

We turned into the hallway leading to the restrooms. Just before the bend in the corridor, a woman in a housekeeping uniform was struggling to get a door open. She yanked at the doorknob, gave the bottom of the door a solid kick, and cursed loudly. She sucked in a breath when she saw us heading her way. "Sorry. This door won't open." She twisted the key and shoved at the door.

I was about to go into the restroom, but Aunt Joyce went to see what was going on, and I followed. "Are you sure you have the right key?" she asked.

"Absolutely. They're labeled, see?"

"Would you like me to give it a try?" Joyce asked.

The housekeeper stepped back. "Help yourself. The key doesn't seem to want to go all the way in."

"What's kept in here?"

"It's nothing but a small storage closet. Plumbing stuff mostly. There's a problem in one of the rooms, and I was sent to get what's needed."

Aunt Joyce wiggled the key. "Reminds me of my misspent youth," she said to me. "I'd like to be able to say I did some housebreaking when I was younger, but it was more a matter of living in the sort of Village accommodations that were virtually falling down around me, and improvision was sometimes necessary. Hmm . . . something seems to be shoved into the lock. The key won't go in all the way. Lucy, do you have a hairpin?" Aunt Joyce dropped to her knees and put her right eye up to the keyhole.

"A hairpin? Sorry, no. I did last night."

"That's no help to us now, is it? Tweezers, perhaps?"

"I can try and find something like that," the housekeeper said.

"That's what you'll need," Aunt Joyce said.

"What's going on here?" A large man in an ill-fitting blue suit approached us. His name tag read DAVID WILLSHAW, MANAGER.

"Sorry, Mr. Willshaw, but I can't get this door open," the housekeeper said. "Maintenance sent me to get something."

He looked at me, and then he looked at Joyce, crouching on the floor. Joyce smiled up at him. She was a woman who liked to have a purpose, I realized. Her earlier mood, when she had to confess she'd lost track of Wayne, vanished when she'd encountered a problem she might be able to help solve.

David leaned over her and wiggled the handle. No surprise that the door didn't magically fly open. "It's locked."

"We know it's locked," Aunt Joyce said. "That is the entire point. Something's jammed into the keyhole, and the key won't work. If you can find me a pair of thin tweezers, I might be able to get it out."

"It's Sunday," he said. "I'm paying time and a half for a service call as it is. Let me see."

Aunt Joyce wiggled over a few inches, and David bent down. He also put his eye to the keyhole. "Something's in there."

"You don't say," Aunt Joyce said.

Connor came down the hallway with Kevin. "What's going on?"

"Are you a locksmith?" the housekeeper asked.

"No," Connor said.

"Me neither," Kevin said.

"I'm not paying Sunday rates to get a locksmith in here." David stood up with a grunt. He was a big man, maybe about 250 pounds, of which only a small amount was held in his belly. His head was bald, and he sported a neat goatee. His shoulders strained against the poor-quality fabric of his suit. "Stand back."

"What?" Aunt Joyce said.

"Stand back. I'll get this door open fast enough."

Joyce wiggled her eyebrows at me as she struggled to her feet. Connor gave her a hand, and then we all, except David Willshaw, stepped aside.

"Are you sure there isn't a better—" Connor began as David took two steps backward, braced himself, lifted his right foot, and charged.

As Louise Jane had noticed, the walls in this hotel were so thin they might as well be made of tissue paper. That appeared to be the case for the door also. It came completely off its hinges and crashed backward.

The storage room was small, more of a closet than a room. The overhead light was off, but I could see shelves of cleaning equipment and various jugs of liquids and powders.

"There you go," David said with a satisfied smirk. "No locksmith needed. I'll get maintenance to prop the door back up, and the locksmith can replace it tomorrow at regular rates."

He turned to leave, but Connor put up one hand. "Hold on a minute, Mr. Willshaw. Something seems to be under that door. It didn't land flat on the floor like you'd expect. We need to move it before anyone tries to walk on it and tips it over."

Connor was right: the door hadn't fallen flat onto the floor but stopped against something. I leaned over and peered at it, and then I grabbed Connor's arm. "Someone's trapped there."

A hand, palm up, protruded from under the door. Nothing moved.

The housekeeper squealed and grabbed Aunt Joyce's arm.

"Lucy, call 911," Connor yelled. He, along with Kevin and David, scrambled to drag the broken door away from the closet as I fumbled for my phone.

"What is the nature of your emergency?" the calm voice asked.

"I . . . I don't know. It's Lucy Richardson here. I mean, Lucy McNeil. The mayor's . . . wife. I'm at the Ocean Side Hotel."

"How can we help you, Mrs. McNeil?"

The three men slowly pulled the door out of the way. Aunt Joyce and the housekeeper watched, their eyes widening with horror as what lay beneath was revealed. Short gray hair, the back of a head, then the neck and shoulders of a man in a suit and eventually the full body, lying very still.

Aunt Joyce let out a moan, and her legs buckled. She staggered against the wall and would have fallen had not the housekeeper caught her.

"Ambulance," I said into the phone.

Connor dropped to his knees beside the body. He put his fingers on the neck, checking for a pulse. He looked up, caught my eye, and gave his head a slight shake.

"And the police," I said. "He's . . . I'm pretty sure he's dead."

Aunt Joyce pushed the housekeeper aside and took a step forward. "Wayne," she yelled. "What do you think you're doing down there? Get up!"

Chapter Three

"Déjà vu all over again."

"Looks like it," Connor said.

The police, in the person of none other than our friend Butch Greenblatt, responded quickly to my 911 call.

Connor and David had rolled the body over, checking for life signs, but Wayne did not move. He stared up at the ceiling, seeing nothing. He was still dressed in the shirt and pants he'd worn to our wedding, although his jacket and tie were missing.

Once the police arrived, Connor, Kevin, Aunt Joyce, the housekeeper, David, and I were hustled into a meeting room farther down the hallway and told to stay put.

After her brief outburst, Aunt Joyce had stared at the lifeless body on the floor, seemingly in shock. Connor and I had each taken an arm and led her away.

"He's not pretending, is he?" Her voice quavered.

"I'm afraid not," Connor replied.

I'd asked Butch if I could call my mother to take Aunt Joyce to her room to lie down, but my aunt soon recovered and declared that she wanted to stay with us and would talk to the police when needed.

We took seats around the big conference table. Someone had ordered drinks to be provided for us, and coffee, tea, and water were soon brought in. I sipped on a glass of water and held Connor's hand. Butch stood quietly by the door, not saying anything, just watching. Noise from the hallway increased as more police arrived and hotel employees gathered, demanding to know what was going on.

"I need to see to my staff," David said.

"Please wait here, sir," Butch replied. "Detectives will be arriving in a couple minutes."

David poured himself a coffee. He didn't offer to serve anyone else.

"What does that mean?" Kevin asked me. "*Déjà vu*?"

"Nothing," Connor said.

"It means one is experiencing something that may have happened before," Aunt Joyce said. "A familiar feeling. Are you saying you knew Wayne, Lucy?"

"Lucy wasn't saying anything," Connor said.

"That door," I said to David, "had a normal key-operated lock, from what I saw. Is it possible to lock it from the inside without a key?"

"Yes. No reason anyone would ever want to lock it while they're inside, but that's the way it came, I'd guess. Before my time. I haven't been here for long. I hope my staff don't slip into cleaning closets in pairs for some quiet time when they should be working." He glanced at the housekeeper, whose name, I'd finally learned, was Sophia. She stared into the distance and didn't reply.

"The lock can be set and then the door pulled shut," I said. "Meaning a key isn't needed to lock it."

"I guess," he said, without much interest. "Like I said. Before my time, and I didn't install new locks when I arrived. What are you getting at?"

"Nothing," I said.

Connor and I exchanged glances, both of us knowing that this had to have been a murder. Wayne might have locked the door from the inside before dying, for some inexplicable reason, but he hadn't stuffed something into the lock to ensure the key couldn't open it from the outside.

Butch caught my eye and gave me a small nod. He knew what we were thinking, and he agreed with us.

We jumped as the door opened. Detective Sam Watson came in, accompanied by Officer Holly Rankin and a man I didn't know. The last time I'd seen Detective Watson, he'd been showing off his dance moves at my wedding. "Lucy, Connor."

"Good afternoon, Detective," I said. I politely made the introductions. "This is my brother Kevin, and the lady is my aunt Joyce."

Kevin said nothing, but Joyce said, "Didn't I see you at the wedding, Detective? Your wife was in a silver gown. Most attractive, I thought."

"Uh, yeah, thanks," Watson said. "Butch, the forensics people are arriving. Can you see if they need anything?"

"Sure." Butch left, closing the door behind him.

The man who'd come in with Watson studied us all. He was in his late thirties, about six feet tall, thin and rangy with long arms and legs. His dark hair was cut almost to his scalp, and his face was freshly shaven. His brown eyes moved between everyone in the room, and not in a friendly manner. He wore dark jeans and a dark shirt under a black leather jacket. It didn't take much imagination on my part to guess he was a detective.

Watson confirmed my guess. "This is Detective North, newly transferred in to the NHPD. He'll be helping me with this case."

"Pleased to meet y'all." North's accent was pure North Carolina, but his tone indicated he wasn't pleased to meet us in the least.

"Mr. McNeil here," Watson said, "is the mayor of Nags Head. Sorry you two had to meet this way."

Connor stood up and held out his hand to Detective North. The two men shook. "As am I. I'm looking forward to hearing how you like working in Nags Head. Local boy, by the sounds of it. Are you?"

"I'm from Duck originally. Born and raised on OBX."

Connor indicated me. "My wife, Lucy McNeil."

I mumbled some sort of greeting.

"Okay," Watson said. "Let's get on with it. Mrs. McNeil here made the 911 call. Were the rest of you with her when she came upon the scene?"

"Yes," they chorused.

"Are you the hotel manager, sir?"

David extended his hand to Watson. "Dave Willshaw, and yes, I am. All I know about this business is that I knocked down a stuck door and we found some guy in a storage room. I don't know who he was, and I'm positive I've never seen him before."

"Do you also work at this hotel, ma'am?" Watson said to Sophia. "What's your name?"

"Sophia Montclair. I'm a housekeeper here. I was trying to get into the storage closet. The key wouldn't work." She waved her hand to take in the circle of watching faces. "Mr. Willshaw and all these people came to see what was going on."

"Were either of you in the hotel last night? Say, after seven o'clock?"

"No," David said. "I don't work Saturday nights." Sophia shook her head.

"Did you know the dead man?"

More shaking of heads. "Never seen him before," David said. "If he was a guest here, no reason I should have. I don't normally meet with the guests. Not unless they have a complaint." He chuckled. "I guess that guy has a complaint now, wouldn't you say? Sorry. Not funny."

"Ma'am?" Watson asked Sophia.

"I . . . I didn't take a close look, but like Mr. Willshaw, I don't think I've seen him before. If he was a guest here, I wouldn't speak to him unless we passed in the hallway, and even then I scarcely ever look at them."

Watson spoke to Holly Rankin. "Will you take Mr. Willshaw and Ms. Montclair's statements, please. Then they can continue with their day."

David and Sophia needed no excuse to hurry away, both of them giving us suspicious looks over their shoulders as North closed the door behind them and Officer Rankin. North planted his feet far apart, crossed his arms over his chest, and faced us.

Sam Watson was in his fifties, about six feet tall, not an ounce of spare fat on his body, with a thin, square face, nose like a hawk's beak, and intense gray eyes. He let out a sigh. "I had a quick look at the man when I got here. I recognized him from last night. He was a guest at the wedding, right? I didn't speak to him though. I believe he was with you, Mrs. . . . ?"

"Joyce Mary Richardson Gomez Ridley O'Riordan, now plain old Joyce Richardson once again and intending to remain so to last out my days. I'm Lucy's aunt. Her father's sister. The . . . deceased . . . is . . . was Wayne Fortunada."

"Your husband?"

"My boyfriend, for lack of a better word." She'd taken a lace-trimmed handkerchief out of her skirt pocket, but she didn't appear to need it. After the initial shock of finding the body, Joyce had pulled herself together remarkably well, and she shed no tears.

"Where do you and Mr. Fortunada live?" North asked.

"In Manhattan. But not together. I haven't known him for long, Detective. A matter of a couple of weeks. I called him my boyfriend, but he was no more than a temporary companion. A brief fling, if you must. It wouldn't have lasted. I asked him to accompany me to Lucy's wedding on a whim. Some people in my family, my sister-in-law most of all, disapprove of my lifestyle, and I didn't want anyone to feel sorry for me if I showed up alone to the wedding."

"Did you"—Watson cleared his throat—"pay for this companionship?"

Kevin chuckled.

"As I said, some people in my family do not approve of my lifestyle. Isn't that right, Kevin?"

"Whatever you say, Aunt Joyce."

"Ms. Richardson?" Watson prompted.

"You're asking if Wayne was a gigolo? In a way, I suppose you might say that. I paid for all the expenses incurred for this trip, as I did for things we did together since we met. I did not, however, provide him with housing or an income or anything beyond the cost incurred by accompanying me: accommodation, restaurant meals, theater tickets, and the like. I do not, Detective, travel cheap. I am long past that."

"Do you know of anyone, either in Manhattan or here in Nags Head, who might have meant him harm?"

"I do not. I hadn't known him for long, and I have never met any of his friends or family. I will say, however, that I wish I hadn't invited him to the wedding."

"Meaning?"

"He did not appear to be having a good time. Not last night, at any rate. I didn't care if he was having a good time or not—not everyone loves weddings—but I expect not to be embarrassed by my companion's behavior."

"Can you expand on that, please? Was there a specific incident you found embarrassing?"

"To begin at the beginning . . . We arrived in your lovely town on Thursday evening. We're staying here, at this hotel. Friday morning we enjoyed a long walk on the beach, and then we went to tour the Elizabethan gardens. We lunched in Manteo and joined the family that evening for dinner at a restaurant not far from here. Wayne was pleasant company the entire time. His usual charming self. Did you find him so, Lucy?"

I'd thought he'd been trying too hard, but I gave him some credit because it was never easy being the odd one out at a family gathering. I nodded.

"He might have paid more attention to Suzanne than I thought proper, but I let it go. Men do like your mother, don't they, Lucy?"

"I . . . I don't know about that."

"After dinner," Joyce continued, "he and I returned to the hotel and had a few drinks in the bar before retiring. We spoke to no one except the waitress, and that only to place our order. On Saturday we breakfasted here, at the hotel. After that, it was warm enough to lie in the sun by the pool. I didn't go for a swim, but Wayne did. Then we dressed for the wedding, had the doorman summon us a taxi, and we were at the church at three o'clock as ordered. All perfectly normal activities."

"I don't understand," Watson said. "If he was perfectly normal, as you put it, what was embarrassing about that?"

Aunt Joyce stared off into the distance for a few moments. North shifted from one foot to the other, but Watson gave her the time she needed to gather her thoughts. Kevin poured himself a coffee.

"It's hard to describe, Detective," she said, "but I'll do my best. From the time we arrived at the church, his mood abruptly changed."

"In what way?"

"He became out of sorts. Sullen. I dropped my phone when I was making my way to our seats, and he snapped at me. Quite uncharacteristic of him. From that moment on, he was in a foul mood."

"You don't know why the change?"

"He wasn't a religious man, and at first I put it down to him not being comfortable in a church, but the mood didn't end when we left."

"I noticed him at the reception," Connor said. "I even said to Lucy that he didn't seem to be having a good time."

"That he wasn't," Aunt Joyce said. "The bad mood continued into the evening. He didn't eat much of the meal. He drank too much. He barely spoke to our table companions, was morose to the point of rudeness to me. Out-and-out rude to some of the men in my family."

"Guy was a jerk," Kevin said. "I know we're not supposed to speak ill of the dead, but he was. He sat by himself when people were up dancing, drank a lot. I tried to talk to him, and he pretty much told me to get lost. My dad said the same."

After his initial question to Joyce, North said nothing, leaving the questions to Sam Watson. He shifted his feet and his eyes moved constantly, watching us, taking it all in. If he was a newly promoted detective, he was lucky to have been assigned to shadow Sam Watson. Watson had spent twenty years in the NYPD as a homicide detective and had returned to his hometown of Nags Head to finish up his years before retirement. I knew, because his wife, CeeCee, had told me, that retirement was imminent. Imminent in her mind, anyway; she wasn't so sure about her husband's intentions.

"I left the reception early," Joyce said. "I suggested to Wayne that he'd had enough to drink. He didn't take my comment well, and he snapped at me not to be a nag and leave him alone. Although he didn't use such polite words. I didn't want to create a scene, which would have happened if I'd insisted, so I asked Millar to keep an eye on him, and I left."

"Who's Millar?" North asked.

"My brother, father of the bride, Millar Richardson."

"Were you and Mr. Fortunada sharing a room?" Watson asked.

"We were. He did not come to bed. He wasn't there in the morning, and he didn't appear to have come in while I was asleep. I went to brunch with my family by myself and made some excuse about him going for a run on the beach. No one believed me, and I found that far, far more embarrassing than if I'd come to the wedding unaccompanied." She turned to me. "One thing I can say for myself, Lucy, is that I learn by my mistakes. I will not make that one again."

"What did you think had happened to him?" Watson asked. "Did you try to find him?"

"I assumed he'd met a lady and persuaded her to take him home with her. Either that or he'd made a nuisance of himself and spent the night in the drunk tank. I did not try to find him. I don't care to be humiliated." She sighed. "It would appear I was mistaken. Instead of simply embarrassing me, he . . . died."

She was seated across the table from me. I stretched out my arm and held out my hand. She took it in hers and gave me a sad smile.

"Connor, did you notice anything else about this guy?" Watson asked. "Did anyone see when he left the reception?"

Connor and Kevin spoke at the same time. "No."

"I didn't see Aunt Joyce go," Kevin said. "And I can't say I paid any attention to Wayne again. My brothers and my dad and I were just about the last people to leave."

"He wasn't wearing a suit jacket or tie when . . . when we found him," I said. "But he had those on last night. It was a nice suit too." I remembered what I'd heard him say to his unseen companion in the hallway. Something about his *lady friend* picking up the bill.

Watson turned to Officer Rankin. "Check the hotel's lost and found."

She slipped out.

"What about you, Sam?" Connor said. "You remembered him. Did you notice anything in particular about this guy?"

"I noticed a man drinking too much and exchanging harsh words with the woman he was with." The detective nodded at Aunt Joyce. "I noticed Millar Richardson having a quiet and not entirely friendly word with him. I kept a half eye on him, thinking there might be trouble. But that didn't materialize."

"He was still there minutes before Connor and I left," I said.

"Are you sure of the time?" Watson asked.

"Positive. The dessert buffet was due to come out around midnight. Connor and I were ready to go, but I went to the ladies' room first. When I came out, I heard people talking, but I couldn't tell what they were saying. You saw how that hallway takes a bend to the left after the restrooms and the closet?"

"Yes."

"They were there, around the bend. I couldn't see who was speaking, but I could hear the murmur of voices. One was clear, but the other wasn't. I didn't hear much, and then Wayne came around the corner. He looked . . . thoughtful. Maybe even a bit sad. I don't really know. He saw me, said something along the lines of 'Nice wedding,' and walked right past me. He was wearing his suit jacket."

"You didn't see who he'd been talking to?" Watson asked. "Or recognize the other voice?"

"I didn't see anyone, and as for the voice, it was low and the words muffled. That person was likely facing away from my direction. I can't even say if it was a man or a woman."

"Ms. Richardson, do you know who Wayne might have been talking to, or what about?"

"I'd left by midnight," Aunt Joyce said. "Having been embarrassed enough by Wayne, I was no longer in the mood to continue with the party. As far as I know, he wasn't acquainted with any of the people at the wedding, not until this week anyway.

He never said anything that would make me think he'd seen someone he knew."

"He was a heavy smoker, wasn't he, Aunt Joyce?" I said.

"He sure smelled of it," Kevin said.

"He was," Aunt Joyce said. "He slipped away a couple of times for a cigarette, as was his habit, but as I don't smoke myself, I didn't join him."

"Mr. Richardson," Watson asked Kevin, "had you met Mr. Fortunada before this week? You said he was a jerk."

"He acted like a jerk at the wedding; that's all I meant. I'd never set eyes on him before dinner on Friday. He seemed okay then. He didn't drink too much, he didn't talk too much, but he was friendly enough when he did. He was super snobby about the wine Dad ordered, though."

"Wine?"

"Yeah. Dad was paying for the dinner, so he ordered several bottles of wine for the table. Wayne said they were not of the best vintage and couldn't the restaurant provide anything better. My dad, who knows his way around a wine list, brushed him off."

"Wayne considered himself to be a wine connoisseur," Aunt Joyce said. "When someone else was paying, at any rate. I gave him a good solid kick under the table when he made that comment, and he let it go. As he usually did when I told him to behave himself. Which is why his behavior on Saturday was so unexpected."

"Connor? Lucy?" Watson asked.

"Never seen the guy before we met on Friday at Jake's," Connor said.

"Nor had I, Detective," I said. "He was a good-looking man, for his age, and didn't he know it. I would have remembered if I'd met him previously."

Aunt Joyce let go of my hand. "Modesty was not one of Wayne's virtues."

"That name, Fortunada," North said. "It's unusual. Is it his real name?"

"Likely not," Aunt Joyce said. "Wayne was an actor at one time. He had a few minor roles on Broadway, but not for a long time. It's highly possible that's a stage name, but it is the one on his driver's license and passport."

"If he changed his name to Fortunada, I have to assume he didn't read Poe," I said.

"What does that mean?" Watson and North said at the same time.

"The victim in 'The Cask of Amontillado' by Edgar Allan Poe is named Fortunada. He's the one who's bricked up in a wine cellar." I felt a sudden shiver run down my back. Connor noticed, and he laid a warm hand on my arm. North snorted in amusement.

A light knock at the door, and Holly Rankin slipped in. "A suit jacket and tie were left on a chair in the ballroom last night and found by the cleaners this morning. I took a picture."

Watson nodded toward Aunt Joyce, and Rankin showed my aunt the photo.

"That looks like his, yes."

"Thanks," Watson said. "I won't read much into it. As soon as the formalities are over, suit jackets and ties come off awful fast. Lucy, Connor, Mr. Richardson, thank you for your time. Ms. Richardson, I'm going to have to ask you some more questions about Mr. Fortunada's life in Manhattan and what you know about his past."

"I'm happy to help," Aunt Joyce said, "if I can. But I know little to nothing about his past. Ours was not a relationship based on trust or even respect. He told me some stories, mostly about his days on Broadway. I listened intently, nodded enthusiastically at all the right places, and didn't believe a single word he said."

"When do you plan to leave Nags Head?"

"I might stay for a few days and enjoy the hospitality of your lovely town. I have nothing in particular to hurry home for. That had been our original plan, but last night Wayne changed his mind."

"Changed it in what way?" Watson asked.

"He told me last night, as I was leaving the reception, that he'd decided to go back to New York City today. I replied that he could do whatever he wanted."

"Did he say why the change?"

"No. I brushed off what he said at the time, thinking it was just something he said because he'd fallen into a sullen mood. If he went back early, he'd have to pay his own way. I reminded him of that before I left."

"How did he react to that?"

"I didn't remain in his company long enough to notice. But that reminds me of something else. He'd never been to the Outer Banks before. Not anywhere in North Carolina. So he said, anyway. When I first invited him to accompany me to Lucy's wedding, he mentioned that. Which is what made me think spending a few extra days here would be nice."

Connor stood up. He held out his hand, and I took it as I got to my feet. "Would you like me to stay with you?" I asked Aunt Joyce. "I can keep you company while you're talking to the detectives?"

"That won't be necessary, dear. I am, as you can see, quite recovered. It was a shock, yes, but truth be told, I wasn't all that fond of the man to begin with, and I was becoming less so as time passed."

"I'll need to speak to your parents and the rest of your family, Lucy," Watson said. "Can you ask them to remain in the hotel, please? And then, I'm afraid, I'll need a full list of everyone who was at the reception along with their contact information."

"I can get that to you, Sam," Connor said. "I have access to it on my phone."

"Thanks."

Connor opened the door. I hesitated before going through it, and he asked me, "Lucy, have you thought of something?"

"No. Nothing. My mom's not going to be pleased at having to stay in the hotel. She was planning on hitting the outlet shops this afternoon."

But I had thought of something. I needed to call Bertie ASAP and ask her if Eddie had been located.

Chapter Four

"Would you mind going to Mom and Dad's room to fill them in on what's happening?" I asked Connor. "I need to make a quick phone call."

He eyed me suspiciously. "What sort of phone call, and why now?"

I gave him my sweetest smile. "Please? I have to check in with someone, and I'll tell you what I learn if it's significant. Promise."

"Lucy, I—"

"No secrets. This might have nothing to do with what's happened here, and if so, I'll forget about it. Otherwise . . ." My voice trailed off. I'd been involved in police investigations before, although never willingly. Connor thought I took undue risks, so I hadn't always told him what I got up to. I'd promised myself I'd be open and honest with him now that we were married. And I would. But if Eddie had gone on a bar crawl last night after dropping Bertie at her house, and if he decided he didn't want to see her again, that was none of Connor's business. It was none of my business either, but Bertie had called me.

Connor kissed the top of my head. "Okay. I'll meet you in your parents' room. Don't be long."

"I won't."

Bertie answered before the first ring died away. "Lucy?"

I could tell by the strain in her voice she hadn't heard from Eddie. "I'm at the hotel. The Ocean Side. Do you have any news about Eddie?"

"No. I've been calling his number and leaving messages. He doesn't answer, and he doesn't return my calls. I'm starting to get seriously worried, Lucy. I was thinking of coming to the hotel to ask if anyone saw him after he and I left, but I'm hesitant about leaving the house in case he comes here. Would you mind asking around for me? Maybe he . . . couldn't get another taxi and took a room at the hotel."

"I can ask, yes. Something's happened. I don't know if it has anything to do with Eddie, but . . ."

"But? But what?"

"Did you speak to a man named Wayne last night? Wayne Fortunada. Sixtysomething, silver hair, nicely dressed, not bad-looking. He was with my Aunt Joyce, and they were at the table in the back of the room near the kitchen entrance."

She paused before saying, "Not that I recall. Eddie and I mostly spent time with the library group and my other friends from the area."

"Did you notice if Eddie talked to him at all? Or to my aunt Joyce? Did you meet Aunt Joyce?"

"I must have, but I don't remember specifically. Lucy, what does this have to do with Eddie?"

At midday, the lobby was busy. People checking out, a few arriving. Families leaving the restaurant, having finished their Sunday brunch, and others heading out for the day. The police had sealed off the hallway, and more than a few people tried to peer over the yellow tape. The officer guarding the scene politely told them to continue on their way. A couple of preteen boys, all wide eyes and mischievous expressions, lurked behind a potted plant, hoping the cop would turn away and they'd grab the chance to dash past the barrier.

"It might have nothing to do with Eddie, but Bertie, you need to know. This Wayne Fortunada was found dead this morning. Here, at the hotel."

"I'm sorry to hear that, but I don't understand what it has to do with Eddie or me."

"He died from . . . not natural causes. He was left in a storage closet, and the closet door had to be broken down."

"Surely you don't think Eddie had anything to do with that! We're talking about Professor Edward McClanahan here. The most laid-back, absent-minded, mild-mannered man I've ever known."

"Bertie, we have to consider the possibility that Eddie saw something and . . . decided he needed to get away for a while. Detective Watson's on the scene. You need to speak to him."

"I can't report a man missing when it's barely been twelve hours since I last saw him. They'll tell me he's a grown man who doesn't even live with me and if he wanted to leave town without telling me, that's his right."

"I know that. But in light of this recent death, I'm pretty sure Detective Watson will want to be informed."

"I . . . I don't know. Is he, Sam, at the hotel?"

"Yes. He's interviewing people about Wayne." Butch came through the door behind the reception desk. He saw me and gave me a wave as he crossed the lobby floor, heading for the hallway to the business offices. "Hold on a sec, Bertie." I gestured for Butch to join me. "I'm on the phone with Bertie. She seems to have . . . misplaced her friend, Eddie. Edward McClanahan. Can you ask the reception if he took a room?" A small line had formed at the reception desk, and Butch would get seen to a lot faster than I would.

"Sure." He went up to the desk and leaned across it. The woman helping guests check out excused herself and gave him a bright, and not at all fake, smile. He spoke to her; she typed a few words into her computer and gave her head a shake.

Butch turned, glanced at me, gave me a similar shake of the head, and continued on his way. At that moment the elevator pinged, the doors slid open, and a group of teenage girls—short shorts and tight T-shirts or short swirling sundresses, all of them clutching their phones—emerged. As one they gaped at Butch. My friend was a good-looking man, and at six foot five and two hundred pounds, he filled his uniform out very well indeed. He and I had dated for a short while when I first arrived in Nags Head to take the job at the library. We liked each other a great deal, but romantically we simply hadn't clicked. Which was just as well, as he fell in love with Stephanie Stanton the moment he laid eyes on her, and I realized the only man for me was Connor, whom I'd first met when I was fourteen years old.

Oblivious to their stares, Butch exchanged a couple of words with the officer on guard and then slipped past the yellow tape. The girls let out a collective sigh.

I returned my attention to my phone. "Eddie hasn't checked in here. I don't suppose that means much; there are a lot of hotels in this part of Nags Head."

"Will you tell him?" Bertie asked.

"What? Oh, you mean will I speak to Sam. Yes, I can do that, if you want me to, but—"

"Thank you, Lucy. Call me if you learn anything. I'll let you know if . . . when I hear from Eddie." She hung up.

". . . can slap me in handcuffs anytime," one of the girls was saying to her friends as they passed me. The others shrieked with laughter, earning them a disapproving glare from an elderly lady ensconced in a threadbare chair next to the windows overlooking the pool area.

Bertie was right that in most cases the police wouldn't have any interest in searching for a man who'd been at a party the night before and had not shown up at his lady friend's the morning after. But Eddie's disappearance—if not answering his phone after less than twelve hours even counted as a disappearance—could be significant in light of the death of Wayne Fortunada. That Eddie might be involved in the matter was clearly something Bertie didn't want to consider. The police, however, would very much want to consider it.

I sent a quick text to Connor: *Be a few minutes more. If you need to go home I can get a lift*

Connor: *I'll wait*

The elevator pinged once again, and the doors slid open. Olivia and Ashley, two of my friends from when I'd worked at Harvard, stepped out. They'd linked their arms together and were dressed for a day of playing tourist in white jeans, brightly colored T-shirts, and sandals. They spotted me and headed my way.

"I did not expect to see the bride standing in a hotel lobby all alone on her wedding morning," Olivia said.

"Is everything okay, Lucy?" Ashley asked. "You don't look like a blushing bride should on the morning after her wedding. Unless you've got a hangover, I suppose. I guess that's allowed."

I gave them a smile. "I'm perfectly fine. Not even a hangover, just a pleasant glow. Connor and I had brunch with my family, and they went upstairs while I made a quick phone call."

"Whew!" Ashley said. "That's good to know. I was worried for a moment."

"Fabulous wedding," Olivia said. "We had such a great time."

"Speaking of husbands," I asked. "Where are yours?"

"Fishing. Of all the boring things. They went out on a charter first thing. We, on the other hand, lazed in our beds and then met for a room service breakfast complete with a mimosa."

"Or two," Ashley added.

"We're going to work off that breakfast with a walk on the beach. The sun's out, but that water's still too cold for swimming for me. Then we're going for lunch and see what other fun we can get up to."

"We'd love it if you could come with us, Lucy, but we didn't even think to ask. We assumed you had more important things to do today." Ashley gave me a broad wink.

"Thanks," I said. "But I plan to spend the day with . . . my husband."

My friends burst out laughing. "We bet you do, honey. As much as we'd like to stay a while longer, we have to go home tomorrow, and then it's back to work."

They both wrapped me in hugs that I happily returned.

"Now remember, we don't want to be forgotten. Next time you're in Boston to see your folks, give us a call. We'll dump the husbands, and it can be like old times again."

"For sure," I said, meaning it. I'd been losing touch with my Boston friends since moving to the Outer Banks. It had been great to see them again.

They wiggled their fingers at me and skipped off. I watched them go with a pang of regret.

Ashley and Olivia had been right that I had more important things to do than spend a fun day with old friends. But it didn't have anything to do with enjoying the day after my wedding. I needed to speak to the police.

I approached the young officer guarding the hallway. He must be new—I didn't recognize him. "Hi," I said, trying to sound cheerful, but not too cheerful considering the circumstances, and helpful. "I'm Lucy Rich—Lucy McNeil. I was talking to Detective Watson a short while ago, but there's something I forgot to mention. Can I go back in?"

"Let me check." He spoke into his radio.

Butch's deep voice replied, "Send her in."

The officer lifted the yellow tape for me. Farther down the hallway, men and women in white overalls and their equipment were clustered around the storage closet. It would be difficult, I thought, for them to do what they needed to do in that small space. I averted my eyes as I passed.

I went around the bend. Butch was standing at the door of the meeting room as Aunt Joyce left.

"Everything all right, dear?" she asked me.

"Yes, fine. I remembered something, that's all."

She touched my arm lightly as she passed, and Butch and I went into the room. Sam Watson had taken the chair at the head of the conference table, and he was checking his phone. Detective North stood at the window, gazing out onto the parking lot. He didn't turn as I came in.

"Lucy. What's up?" Watson put his phone away.

"I've learned something that might, or might not, be relevant to what happened here."

North turned from the window.

"Go ahead," Watson said.

I took a breath. "Did you talk to Eddie McClanahan last night? Bertie's friend?"

"Briefly. CeeCee wanted to visit with the folks at the library table for a while, so we stopped by after dinner was over. As I recall, I said hi to the guy but not much more."

"Why are you asking?" Detective North asked.

"He's . . . I guess the best word is missing."

"Missing?" the detectives chorused.

"Missing?" Butch said. "What does that mean?"

"Bertie—that's my boss," I explained to the new detective. "Albertina James. The director of the Bodie Island Lighthouse Library."

"You're a librarian?" North didn't look impressed. A lot of people don't. Librarians still have a certain reputation.

"Yes, I am. Bertie called me this morning to say Eddie hadn't come home—to her house, I mean. He doesn't live there."

A spark of interest lit up Detective North's face. "Is that so?" he said slowly.

"She doesn't know where he is?" Watson asked.

I shook my head. "She's been calling him, but no answer."

"Why are you telling us this and not her?" North asked.

"Because I happen to be here, and she isn't. She doesn't want to leave the house in case he arrives when she's out."

"I'm well acquainted with Ms. James," Watson said to North. "She's not a fanciful woman."

"Seems to me you're too well acquainted with this bunch," North muttered.

Butch caught my eye. Neither of us said anything.

"Step back a minute here, Mrs. McNeil," North said. "Considering I wasn't invited to this party, I want to be sure I follow. This McClanahan guy was at the wedding reception at this hotel last night, and he hasn't been seen since."

"So I've been told," I said.

"Did Bertie say what time they left last night?" Watson asked. "Did she say anything about Mr. Fortunada?"

I told him everything Bertie had told me, adding, "Eddie's in his late fifties, Detective North, a professor of languages at Blacklock College in Elizabeth City. He's not the sort to decide to go barhopping late at night. In my opinion, anyway, for what that's worth."

"It's worth a lot, Lucy," Watson said.

North didn't look so sure, but he said nothing.

"Okay. I'll give Bertie a call later," Watson said. "If you hear from her, let me know right away."

"I will."

"Connor sent me a copy of your guest list, and I've got officers making calls to the people on it as well as hotel staff working the reception. Maybe someone saw something. In the meantime, I want to talk to your family next." He stood up. "You might as well come with us."

"Why?" North asked.

"Why what?" Watson said.

"Why are you going to them? Tell them to come here."

Watson's face tightened, only slightly but I saw it. Butch and I exchanged another glance. "I know the Richardson family personally, and I'm willing to extend them this courtesy. I trust that's all right with you, *Detective*."

"Just askin'." North brushed past me on his way out the door. Butch followed, but I hesitated.

"Lucy?" Watson asked.

"Are you sure . . . I mean, are you sure it was murder?"

"No doubt about it," he said in a low voice. "And not only because of the disabled lock. Wayne Fortunada was strangled."

I dipped my head.

"Detective?" North called.

"Coming," Watson said.

* * *

We found Connor and my mother and father in my parents' suite. Aunt Joyce was there, as were all three of my brothers, Kevin, Luke, and Lloyd, Luke's wife Barbara, and Lloyd's wife MaryBeth. Lloyd, who'd missed the brunch because he was hungover, still didn't look all that well. His eyes were red and his skin had an unpleasant greenish tinge. I assumed he'd only joined us because he'd been summoned by Dad. MaryBeth wore a floor-length beach wrap over her bathing suit and didn't look in the least pleased at missing her pool time.

A tray on the sideboard held a silver carafe of coffee along with a cream pitcher, sugar bowl, and several mugs. Aunt Joyce was squeezed between my mother and Barbara on the sofa, cradling a glass of wine. Kevin had helped himself to a beer from the bar fridge. MaryBeth and Dad sipped orange juice. Mom and Barbara had coffee, and Lloyd gulped water. Dad sat in the chair in front of the desk, Connor stood by the window, and Luke and Kevin paced the room. Lloyd huddled in an armchair.

"Detective Watson." My mother rose from the sofa in one fluid movement. She'd dressed for brunch in wide-legged white linen pants and a blue silk shirt. A silver necklace hung almost to her waist, and long silver earrings dangled from her ears. Her artfully highlighted blonde hair, a few traces of silver showing, was tied behind her head in a loose chignon. She was, as usual, the very picture of old-money grace and elegance. Her Nags Head fishing family roots had been abandoned long, long ago. "I believe I said last night that it's always a pleasure to see you, but I regret these circumstances have brought you here today. I did enjoy meeting your lovely wife at the party. Please give her my regards." My mom sounded as though she were welcoming guests to a garden party.

"I will," Watson said. "Sorry to interrupt your day like this. I appreciate y'all taking the time to meet with me."

"We'll do what we can to help, Detective," my dad said. "I won't offer you a beer, as you're on duty." He waved his glass in the direction of the sideboard. "But we have coffee and juice."

"Not for me, thanks. You know Officer Greenblatt. This is Detective North. He's newly arrived in Nags Head, and he'll be helping me with this case."

The men grunted greetings.

"I heard on the radio you had a robbery in town on Saturday," Dad said. "No arrests yet, the report said. That must be keeping you busy."

"We can handle two cases at once," North snapped.

My father was a corporate lawyer, head of a huge firm. He spent little or no time in a courtroom these days, but the look he gave the younger detective was well practiced to put rookie cops firmly in their place.

North glanced to one side and said no more while Watson took the lead on asking the questions.

My family couldn't add much to what had previously been said about Wayne Fortunada. No one, other than Aunt Joyce, had met him prior to the rehearsal dinner on Friday night. As no one knew him, they couldn't say if he'd been acting out of character on Saturday. The edges of my mother's perfectly lipsticked mouth might have turned up when she referred to him as Joyce's "close companion," in response to which Joyce simply poured herself another glass of wine.

"You had words with him, Mom," I said. "Not long before Connor and I left. What was that about?"

"I'd hardly call that brief exchange having words." She sniffed. "I mentioned to Joyce, in his presence, that an open bar doesn't always require guests to take full advantage."

"What did he say to that?" Watson asked.

"Nothing. The man was in a strange mood last night. Not combative or argumentative, yet not friendly either. I'd say he was thoughtful, wrapped within himself. I said my piece and left him and Joyce to enjoy the remainder of their evening."

"Wayne drank a lot, I'll agree," Aunt Joyce said. "I admit to not knowing him well, but he was never, in my presence anyway, an angry drunk. He was the sort whose inhibitions were loosened by drink, and he'd want to make lifelong friends with everyone he met."

"But not last night?" Watson said.

"Definitely not last night."

"I sat next to him at dinner on Friday," Barbara said. "We had a long, pleasant chat. I enjoyed his company. At the reception on Saturday, Joyce disappeared somewhere, and Wayne was left by himself at their table."

"I didn't disappear, dear," Aunt Joyce said. "I was being friendly and enjoying the party."

"I didn't mean disappear as in vanish. All I meant was you'd left him alone."

"And . . . ?" Watson prompted.

"I asked him if he'd like a dance, but he said no, so abruptly it verged on rude."

"You have no idea why the change between Friday and Saturday?"

"Not in the least. Like I said, we sat together at dinner on Friday, and I thought he was interesting. We had a great talk. He was a singer and a dancer, and he'd been in lots of big Broadway productions. I was a theater major in college. I gave up the bright lights and greasepaint when I married Luke. I always intended to go back to it, but then . . . well, I had the kids and life happened. Anyway, he, Wayne, had had some big parts once—not so much lately, he told me, as age crept up on him. Is that right, Aunt Joyce?"

"Big parts, no. He'd been in the chorus a few times, in a handful of major musicals. He had the looks for the front row but only a moderate amount of talent. He hasn't had a role in years. These days he hangs around the outskirts of the old crowd, always nattering on about their glory days. I told you this, Detective."

"We'll be following up with his contacts in New York City," Watson said.

"I wondered if he was ill Saturday evening," Barbara said. "I asked him if he was okay, and he snapped yes. That was the end of that, so I left him to it and went to find more amiable companionship. Sorry, Aunt Joyce."

"I told the police Wayne and I had come to a parting of the ways." Aunt Joyce chuckled. "By one means or another."

My father gave her a disapproving stare. She waggled her eyebrows at him and lifted her glass in a salute. The intensity of his stare increased. He was telling her it was never a good idea to make jokes or to be appearing to take these things lightly. But, as the family always said, Aunt Joyce did things her own way, regardless of the consequences.

"Lucy, any further comments?" Watson asked.

"I can't say much about him," I said. "I spoke to him briefly on Friday, and he was friendly enough, but I didn't sit near him at dinner, so we didn't talk much. Now that I'm thinking of it, I don't think I spoke to him at all yesterday. He didn't even offer me his best wishes, not until he passed me in the hallway around midnight. That is sort of unusual, isn't it? To not say anything to the bride at a wedding you've been invited to."

"Might be because he couldn't get the chance. You didn't sit down all night," Connor said with a smile.

"Did you speak to him, Connor?" Watson asked.

"No, I didn't. Can't say I even noticed the man, not after dinner was served."

"He was," my mother said, "seated at the far side of the room."

"Ah, yes," Aunt Joyce muttered. "The outcast table."

"You might want to have a word with Kristen," my brother Kevin said.

"Kristen?" Watson said.

"Kristen ex-Richardson. My wife, soon to be my ex-wife, and not a moment too soon."

"We'll be getting in touch with all the wedding guests. Is there a particular reason you think your wife might know something?"

"She brought her own fancy man." Kevin rummaged in the small fridge for another beer. "She shouldn't have come to this shindig in the first place. It's not as though she and Lucy had been fast friends, is it, Luce?"

I said nothing. I'd never been able to stand Kristen, but that was irrelevant. I didn't get on all that well with any of my brothers' wives. Social climbers, the lot of them, as far as I was concerned. Kristen in particular—so I'd been told—had lunched out for months on the juicy details of how I'd humiliated Ricky Lewiston, son of my father's law partner, and disgraced my family when I abandoned Ricky, left him on bended knee midproposal in full view of everyone in a busy restaurant, and fled Boston in the middle of the night. That wasn't true—I'd waited until the next morning before packing up my Yaris and fleeing Boston for the arms of my aunt Ellen and my beloved OBX and eventually a job at the Lighthouse Library.

All of which was neither here nor there. That Kristen didn't like me, and I didn't like her, didn't make her a murderer.

"She and her date—I'd use another word, but my mother is present—" Kevin began.

"Don't mind me," Mom said.

MaryBeth laughed.

"—were seated at Aunt Joyce's table," Kevin continued. "The table for the not-quite-respectable Richardsons and their various hangers-on."

"Careful, son," my dad warned.

Aunt Joyce lifted her glass toward him. "Respectability, Millar, is a goal I gave up many long years ago."

"So I see," Dad said. Mom caught his eye and gave her head a sharp shake of warning.

"Okay," Watson said. "I'll talk to this lady and her friend. Anyone know what room they're in?"

"Three ten," Kevin said.

My mother gave him a look.

"Keep your friends close and your enemies closer, isn't that what they say?"

"Anything else you think I need to know?" Watson asked.

My family shook their heads.

"When are y'all planning to leave Nags Head?" Detective North asked.

"My wife and I are going home Tuesday morning," Dad said.

"First thing tomorrow," Lloyd said, from the depths of his chair.

"Barbara and I are continuing on down to Florida," Luke said. "The plan's to leave tomorrow morning, first thing. Barbara's parents live in Jacksonville, and we thought as long as we were coming this way, we'd go there for a few days."

"You, sir?" Watson asked Kevin.

"I have no concrete plans. I told my office I'd be out of state for most of the week, but I'm on call if anything comes up. I thought I might hang around a bit, enjoy the sea air."

"You don't get sea air in Boston?" North asked.

"Different sea air."

"I hope," my mother said, "your plans have nothing to do with Kristen's."

"Kristen? Is she staying on? I don't know anything about that. Although I do know she doesn't have a job to go back to. Things being somewhat uncomfortable around the office these days."

"You have two children to think of," my mother said.

"Let's not talk about this right now, Mom," I said. "Detective Watson, is there anything else we can help you with?"

"What are your plans, Ms. Richardson?" Watson asked Aunt Joyce.

She waved her wine glass in the air. "My original intention was for Wayne and me to stay on for a few days, see the sights, enjoy the sea air, as Kevin put it. I have my room booked in this hotel until the end of the week. I'll decide later how I feel, but at the moment I expect I'll stick to that plan. As there's apparently no one else to take care of it, I'll do what I can to help with Wayne's . . . arrangements. Shall I assume you'll be holding the body for a while?"

"For now," Watson said. "I'll let you know when I know more."

"Can y'all give Officer Greenblatt here your contact information," North said.

Everyone mumbled some sort of agreement.

"One more thing," North said. "Did any of you speak to a Mr. McClanahan last night? Eddie, I think's his name. Edward McClanahan."

"I did," Connor said. "He came with Bertie, from the library."

"Not that I recall," said Dad. "Hard to remember who I spoke to. So many people."

"You've met him before, dear," Mom said. "He came with Bertie to Lucy's engagement party. We spoke briefly at the reception, but no more than passing greetings. He's around our age. A university professor, for all that the man resembles an unmade bed."

"Why are you asking about him?" Dad said.

"Did he seem to be concerned about anything last night?" North asked.

"Concerned? I can't say." Mom's face crinkled in thought. "Bertie and he extended their congratulations, and we had a few moments of aimless chitchat, as one does. Come to think of it, I don't know that he and I exchanged any words beyond 'Pleased to see you.' Bertie did all the talking. I thought him taciturn."

That didn't sound like Eddie. He didn't go in for a lot of small talk, but he was friendly enough. Particularly, I'd have thought, to a woman like my mother, who as a consummate hostess always managed to make people believe she was simply dying to hear all about them. Eddie loved nothing more than to talk about his work. That not a lot of people were interested in the sentence structure of Ancient Greek or the Latin origins of many of the words we use today had never occurred to him.

"Anyone else talk to this McClanahan guy?" North asked.

My brothers and sisters-in-law all muttered something along the lines of "No."

"Why are you asking about him?" Connor said. "Surely you don't think Eddie had anything to do with this?"

"I'll fill you in later," I whispered.

"I do not like the sound of that," he replied.

"Thank you for your time," Watson said. "If you can think of anything at all, please get in touch."

"We will," my dad said.

Butch opened the door, and the police left. I hadn't taken a seat, and I edged toward the door. Connor threw me a look I pretended not to notice.

"This Eddie guy concerns me," I heard North say.

"Yeah," Watson agreed. "We need to find him. It's time to split up. I'll pay a call on Bertie James while you speak to Kristen Richardson and her friend."

"Better if I take the professor guy."

"No," Watson said. "I know Bertie."

"That's why I should talk to her. You're too close to these people."

"This is my case, North. I'll run it my way. After you've spoken to Kristen, you and Butch check in with the forensic people. We'll meet up here later. In the meantime, what's happening with that robbery?"

"It appears to have been strictly an amateur effort, and he'll be anxious to dump the goods fast. I've sent descriptions of the items taken to secondhand jewelry stores, antique dealers, et cetera. We'll get him soon enough."

"Keep me posted." Watson walked away.

North turned to speak to Butch and caught me eavesdropping. The look he gave me was not friendly.

Chapter Five

Before Connor and I bought a house together, I lived in a tiny apartment on the fourth floor of the lighthouse, which I called my Lighthouse Aerie. One of the things I loved most over those years was being alone in the library at night. I never felt as though I was alone: I was surrounded by centuries of great minds and beloved fictional characters. I love living in the beach house with Connor, but I miss the comfort of the library sometimes. Today, I'd been the first to arrive at work, and I was able to recapture a tiny portion of that feeling as I let myself in, freed Charles from his cat carrier, and began switching on lights, watched over by the silent shelves of books. I refrained from calling out a cheerful good-morning to them as I went into the break room to get the coffee on, put my purse away, and charge up the library's Wi-Fi. I was switching on the computer at the circulation desk, and Charles was settling himself into the comfortable wingback chair in the magazine nook for the first of the day's naps, when I heard footsteps skipping down the spiral iron staircase that twists upwards to the additional floors of the library, beyond that to the Lighthouse Aerie, and then to the thousand-watt light at the top of the tower itself. Although it's now been repurposed as a library, the Bodie Island

Lighthouse is still a fully functioning lighthouse. The great first-order Fresnel lens flashes all through the night in its regular rhythm of 2.5 seconds on, 2.5 seconds off, 2.5 seconds on, and 22.5 seconds off, guiding ships through the Graveyard of the Atlantic as it has for so many years. When I moved out, Louise Jane couldn't move in fast enough.

Charles opened one eye, saw it was only Louise Jane, and returned to his nap.

This morning her eyes were wide with excitement as she leapt off the bottom step and skipped across the room toward the circulation desk. She'd had a visit yesterday from the police, she told me, but for once she wasn't interested in drawing out every detail of the investigation from me. "That new detective, Kyle something—I don't suppose you know if he's married, Lucy?"

"I didn't think to ask. He doesn't wear a wedding ring. His name's Kyle North."

"Some men don't. Wear a wedding ring, I mean. More's the pity. They should be forced to wear a sign around their necks warning unattached women to stay clear."

"Good morning, all." Denise came in, carrying her ever-present laden briefcase. "It's going to be a lovely day. Lucy, words cannot express what a marvelous time I had on Saturday. One of the best weddings I've been to in years. I loved meeting your family. Your father's such a charmer. Louise Jane, I want to get that response to Duke finished and sent off today." Denise was our academic and research librarian. She worked part-time, and Louise Jane was her assistant.

"Yes, yes," Louise Jane said. "Won't be a minute. This is important. Did the police speak to you yesterday, Denise?"

"A uniformed officer came to my house to ask some questions about something that happened at the hotel. I heard on the news they'd found a man dead at the Ocean Side yesterday, and the police were investigating. I hope that wasn't anyone you were close to, Lucy."

"He was a guest at the wedding, but only because he came with my aunt. I'd never met him before."

Louise Jane laughed. "Denise got a uniform. Ha! I got the new detective."

"I don't think that's a one-up, Louise Jane," I said. "Maybe they sent a detective because they suspect you're guilty."

"Most amusing. Anyway, I couldn't help them, much as I'd have liked to. Kyle—that is, Detective North—showed me a picture and asked what I knew about the man in it." She shrugged. "I knew nothing, and I told him so. You had, what? A hundred people at your wedding? I didn't speak to most of them."

"I'm so sorry this happened to you, Lucy," Denise said. "Louise Jane should be sorry also, rather than looking at it as an opportunity to get a date."

"I am sorry," Louise Jane said. "I can think two things at once, you know."

"Right now you should be thinking about those maps Duke wants."

"I can think three things at once," Louise Jane said.

Denise hid a smile. Louise Jane wasn't exactly a model employee. She took her assigned hours as more of a suggestion, decided what she wanted to work on and what she didn't, and was straining at the bit to be allowed to take her research in unauthorized paranormal directions. But she was passionately devoted to Outer Banks history, knew just about everyone belonging to the old-time families (and was related to just about everyone), and when she did (finally) get down to doing her duties as assigned, her work was exceptional. Or so I'd once overheard Denise telling Bertie.

"Bertie told me Lucy had a habit of getting herself involved in police business," Denise said. "I didn't realize that meant at your wedding too."

"It didn't disrupt my wedding at all, thank heavens. And unlike that last time, I didn't discover a body in my own house, so there's that. I'm only sorry the police had to disturb the Sunday of our guests."

"Added a spark of interest to my day," Denise said.

"What did you tell them?" I asked.

"I recognized the man from the picture the officer showed me, but I hadn't spoken to him. He was with your aunt, and I thought there seemed to be some tension between them, but I couldn't add anything more." She sucked in a breath. "Your aunt. I hope they're not thinking—"

"No, they're not. He was alive and well when Aunt Joyce retired to her room." No reason Aunt Joyce couldn't have returned to the ballroom, of course, but I decided not to consider that. Not yet, anyway.

"Glad to hear it," Denise said.

The next person to come in was our boss, Bertie James. She's a part owner of and part-time instructor at a yoga studio in town. She leads classes on Monday mornings, so it wasn't unusual for her to arrive at work after the library had opened. What was unusual was the drawn expression on her face and the darkness behind her eyes. I could immediately tell she hadn't heard from Eddie. "Good morning, all," she said.

"Morning," we chorused. Charles roused himself and jumped onto the circulation desk. Bertie gave him an absent-minded pat, and he rubbed himself against her arm. Charles always seems to know when people need comforting.

"Is everything okay?" Denise asked. "You don't look too well, Bertie."

"I'm fine. Tired. I had two classes this morning. Increasingly, that takes a lot out of me. I'm not getting any younger."

"So say we all. Come on, Louise Jane," Denise said. "Let's get to work."

"*I owe, I owe. It's off to work I go,*" Louise Jane sang as she ran lightly up the stairs.

"I do not know," Bertie said to me as she watched them go, "where she gets that energy. Louise Jane's not getting any younger either."

"I assume you've had no word from Eddie."

"Nothing. I keep phoning, but no answer. He has no classes until Wednesday, so there's no point in phoning Blacklock to ask if he's come to work."

"Did Sam Watson call on you yesterday?"

"Yes. He didn't come right out and say it, but I could tell he thinks it suspicious that Eddie disappeared around the same time that man was killed. The other detective, the new guy, dropped by last night with the same questions, but I had nothing to tell either of them. Charles, did I not say good-morning to you? My apologies. Good morning." She gave him a rub on the head, and the big cat purred.

The library was empty at this time on a Monday morning. It was a lovely spring day, full of the promise of summer to come, and we had no children's programs scheduled, so I expected it would be quiet all day.

"I'm so dreadfully worried, Lucy," Bertie said. "Not that Eddie killed a man, as the police seemed to be suggesting, but that he . . . got in someone's way and . . . had to run away."

"Surely you don't think Watson suspects Eddie?"

"Sam? No, he seemed more concerned that Eddie might have seen something he shouldn't. Which is what has me worried. The new detective—he was, shall we say, blunter. Questions as to if Eddie had a police record or a history of violence."

Bertie shook her head. "Nothing, I told him, could be more unlike the man I know."

"Eddie is, as you yourself have said many times, something of a scatterbrain. It's possible he decided to leave early and didn't want to bother you."

"It's possible, Lucy. Anything's possible. He left the clothes he'd brought for the weekend at my house, but possessions, to Eddie, are always an afterthought. It's entirely possible someone spoke to him in Latin Saturday night and an entirely new line of research opened up for him on his new book. He's having trouble with that book." She gave me a smile so weak it broke my heart. "I don't suppose anyone in your or Connor's families speaks Latin or Ancient Greek?"

"Not that I know of. Then again, my mom can surprise me sometimes. Eddie told you he wanted to go back for his tie. Did you tell Sam that?"

"I did. He checked with the lost and found at the hotel, but it hadn't been turned in."

"Did you and Eddie spend any time at the party with the man who died?"

"Sam showed me a picture of him. I didn't speak to him at all, although I had noticed him. Nicely dressed, well groomed, reasonably good-looking. He spent most of the time just sitting at their table, drinking. Your aunt didn't seem pleased about that. Sam said his name was Wayne Fortunada. I'd never heard of him, and that's such an odd name I would have remembered if I had."

"Likely his stage name. He used to be a singer and had some minor roles on Broadway."

"Nothing to do with Eddie's or my world. It's been years, decades, since I was last in New York City. Same for Eddie, far as I know. He lived in New York for a short while, but that was a long, long time ago. He got his master's degree from Columbia, but I can't see him having had any interest in hanging around the theaters."

"Did you happen to notice if Eddie spent any time with Wayne? Maybe he saw something or overheard something and had to . . . get away."

"Not so I noticed. Then again, I was having such a good time. It was a marvelous wedding, Lucy, and I'm sorry if I forgot to say so. I haven't danced so much in years."

"Sounds like everyone else," I said.

"Eddie's not much of a dancer, never has been, but he usually can be persuaded to take a few turns around the floor. Ronald and Teddy and even Connor and your dad stepped in when they saw me unpartnered. Eddie wasn't feeling well that night, I think I told you that?"

"You did. That's why you left early, right? Maybe he felt ill and went to the hospital. Did you call around?"

"I did. Nothing."

"That's good, Bertie. That he's not in the hospital, I mean. What about contacting his family to see if they've heard from him?"

"His parents are dead. He has a sister in California, but she's married, and I don't know her last name. Her first name's Jane. Not much to go on, I'm afraid. When Eddie and I did things together, he always came here. I don't know his friends at the college, or even if he has any. No one he's particularly close to, at any rate."

"Dare I mention Professors McArthur and Hoskins?"

"Eddie's nemeses. Is that a word? What's the plural of nemesis?"

"I've no idea."

"If they have him, they have him locked up in a deep, dark dungeon somewhere in the manner of *The Count of Monte Cristo*. How's that book working out for the book club?"

"It's not. No one has the time to read it. Except Theodore and he reluctantly admitted to me that he's struggling. We've chosen Poe instead. 'The Cask of Amontillado' and—"

I broke off at the look on Bertie's face. She'd tried to make a joke about *The Count of Monte Cristo*, but mention of Poe's tale of revenge and kidnapping had been a step too far.

"I'll be in my office most of the day." She walked slowly away, looking so defeated. Poor Bertie. Charles followed her. He might not be able to stop Bertie from worrying, but he'd do his best to offer her comfort.

Bertie and Eddie had met when they were both graduate students. She'd finally broken off with him when, one time too many, he'd forgotten plans they'd made in the furor of a new linguistic discovery. They'd reconnected a couple of years ago when Bertie and I went to Blacklock College in pursuit of a clue regarding a murder that had happened here, at the library.

They'd both mellowed a lot since their college years, and she'd told me, with a laugh, that this time she fully knew what she was getting into with Professor McClanahan. She had to be concerned that either he'd come to harm on Saturday night or he'd spontaneously left town without considering her feelings.

"Mrs. McNeil! What on earth are you doing here?" I was startled out of my thoughts by the arrival of a patron. She dropped a stack of books onto the returns cart and wagged her finger at me. "I'd have thought you'd be sunning yourself on a beach somewhere or enjoying the great museums of Europe. Not working!"

I smiled at her. "The honeymoon has been temporarily postponed. Connor and I are going to Paris next month."

"Paris. How marvelous. I'm relieved to hear that. How was the wedding, dear?"

"Fabulous."

"I'm glad." She headed toward the stacks.

* * *

Our house boasts a spacious garage, but it's still packed to the rafters with construction supplies and equipment, leaving no room for cars. Connor's BMW was in the driveway when I got home, and I pulled my teal Yaris next to it. I turned off the engine but made no move to get out. I liked to sit here and enjoy a moment of quiet and simply admire the house. My house. Our house. Although the quiet was only temporary, as Charles howled from the cat carrier in the back seat, reminding me he was trapped inside.

The house is almost a hundred years old and is what in Nags Head is called one of the "unpainted aristocracy," so named because the time- and weather-worn shingles are not painted. The house is built on stilts, being right on the beach, with two levels, numerous entrances, outdoor staircases, and a porch that wraps around three sides.

It had long been Connor's dream to own such an important part of Outer Banks history, but these properties don't come up for sale often, and when they do, they are not going cheap. We got a deal because the house hadn't been lived in for fifteen years, and although the owners kept an eye on it, they did only critically necessary repairs, and it needed a lot of work to be habitable once again. Connor's dad, restless in his retirement, leapt eagerly into the task, and Connor worked alongside him all the previous winter as his schedule permitted. I was incredibly proud of what they'd done. The upstairs was still sealed off—it would be the last section to be renovated—but we had a gorgeous, spacious home with a deck that opened directly onto the beach and fabulous sea views. The McNeil men had done a superb job of maintaining the historic charm of the house while updating it with modern touches, including ripping down the non-load-bearing walls between the kitchen, dining room, and living room to open the space up to the gorgeous ocean light.

I pulled myself away from admiring my house, got Charles out of the back seat, and climbed the side stairs to let us in through the kitchen door. Just about the last thing I felt like doing after a day at work following a whirlwind weekend was have dinner with my family, but Mom and Dad were going home tomorrow, and so Aunt Ellen had invited us all to the beach house.

I put the cat carrier on the island and opened the door. Charles shot out, flew across the room, landed nimbly on the floor, and disappeared around a corner. Poor Charles. He hated the cat carrier, but he knew that if he was to come to work with me every day, he had to travel safely in the car. Charles—named in honor of Mr. Dickens—had proudly served as library cat since before I got the job. When I moved into the Lighthouse Aerie, he'd followed me upstairs one night and settled in. When I moved out, he'd simply followed me once again. Now he lived here, with Connor and me, but he still had his job to do.

"Are you ready to go?" I called.

"Do we have to?" came a plaintive voice from the dining room.

I peered over the countertop. "I suppose we can come up with some excuse."

Connor was seated at the dining room table, laptop open in front of him, papers scattered across the surface. The table, handmade of red oak, extendable to seat twelve, had been our wedding gift from my parents. He was dressed in the suit he'd put on this morning, but his jacket was draped over the back of the chair, his tie lay crumpled on the table, and the top button of the shirt was undone. "Probably not the best way to start life as Suzanne Wyatt Richardson's only son-in-law."

"You got that right." I went into the dining room and picked a sheet of paper off the floor and put it on top of a pile. "We're due there at six. I'm going to have a shower and change."

He looked up from the screen in front of him and gave me a smile that had my toes tingling.

"What?" I asked.

"Nothing. I'm happy you're home. I'm happy this is our home. I'm happy you're my wife and I am your husband."

I kissed him lightly. "I'm happy about all those things too. I'd like to say everything in our life is perfect, but I'm worried about Bertie."

"Still no word from Eddie, then?"

"Nothing."

He took his hands off the keyboard and focused his attention on me. "What do you think happened, Lucy?"

"I have no idea. I don't know much, if anything, about his personal life. Did someone follow him here, to the Outer Banks, and persuade him to leave for reasons unknown? Did he see who killed Wayne Fortunada and have to run for his life? Does he care so little about Bertie that it wouldn't cross his mind to tell her he was leaving town early?"

"None of those are good options."

"No. I've been racking my brains all day, trying to remember what happened Saturday night. If I saw anything. It's all such a blur. So many people, every one of them wanting to talk to me. To us. To dance with us and wish us well. Toast after toast."

Connor took my hand and guided me to a seat on his lap. I snuggled in comfortably. "I don't know Eddie well . . ."

"None of us do," I said.

"True. I joined the group at the library table for a while, not long before we left. I don't remember Eddie saying much at all, if anything. Bertie and Denise were up dancing, but Ronald and

Nan were sitting that one out. They had the chairs across from me. Eddie was on one side of me, Louise Jane on the other. Louise Jane wants the town to give the library a grant for a research project she's proposing."

"She did not try to talk to you about work at our wedding!"

"You know Louise Jane. Subtle is not her strong suit. She did. That's why I didn't stay long at the library table. I thought she was going to whip out her written proposal, along with all the accompanying documentation, on the spot. As for Eddie . . . I didn't think he looked all that well, and I told Sam that. A bit gray around the gills, so to speak. I didn't notice him drinking an excessive amount. Did he?"

"Bertie said no. He's not much of a drinker. He's a big dessert lover, though, and when he said he wanted to leave before Josie's pecan squares arrived, Bertie thought he must have been feeling mighty sick."

"As for Wayne . . . I talked to him for a while at dinner on Friday. He seemed nice enough, apart from needling your dad over his choice of wine."

"Which, considering Dad was paying, was rather out of line."

"I didn't get the impression he was trying to be rude. Just taking the opportunity to show off his knowledge and not realizing it was inappropriate under the circumstances. We chatted for a while, but he said nothing I could tell the police. Former Broadway star, or so he said, now enjoying his time as a"—Connor made quotation marks in the air—"'patron of the arts.'"

"Meaning scrounging off rich divorced women like Aunt Joyce."

"Who has never pretended their relationship was anything more lofty. As I said, nice enough guy on Friday. Sullen, morose, verging on rude on Saturday."

"Something happened to him between dinner Friday and our wedding on Saturday. Aunt Joyce said he turned moody when they arrived at the church."

"Or he was playing a part—stage background, remember—on Friday, and on Saturday he reverted to type and didn't want to pretend anymore."

"Aunt Joyce says—"

Connor held up a hand to interrupt me. "For all your aunt wants everyone to believe she had no emotional connection to the man, she's not exactly a disinterested party."

"True enough." Reluctantly, I jumped off Connor's lap. "If we don't want any snide insinuations as to why we're late, I need to get ready. Half an hour?"

I glanced through the dining room windows as I left the room, wondering what to wear. The sky was clear and the ocean calm, so we'd probably sit outside for dinner. It could get chilly when the sun went down, particularly if a breeze came up, so I decided on slim-legged white pants and a patterned blouse under a blue denim jacket.

Charles appeared out of nowhere and followed me to the bedroom.

* * *

As expected, Aunt Ellen had laid the glass-topped table on the deck next to the kitchen for dinner. Besides my parents, she'd invited Kevin and Aunt Joyce. Luke and Barbara as well as Lloyd and MaryBeth had left Nags Head this morning. Josie bowed out, saying she was simply too tired, and Jake had to work. Gloria was still staying at the beach house.

Uncle Amos answered the door. He gave me a big hug and Connor a hearty slap on the back. "The guests of honor. Welcome. I'd ask how married life is treating you, but I don't have to. It's written all over Lucy's pretty face."

I blushed to the roots of my hair, and Connor laughed. "Is that decades of courtroom experience talking, Amos?"

"Can't say I ever saw such happy faces in court. Come on in. It's a nice night, and we're sitting out."

We followed Amos up the stairs to the main level and then the sound of voices through the comfortably furnished house. "Go on out, you two," Uncle Amos said. "Make yourselves comfortable. What can I get you?"

"I'll have a beer, thanks," Connor said.

"Just tea for me, please," I said. "It's my turn to drive tonight."

We settled ourselves around the big table, the focus of many a family gathering, already set with cocktail napkins, a breadbasket, and a rustic wooden platter bearing an arrangement of cheeses, pâté, thinly sliced salami, and olives. The lid was up on the big grill in the corner of the deck, cooking implements laid out next to it.

Gulls swooped overhead, and at the ocean's edge, sandpipers darted in and out of the surf. No one was in the water, but a few people were enjoying an evening stroll, and a handful of fishermen had settled into their camp chairs, coolers close by, the long poles arching into the water.

We exchanged greetings with everyone, accepted frosty glasses from Uncle Amos, and took our seats.

"Any recent news from the police, Lucy?" Dad asked me.

"I didn't hear from them today. Did you?"

"No. I saw Sam Watson at the hotel earlier, but he didn't speak to me."

"And thank heavens for that," Mom said. "Your Detective Watson is a nice enough man, but we don't need to be involved in his professional affairs."

"Be that as it may," Aunt Joyce said, "someone killed Wayne. I might have decided to have nothing more to do with the man, but I didn't intend for it to end that way. I have to say, I don't care for that younger detective. Yesterday he just about came right out and accused me of killing him."

"That's a reasonable assumption," Gloria said. "You are obviously the prime suspect."

"I am not!" Joyce bristled. "That's a preposterous allegation. I had nothing to gain by his death."

"I'm not accusing you of anything. As for gain . . . the police will be looking into all angles."

"I have no angles to look into!"

"I am attempting to think like the police do." Gloria poked at the olive in her martini.

"Mother," Uncle Amos warned.

She ignored him. "As, I am sure, is Lucy. What have you uncovered, dear?"

"Me? I've uncovered nothing. I'm not involved. I didn't even know the man."

"You were so helpful when I was here that other time," Gloria said. "You caught the killer single-handedly. If it hadn't been—"

"What are you talking about?" Aunt Joyce asked.

"Lucy," Gloria announced, with a considerable amount of pride, "has been of help to the police more than once. In my own case—"

"Enough, Mother," Amos said. "We don't need to go over that again."

Gloria was right that I'd discovered what happened at the time of Josie's wedding, but I was surprised she was bringing it up. What I learned didn't paint Gloria in a very flattering light. Then again, Gloria had a way of twisting reality to suit her ideas of what things should be. She continued to insist that her ancestors had been the owners of a grand Louisiana plantation that they'd lost during the Civil War. That (1) they'd been nothing of the sort, according to Uncle Amos, and (2) most people these days didn't like to brag about having been southern plantation owners didn't matter a whit to Gloria.

"You must tell me the story, Lucy," Aunt Joyce said. "You have hidden talents."

"I do not." I cut myself a hunk of cheese and added it to a slice of the soft, warm baguette. Made by Josie herself, was my guess.

Connor gave me a fond look over his beer glass. "Lucy's the curious sort. When she gets curious, she tends to go to great lengths to satisfy that curiosity."

I made a face at him.

"She's been like that all her life," Mom said. "Naturally, her father and I encouraged her curiosity, but it can be carried to extremes. All of this is none of our business, or of Lucy's. I intend to keep it that way. Gloria, will you be staying in Nags Head for long?"

"I haven't yet decided," the matriarch proclaimed. "My ticket home is for Wednesday, but I purchased a fully refundable fare in case I decide to extend my visit."

Aunt Ellen's eyes widened in despair. She stumbled to her feet and said, "I have to check on dinner."

"Let me help," I said.

Plump pork chops were soaking in a spicy marinade on the kitchen table. Bowls containing a variety of salads were ready to be taken out, and plates, cutlery, and napkins had been arranged on a tray.

Aunt Ellen gave me a rueful smile. "I've nothing in particular to do. Everything's ready for Amos to put the chops on the grill. I was afraid if I stayed out there, I'd end up telling Gloria she has to leave because I've rented out her room."

I laughed. "She isn't one to take a hint."

Ellen poured herself a glass of tea and leaned against the counter with a sigh. "Any news about Eddie's whereabouts?"

I shook my head, and a cloud passed over her face. Aunt Ellen was a regular volunteer at the library, and she and Bertie were good friends. It was through that friendship that I'd landed the job at the library.

"You don't think his . . . whatever . . . had anything to do with what happened to that man? Your aunt's friend?"

"I don't know what to think. But—I hate to say it, and I won't say it to anyone but you—it would be a heck of a coincidence if it didn't. Still, coincidences do happen. Have you spoken to Bertie?"

"She called me Sunday morning, wondering if Eddie might have come here for some reason. She made it sound as though he'd temporarily misplaced himself, but I could tell how worried she was. It came through loud and clear in every word."

"She came in to work today, but she stayed in her office all day. I popped my head in to tell her I had a few errands to run in town over my lunch break and ask if she wanted anything. Her eyes were red and her voice broke."

"Poor dear. What exactly happened, Lucy? When did she see him last?"

"Eddie was not having a good time at our wedding, because, he said, he felt ill."

Aunt Ellen nodded. "He didn't look well, and they left early. Bertie made their excuses, saying Eddie appeared to be coming down with something."

"Nothing out of the ordinary about that, it happens. He and Bertie left, without even having a pecan square, but Eddie didn't get out of the cab at Bertie's. He said he'd left his tie and wanted to go back for it, although he could have picked it up the next morning. I'm sure the staff find all sorts of discarded objects when they clean up after big parties." Wayne's suit jacket and his tie came to mind. "They left shortly after twelve. Meanwhile,

I know for an absolute fact that Wayne was alive only minutes before, because I saw him myself."

"Surely you're not suggesting Eddie returned to the hotel and murdered this Wayne person?"

"Like I said, I don't know what I'm saying. You didn't see Eddie, did you? After he and Bertie left, when he supposedly came back to the hotel?"

Ellen shook her head. "Bertie said a quick good-bye to us, so I likely would have noticed Eddie if he returned later. The room was thinning as the older people began to leave."

We stopped talking as the sliding doors opened and my mom came through. "Putting the finishing touches on dinner or escaping for a private chat?"

"Caught red-handed," Aunt Ellen said.

"The men are getting restless, and Amos was about to come in for the meat. I said I'd get it."

"I haven't had a chance to ask you how Kevin's managing," Ellen said in a low voice. "What with the pending divorce and all."

Mom sighed. "He is not handling it well. He's telling everyone he's happy to be rid of Kristen, but a mother can tell. He's devastated. And, as happens when men can't express their feelings, he's out for vengeance. He's going to make the divorce as drawn-out and expensive as he can, and that never goes well for anyone. Not for Kristen, not for their children, and certainly not for Kevin." She took a bottle of wine out of the fridge and filled her glass. "What Kristen was thinking, showing up here, with her new man in tow, I cannot imagine. Pouring gasoline on the fire is what she's done."

"Did you know about him before?" I asked. "I mean, was she seeing this guy when she was still with Kevin?"

"I don't know, dear. And I do not want to know."

"How about you, Susan?" Aunt Ellen asked her sister. Susan was my mother's birth name. She decided to call herself the more sophisticated Suzanne when she married my dad and tried to fit into his blue-blood Boston family. "Are you okay with it? Were you and Kristen close, as in friends?"

"Friends? Good heavens, no. I never much liked her, to be honest. Somewhat self-centered, I always thought. Still, she gave me two lovely grandchildren, and as far as I could tell, she and Kevin were excellent parents. Are excellent parents. Although I worry what a drawn-out, bitter divorce is going to do to them."

Out on the deck, people laughed.

"We should join the others," Aunt Ellen said.

"You never met Kristen's boyfriend before Friday?" I asked my mother.

"I didn't actually meet him until the wedding on Saturday. They were not invited to the rehearsal dinner, and I didn't encounter them in the hotel."

"Oh, right."

The door slid open again, and this time it was Gloria who came through. "Amos is looking for those chops, Ellen. Can't keep a southern man from his meat. You need to learn that, Lucy."

"Connor's a better cook than I am," I said.

Gloria snorted. "You young women these days. That's no way to keep a husband, let me tell you. In the meantime, I'll have a glass of wine while I'm waiting for my dinner." She opened the fridge and peered in.

"Although," Mom said, "there was something familiar about him."

"Familiar? About Kristen's friend?" Ellen asked.

"I had the feeling I'd seen him somewhere before, but I can't be sure. I never did get his name. Did either of you?"

"No," Aunt Ellen said.

"The unknown guest," I said.

"Ray. Ray Croft." Gloria produced the wine bottle with a flourish. "That's the name of the man who accompanied your daughter-in-law, Suzanne."

"How do you know that when we don't?" Aunt Ellen asked.

"Because I, my dear, make it a point to make the acquaintance of gentlemen at social occasions. He was left on his own for a while, and I suggested he and I have a dance. He was quite a good dancer, too. He knew the proper steps. None of that ridiculous bobbing-up-and-down modern stuff. He told me he'd come to the wedding as the guest of Lucy's sister-in-law. He hurried to assure me that Kristen and your son were in the process of getting a divorce. I replied that I hadn't thought they were bigamists. I know how things work in the modern world, although I have to say I don't—"

Aunt Ellen coughed.

"You think you might have met this Ray guy before, Mom?" I asked.

"I'm not sure. I can't place him. Perhaps he reminded me of someone. I can't put my finger on it. Oh well. No matter."

Aunt Ellen picked up the platter of chops and said, "Shall we join the others?" Gloria preceded her, and Mom and I followed with the place settings. Uncle Amos leapt to his feet and accepted the meat from Aunt Ellen. He put it down next to the grill and grabbed his barbecue tongs.

"Rodanthe might suit," Connor said.

"Suit what?" I asked. "What are you talking about?"

"Your dad's been telling me one of his young lawyers is looking for a place to go for a secluded, but not entirely secluded, beach vacation in July. As much as I'm an enthusiastic proponent of Nags Head, secluded is not a word I'd ever use to describe it. It can get mighty hectic in the summer months. Rodanthe's generally pretty quiet, but it's close enough to Nags Head that you can drive back and forth easily and thus enjoy the amenities of both places. It's far enough away that accommodation's slightly cheaper too."

"Some lovely old cottages in Rodanthe," Aunt Ellen said.

"I'll mention that to him," Dad said. "You need a hand there, Amos?"

"The day I need a New England lawyer to give me grilling tips is the day I hand in my apron," my uncle growled.

Chapter Six

The human mind's an amazing thing. Connor's recommendation of Rodanthe as a good place for visitors seeking some seclusion on their vacation passed straight over my head in the flurry of setting the table, bringing out the side dishes, getting more drinks, and tucking into dinner, never mind trying to follow the various threads of conversation swirling around the table.

It was a nice evening. The meal was, as always, delicious, and finished off with a towering lemon meringue pie Josie herself had dropped off earlier. Shadows grew long on the beach as behind us the sun set over the mainland, lights came on in nearby houses, birds flew overhead seeking a place to nest for the night, and the surf rolled gently onto the shore.

Conversation moved on from Eddie's whereabouts and the mystery surrounding Wayne Fortunada. Gloria mentioned that she had never been to Boston but she'd heard it was very nice. Dad said she'd be welcome to stay with them, and I felt Mom deliver him a solid kick under the table. Kevin tried to ask Dad for legal advice in getting child custody, and Mom sharply reminded him that his children were teenagers and thus old enough to decide for themselves where they wanted to live. Dad asked Amos about his plans for retirement, and Amos was noncommittal, to which Aunt Ellen did not look pleased.

It was a lovely evening, but I was glad no one showed signs of wanting to linger. Except for Kevin, who tried to ask Connor if he'd care to hit some bars in town.

Connor didn't even have to politely decline, as my mom snapped, "Don't be ridiculous. Connor—*and Lucy*—have work tomorrow. Speaking of which—don't you have a job to get back to, or has your staff decided they can get along well enough without you?"

"I've taken some vacation days, Mom. I'll have another beer. Thanks, Uncle Amos."

"I suggest you save your vacation days," Mom said as she stood up. "And save the beer, while you're at it."

"Lucy," Aunt Ellen said. "I got rather carried away last week and embarked on a cooking marathon. I made far more lasagna than we can possibly eat."

"I can always eat lasagna," Uncle Amos said.

"That's true." Aunt Ellen chuckled. "But I can spare a small serving for Lucy and Connor."

"I won't say no to that," I said. No one makes lasagna like my aunt Ellen. She's taught me to make it, but I always seem to miss that indefinable something that makes hers so extra delicious.

She opened the freezer and took out a heavy glass casserole dish wrapped in aluminum foil.

"Only in Ellen's mind," Connor said, "is that a small serving."

She thrust the dish into his arms.

* * *

When Connor and I got home, I put the lasagna into the freezer and then crawled into bed with the collected works of Edgar Allan Poe to prepare for book club, and Connor watched a game of some sort on TV. Charles wandered between the living room and the bedroom, debating which of us deserved the pleasure of his company the most.

"Did you know that Poe's character Auguste Dupin was an early version of Sherlock Holmes?" I asked Connor when he came to bed.

"If I did, I forgot."

"He makes an appearance in the story 'The Murders in the Rue Morgue,' and never again. I wonder if he might have been as famous as Holmes if Poe had kept writing about him."

"Is that suitable bedtime reading, Lucy? It's been years since I read Poe, but as I recall, his stories can be mighty disturbing."

"Fortunately, I am possessed of a singular lack of imagination, so the activities of fictional characters do not disturb my peace of mind."

"You keep telling yourself that, honey."

"I will." I gave him a big smile. "I also know that if I'm disturbed in the night, you're here to keep me safe."

He touched my cheek. "And I always will be."

* * *

I woke suddenly. The drapes were closed. The bedroom was pitch-dark; all was quiet outside. Beside me, Connor snored lightly. After much argument and discussion, Charles had emerged victorious from the fight over who could sleep on our bed. His warm little body was snuggled into my other side, and he also snored. Although not as lightly as Connor. Otherwise, the only sounds were the low hum of the refrigerator and the steady pounding of the surf on the incoming tide.

Rodanthe. *Something about Rodanthe.* I'd been there a few times. A pleasant little beachside community, as Connor had said. I didn't know anyone who lived there, and I'd never stayed overnight. But someone had—

And then I knew what had woken me.

Josie, Steph, and Grace had thrown Connor and me an engagement party at the beach. It had been a wonderful party, spoiled only by the late arrival of my ex-boyfriend Ricky Lewiston and his mother, the overbearing Evangeline, who had, in effect, gate-crashed.

Eddie had come to the party with Bertie. He'd been relaxing under a sun umbrella with the library crowd when I dropped onto the blanket next to him. Bertie, as I recalled, had gone to help Josie pack up the gifts. Louise Jane had, as usual, been entertaining the newcomer with tales of her family's rich and occasionally sordid history on the Outer Banks. I'd heard all her stories before, which is why I paid no attention and instead asked Charlene, at that time our academic and research librarian, about a project she'd been working on.

Yes, the human mind is a marvelous thing. I hadn't been listening to Eddie and Louise Jane, and I hadn't given their conversation another thought. But there it lingered, in the far recesses of my mind, waiting for the moment I would need it.

"A colleague of mine has a place in Rodanthe," Eddie said. "He doesn't use it much anymore, if at all, and his children aren't interested, so he said I'd be welcome to it anytime."

"You should take him up on that," Louise Jane had said. "Rodanthe's not too far from here."

As I lay in the dark between my husband and my cat, I frantically sorted through the nooks of my memory banks. And then I had it.

"What's your friend's name?" Louise Jane had asked. "I know just about everyone who's anyone in these parts."

"Daniel Estevez. Dan."

"Never heard of him," Louise Jane declared, and she went on to talk about people she had heard of.

It was likely I remembered the name of Eddie's acquaintance because one of my first bosses at Harvard was named Danielle Estevez, and she'd been a huge help to me in my career.

I leapt out of bed the moment I remembered that long-ago conversation and ran for my iPad. I plopped myself down at the island in the kitchen and searched for the name Daniel Estevez. A not uncommon name, but fortunately Eddie had mentioned that the man was a colleague of his. I soon found that name listed on the Blacklock College website, mentioning he was a professor of Spanish literature. The only phone number provided was for the college's literature department. I then searched the Elizabeth City area on 411.com but found no number listed for that name or any version of it. Drat! People were increasingly getting rid of their landlines these days, and a directory of cell phone numbers didn't exist. Highly inconvenient for the amateur sleuth. Not that I am an amateur sleuth, but I was interested in talking to this Dan Estevez.

Realizing I could do nothing more tonight, I went back to bed, where I lay staring up into the darkness until the first rays of the rising sun peeked through the blinds. I got up once again, swept my phone off the night table, and tiptoed into the kitchen, followed by a yawning Charles, wondering what I was doing up so early.

I was on the phone to Bertie at six o'clock. Early to be calling, but I figured she wouldn't mind.

She answered quicky. "Lucy! What's happened? Have you learned something?"

"I might have. Do you recognize the name Daniel or Dan Estevez?"

"No. Not offhand. Should I?"

"He's a friend of Eddie's. I remembered last night. He has a place in Rodanthe, which he told Eddie he's free to use anytime."

"Rodanthe? Why would Eddie go to Rodanthe without telling me?"

"That's the question, isn't it?"

"Great. I can be on my way in a few minutes. Make my excuses if I'm late for work, please."

"Hold up, Bertie. It might not mean anything, but it is an avenue to explore."

"I won't get my hopes up. What's the address?"

"I don't know."

"You don't know?" The excitement in her voice faded. "Rodanthe's small, Lucy, but it's going to take me a long time to knock on every door asking if they know someone named Daniel."

"He works at Blacklock College. I looked him up. He's a literature prof there."

"Did you find his phone number?"

"Not his personal one, unfortunately. We'll have to wait until the office at the college opens."

Connor padded into the kitchen, bleary-eyed and tousled with sleep. He lifted one eyebrow in a question, and I mouthed, "Bertie." He yawned and went to put the coffee on.

"Wait," she said. "I'm sick and tired of waiting. I need to be doing something."

"It's a lead, Bertie. It might not amount to anything, but it might."

"Thank you, Lucy. I'll let you know what I find out. If anything."

"Wait! Bertie, I don't want you going by yourself. It might be . . . emotionally difficult." I didn't want to say *dangerous*, but I was thinking it. Connor had frozen in the act of adding ground coffee beans to the pot. I gave him a shrug. "Why don't you come here? We can have breakfast and wait until the college offices open. There's likely to be someone getting in around eight. Even if they give us this Daniel's number, he might not be available or even want to talk to us."

Despite all her worries, Bertie could still remember practical matters. "What about the library?"

"It's Tuesday. Ronald will be in on time to open. We can put Louise Jane on the desk. Other duties as assigned. If we have to go out of town, I can ask Aunt Ellen to get one of the volunteers to help out if necessary, but I'm sure we won't be long." I was sure of nothing of the sort.

"It's worth a try," Bertie said. "I have to confess that I'd appreciate the emotional support. I need to take a yoga class this morning, so I'll be at your place around eight."

"Great. See you then."

"What," Connor said when I'd hung up, "is going on?"

"Bertie's coming over. I have a lead on Eddie, but we can't do anything until his office opens."

"What sort of lead?"

I explained.

"So you're planning to go to Rodanthe in pursuit of a missing man, one whom the police are searching for in connection with a murder?"

"Yup. It's Eddie. We'll be fine."

"You and Bertie are not going alone. I have nothing on this morning I can't cancel."

"You don't need to come."

"Yes, Lucy, I do."

* * *

As long as we were up early and neither of us was rushing off to work, Connor set about getting bacon and eggs out of the fridge while I grabbed the shower first. I debated what to wear, and finally decided to be optimistic and settled on work clothes of dark pants and an ironed blouse. Connor and I ate our breakfast largely in silence, both of us wrapped in our own thoughts. "When we have an address," Connor said at one point, "if we have an address, I'll call the mayor of Rodanthe and ask if there's anything about that house we need to know. Such as any recent police activity."

"Good idea."

Bertie arrived shortly after eight, still in her yoga gear. The shadows under her eyes were deeper and darker than they'd been yesterday.

Connor poured her a coffee and offered to cook more bacon and eggs. She accepted the first, declined the latter, and pulled out a stool.

"That new detective who's helping Sam called me last night," she said. "I wonder if we're getting too comfortable with Sam. The new fellow, what's his name?"

"North."

"Yes, Detective North. He's more . . . *aggressive* might be the word."

"Sam knows us all," Connor said. "He knows he can trust us. North's still finding his way around. New job, new community. He doesn't trust us, and that's fair. We need to earn his trust."

"Perhaps."

"What did he want?" I asked.

"To know if I'd had contact with Eddie. I told him I didn't. He reminded me I was expected to let him or Sam know immediately if I did, and I said I knew that. I then asked why he was so interested in Eddie, and he told me Eddie is a"—she took a deep breath—"person of interest in the murder of Wayne Fortunada." She gripped her mug so tightly I feared it would shatter.

"Did he say why?" Connor asked.

"A hotel waiter told them he overheard Eddie and Wayne arguing on Saturday, at the reception. He couldn't say what the argument was about or how long it lasted. So he told the police, anyway."

"Where was this and at what time?" I asked. "Did North say?"

"The waiter passed them in the hallway outside the meeting rooms. Around midnight, apparently. Not long before Eddie and I left."

I wondered if that was the conversation—I wouldn't have called it an argument—I'd overheard a portion of. The timing was right.

"It'll all get sorted out, I'm sure," Connor said. "Bertie, do you want Lucy to make that call now and we can get started?"

She nodded.

I hoped I wouldn't have to go through a series of beeps and robotic voices instructing me to press one button or another. I did, of course, but eventually I arrived at "Press zero for the operator," and a real person finally said, "Blacklock College. Department of Languages and Literature."

"Good morning. My name's Lucy McNeil, and I'm a friend of Professor McClanahan."

"Professor McClanahan won't be in today. He has no classes or office hours scheduled."

"I know that, thank you. I'm trying to contact Professor Estevez on his behalf. I've lost his cell phone number, and I was hoping you'd give it to me."

"Can't you ask Professor McClanahan?"

"He's not picking up right now."

"I can't give out private numbers. I'm sorry."

"Perhaps I can come around. Is Professor Estevez planning to be in his office today?"

"Just a minute. Let me check."

Bertie and Connor watched me. I gave them a shrug, and the operator came back. "He has consultation hours this morning and a freshman class this afternoon. I'll put you through to his office line, and you can leave a message."

"But—"

Click. Click. I made a face at Bertie and Connor as the professor's voice mail picked up. "Hi. My name's Lucy McNeil, and I'm looking for Eddie McClanahan. I can't go into it over the phone, but it's very urgent, and I believe you might be able to help me. Please call me as soon as you can. Thank you." I rattled off my number and hung up. "Sorry," I said to the two people watching me. "That's the best I could do."

"He might not return your call, Lucy," Connor pointed out.

"I'll keep trying his office number. He's bound to answer eventually if he has students coming in."

Connor cradled his coffee cup. "Bertie, have you considered that Eddie might not want you to find him?"

"I've considered it, yes. But Connor, in all honesty, I cannot possibly think why that would be. Neither of us is making any demands on the other. Nothing's been said about moving in together or, heaven forbid, getting married. He has his life and career and I have mine, and we like it that way. He hasn't been depressed, or even sad, or appeared to be worried about anything. Until Saturday. Something happened on Saturday night. I won't be able to rest until I know what that was."

"Saturday night," I said. "Do you mean specifically at our wedding? How did he seem earlier?"

"Perfectly fine. Normal. He got to town Friday afternoon, and we had dinner out. Breakfast together at my house on Saturday. I had some shopping to do after breakfast and left him researching his new book. He told me he's having trouble getting a focus on what he wants the main thrust of the book to be about, but I didn't get the feeling he was overly concerned about that. Just a minor roadblock that he'd push through eventually, as he always has before. When I got home from the store, we dressed and were at the church by three. He was quiet for the rest of the day, but you know Eddie: he's perfectly comfortable in his own company, and the people at the wedding were my friends, not his. He didn't eat much at the reception dinner, so it was then I first thought he might be coming down with something. The meal was delicious." She laughed without humor. "When he said he wanted to leave before the desserts were brought out, I knew something was wrong."

"Did he say anything to you in the cab on the way back to your place?" Connor asked.

"Not a word. He was," she sighed, "drawn in upon himself. At the time I thought he was sick, as I've said, but looking back on it now, I'd say he was more likely to have been thoughtful, concerned about something. The taxi pulled up in front of my house, and Eddie suddenly announced that he needed to go back for his tie. As far as I know, the tie wasn't anything special. It's just a tie, and Eddie's not the sort to have sentimental feelings about his possessions."

I almost fell off my stool when my phone rang. I threw a quick glance at Connor and Bertie as I checked the display. I didn't recognize the number. "Hello?"

"Is that Ms. McNeil?"

"Yes, it is. Are you Professor Daniel Estevez?"

"I am. I got your message. What's Eddie done now?" His voice was light, tinged with a trace of amusement.

"Nothing really. I'm in Nags Head for a few days. Just a quick visit and I'd love to see him, but he's not answering his phone. He mentioned that he was staying at your place in Rodanthe."

"That's possible. He knows he's welcome to it at any time, although he hasn't taken up the offer before."

I gave Bertie and Connor a big smile and a thumbs-up. Bertie's face lit up.

"You say he's not answering his phone. Cell phone reception can be bad at my place," Daniel said. "It's sort of a dead zone; the signal depends on which way the wind's blowing."

"I'm near Rodanthe now, so I'd like to pop around and say hi to Eddie." I held my breath.

"I guess that'd be okay." Daniel gave me an address.

"Thank you very much." I let out a huge sigh as I hung up. "Got it."

Bertie, Connor, and I ran for the door. "We'll be late going in to work today," I called over my shoulder to Charles.

Chapter Seven

The charming little coastal village of Rodanthe is situated about twenty minutes' drive from the south end of Nags Head.

As Connor drove and the lighthouse in which our library is situated appeared over the top of the trees to our right, I located the address Dan Estevez had given us on my phone's map and Bertie made calls. She told Ronald that she and I would be in to work late. She then asked Louise Jane to fill in at the circulation desk.

This early in the season, the masses of beach-seeking tourists hadn't yet arrived, and traffic was light as we left Nags Head. Dunes rose up on either side of us, part of the long, uninhabited stretch of Highway 12 as it crosses through the Cape Hatteras National Seashore. The land between Nags Head and Rodanthe isn't much more than a thin stretch of sand and rough beach grasses, the wild open ocean on one side, marshes, creeks, and inlets on the other. The road is constantly being covered by drifting sand, and in bad weather it's regularly flooded by seawater.

Gray clouds hung low and heavy overhead, but no rain or high winds were in the forecast for today. The route was clear this morning, but the wind came off the water and sand blew steadily across the road, gathering in the depressions like pale-brown snow.

It wasn't long before the small old cottages and sleek modern rental properties of our destination came into sight.

As Connor drove, he used the Bluetooth on his phone to call the office of the mayor of Rodanthe. The mayor congratulated Connor on his marriage, they exchanged pleasantries, they complained about the county and state authorities, and then Connor said, "For personal reasons, I'm interested in a house on Winthrop Lane. North end of town. Anything about that area I should know?"

"Nothing I'm aware of. Developers have their eye on some of those old buildings, but nothing untoward. Nothing I've heard of, at any rate. Why are you asking?"

"Like I said, personal matter. A friend's interested in a vacation property, just nosing around so far. Thanks." He disconnected the call. "All clear, officially anyway."

I used my own phone to check our destination on the GPS. "Go about another three miles and turn left. Looks like the address we're after is right on the beach. According to the map, it's the last house on the road."

We drove past the bars, restaurants, grocery stores, gas stations, fishing and surf shops, and beach accessory stores of Rodanthe. It was still early, and not many people were around.

"Turn's coming up," I said, and Connor slowed. The edges of the road were indistinct beneath the accumulation of drifting sand; the properties we passed had no lawns, trees, bushes, or flowers at all, just sea oats and tough beach grasses struggling to survive in the shifting sands. Telephone poles, wires drooping between them, rose out of the sand, framed by the overcast sky, giving height to an otherwise flat landscape. This was a street of small old cottages, weatherworn, with peeling and faded paint, some of them poorly maintained. Many had rental information posted on them. At the end of the road, above the rise of the small dunes, the open blue ocean stretched to the horizon. A handful of surfboards rode the waves.

Winthrop Lane not so much ended as faded away, gradually overtaken by ever-drifting sand. The house we were interested in sat at the end of the road, the last one before the beach. Connor pulled up next to it. It consisted of one story built on stilts, as all the houses around here were, with a rickety-looking staircase leading to a narrow balcony running the width of the house. The windows were small, as was the house itself.

We slowly got out of the car and looked around. No garage, no car parked outside. Other than the few surfers on the beach getting ready for another run and a handful of walkers, no one was in sight.

The three of us exchanged glances. "Bertie?" Connor said.

"Let's go." She marched up the steps, and we trailed after her.

Wind blew particles of sand into our faces and whipped at our hair and cheeks. Bertie hesitated at the door, her look almost one of fright, and Connor stepped forward and rapped firmly. Bertie and I held our breath. I gave her a weak smile.

The door opened. Professor Edward McClanahan peered at us through his thick lenses, surprise filling his face. His mass of curly white hair stood on end, a rough beard was beginning to come in, and his salt-and-pepper moustache badly needed a trim. He wore baggy Bermuda shorts showing thin hairy legs, a Blacklock College sweatshirt about three sizes too large for his rake-thin frame, and brown socks without shoes. In an instant the surprise was wiped away by an enormous, welcoming smile. "Goodness, Bertie. Didn't expect to see you here. And Connor and Lucy too. What a pleasant surprise. What brings you lot here? Not much of a beach day, I'm afraid, although the surfers seem to love it. Come in, come in." He stepped back, and we entered.

The cottage consisted mostly of one big room. It was cheapy but comfortably furnished with well-used couches and chairs, overflowing bookcases, thick colorful rugs, and a heavily scarred pine table surrounded by eight chairs. The windows, streaked with salt and sand, gave an unparalleled view of the empty beach and ocean beyond.

"Can I get you something to drink?" Eddie asked politely. "Coffee's ready."

"Eddie," Bertie said. "What's going on?"

He blinked. "Going on?"

Connor and I looked at each other. I lifted my shoulders in a question, and he shrugged in response.

"Yes, going on," Bertie said. "What are you doing here? And why?"

"My friend Dan lent this place to me for a few days. He doesn't come here anymore, and he hates to see it standing empty. I told you about Dan."

"No, Eddie, you didn't."

"I thought I had."

"Before we continue," Connor said, "you look as though you're okay, Eddie. Are you?"

"Yes, I'm perfectly fine. Why do you ask? I'm sorry I left your wedding early, but I had to get away. Come, have a seat. Sure you won't have anything? I have some orange juice."

Bertie's patience finally snapped. "Eddie! I am not going to sit down and have an orange juice or anything else. Do you have any idea at all of how worried I've been? How worried we've all been?"

"Worried? I'm sorry, my dear. Why would you worry? I told you I needed to get away for a while."

"You did not!"

"Yes, I did. Didn't I?"

Connor lifted his hands. "Okay. Let's figure this out. When did you tell Bertie about this and how?"

"And why?" I said.

Eddie dropped into an overstuffed chair covered in a garish homemade afghan in shades of orange, purple, and green. A mug of coffee sat on a side table next to a well-thumbed paperback with a drawing of a dark-haired woman dressed in a toga on the cover. "Didn't you get my text, Bertie?"

"I did not."

He struggled to his feet and went into the single bedroom. We heard muttering and the sound of drawers being opened and then shut.

Bertie put her head in her hands. I pulled my phone out and checked it. No signal. "Are you getting anything?" I asked Connor.

"No."

Eddie came back with his own phone. "I turned this off, not wanting any interruptions. I'm taking advantage of the unexpected seclusion to do some serious thinking about the direction of my next book. I told you about that, Bertie. A critical analysis of *The Iliad* as translated by—"

"I couldn't care less about *The Iliad* if it was translated by Donald Duck," Bertie bellowed in a very un-Bertie-like manner.

"Here we are," Eddie said. "Phone's on now. See, I sent this text to you on Saturday night. Sunday morning, actually. At one forty-five AM." He peered closer at the tiny screen. "What does that little red exclamation mark mean?"

He handed to the phone to Bertie. She didn't take it, so I did. "It means," I said, "the text was not sent. It also says *Not delivered*."

He looked at it again and adjusted his glasses. "I can't quite make out the fine print. Oh, now I see it. Sorry. I wonder what happened."

"Did you send the text when you got here, by any chance?" Connor asked pleasantly.

"Yes. I texted when I got out of the car, and then I turned the phone off. Dan told me the reception here can be poor."

Bertie groaned again.

"Are you aware the Nags Head police are looking for you, Eddie?" I asked.

He looked genuinely confused. "They are? Why?"

"Let's start at the beginning, why don't we?" I settled myself into a chair. "Connor, have a seat."

Connor sat. Bertie dropped onto the brown-and-orange-upholstered couch.

"First, Eddie, Bertie. All of this is probably none of our business, and if you want Connor and me to go, we will. But, as Connor said, the police are interested in events that happened around the time you decided you needed to get away."

"I'm an open book," Eddie said.

"As if," Bertie muttered.

"You felt unwell at the reception and wanted to leave early," I said. "Is that correct?"

"Yes." Eddie sat on the couch next to Bertie. She wiggled over a few inches, putting space between them. Undiscouraged, he took her hand, and she didn't pull it away. "I felt unwell, but not because I was physically ill. I confess that was a small lie on my part. I ran into someone whom . . . I'd have preferred not to see."

"Wayne Fortunada," I said.

"How did you know that?"

"A guess. You say you didn't want to see him, but you went back to the hotel under the pretext of getting your tie. I assume you went back in order to see him."

"I confess that I did. I changed my mind." He turned to Bertie. "Were you able to find my tie?"

"Eddie!"

"No matter. I can always buy another. As for Saturday. I was bothered at having seen the man. It brought up a lot of bad memories. I wasn't in the mood to continue celebrating your wedding, Lucy and Connor, and I was poor company for Bertie. I remembered Dan Estevez and his mention of this place. It was at a staff meeting, I believe. Maybe drinks after." His eyes lost focus as he tried to remember. Bertie was barely holding on to what little patience she had left.

"No matter now," Eddie continued. "I happened to mention on one occasion that I had reacquainted with a lady." He smiled at Bertie. Her look in return could have frozen the seawater outside the door. Eddie cleared his throat. "And thus I found myself visiting Nags Head regularly. Dan told me about this place, and he said I was welcome to use it anytime. I remembered that and decided I could use the time to get away and get some thinking done about my book. It's going to be a seminal study, and—"

"Eddie!"

"Not that it greatly matters in the scheme of things," Connor said. "But how did you get in?"

"Dan told me where he hides the spare key." Eddie's face twisted with remembered pain, and he absent-mindedly rubbed his right knee. "I must admit, I'm not as young as I once was. I thought I'd never be able to crawl back out of that place."

Bertie groaned one more time.

"I'm sorry the text got lost, Bertie," Eddie said. "Perhaps I should have gone back to your house and invited you to come with me. But you mentioned that you had a busy week at work ahead, and I needed some alone time. I had . . . have things to think over. Things aside from the book."

"Tell us about Wayne Fortunada and you," I said.

Eddie's face fell, and his mouth twisted. He hesitated. "You've gone to all this trouble to find me and come all this way because you were worried about me, so you deserve to know the whole sordid story. It was not my finest hour. Wayne and I knew each other a long time ago. We were roommates for a while when I was at Columbia. I was a master's student. He was getting his start—trying to get his start—as a singer and dancer on Broadway, waiting tables between auditions, same as all the other eager young things. I never heard of him after we parted ways, so I assume he never did make it on the stage. I . . ." He stopped talking. He stared out the window, his eyes unfocused.

No one said a word.

"It was a heck of a shock to see him at your wedding, Lucy. I recognized him first. The years have been kind to him, and he hasn't changed all that much." He stroked his moustache. "I . . . should have let it go. Ignored him completely. He likely wouldn't have recognized me. He wasn't paying any attention to those of us seated at the library table, nor to much else, as far as I could see. But I couldn't stop looking at him. Remembering what had happened between us. He caught me looking, and . . . I saw confusion at first and the light dawning. He gave me that grin. That awful supercilious grin of his, the one I knew so well despite the passage of years. He stood up and started to approach our table. I didn't want that—I certainly didn't want to introduce him to Bertie and her friends—so I hastily got up and met him in the middle of the room. He was all hail-fellow-well-met, as though nothing had happened. But he dropped some mighty heavy comments, asking how my career was going and if I'd ever gotten tenure, as had been my dream back then."

"I'm not following," Connor said. "Why would an old friend asking how your life has worked out been threatening?"

"I . . ." Eddie shifted on the couch and moved toward Bertie. He held her hand tightly and stared down at their clenched hands. She did not pull away. We said nothing. We all sensed that this—whatever it was—was hard for Eddie, and he needed time to gather his strength and say it. "I . . . I cheated on my master's thesis."

"You did what?" Bertie said.

"I cheated. I presented someone else's work as my own. When I was an undergrad at Chapel Hill, a girl I knew from my hometown was doing her master's there. She was friends with my older sister, Jane, and Jane, always being overly protective of me, asked her to keep an eye on me. I was shy, a boy from a small town, alone in the big college. Her name was Rose. I can see what you're thinking, but it wasn't like that. Rose was my *in loco* big sister. I wasn't entirely sure what I wanted to study. In my freshman year, I was thinking of getting my degree in ancient history. The heydays of Greece and Rome have always fascinated me. Rose was doing Latin. I've always been good at languages, and Rose herself suggested I might like to pursue that. Poor Rose. She died before she finished her degree."

"I'm sorry," Bertie said.

"Car accident. Terrible thing. Because I was on campus, her parents asked me to pack up her things. I . . . took her thesis."

"Oh no," Bertie said softly. "Eddie."

"I took it to remember her. I decided to specialize in Ancient Greek and Latin in honor of Rose. I was hoping her unfinished paper would inspire me. I never showed it to anyone. I might have, if her parents asked, but they didn't. I kept it. The years passed, and I'd been accepted into the master's program at Columbia, doing Latin and Greek. It wasn't going well. Time, and money, was running out. I had no idea what I wanted my own master's paper to be on. I read Rose's thesis again. I was intending to get an idea from hers, an inspiration, nothing more. It became more than an idea. I . . . tidied it up, added some of my own content. I submitted it as my own. It was very well received, and I was awarded my degree."

"Didn't you have to defend this paper?" Connor asked. "You must have done that successfully."

"A master's degree isn't as intensive as a PhD," I said. "The research isn't required to be entirely original. But it can't be copied without accreditation."

Eddie hung his head.

"Are you saying Wayne Fortunada blackmailed you?" I asked.

"Yes."

"Surely he couldn't read Latin and Greek at that level?"

"He didn't have to. I . . . told him what I'd done. He saw Rose's paper on my desk. She did a lot of her work in longhand, rather than using a typewriter, and the paper was obviously not in my handwriting. He asked me what it was. I said nothing and shoved it into a drawer. Then one night, after I'd submitted my own paper, we went out to celebrate. He'd gotten a call back for a second audition for a big Broadway show. I drank, egged on by my pal Wayne, far more than I was used to. In my drunken stupor, in the company of what I thought was a friend, I confessed to copying Rose's paper. To presenting her work as my own. The next morning I woke up with one heck of a hangover. My desk drawer was open and Rose's paper was gone."

"Oh, Eddie." Bertie stroked his hand.

"I had next to no money, but I still had more than Wayne did. He asked for three thousand dollars, something to tide him over until he landed the part he was so sure was in the bag. Or, he said, he'd take Rose's paper to my professor. The similarities would have been immediately obvious to anyone who could read and understand it. I scraped together the three thousand. He didn't get the part he was so confident of. He didn't get any more auditions. We were still roommates, although no longer speaking, and certainly not hitting the bars together. He wanted five thousand the next time. You get the story."

"Blackmailers never quit," Connor said.

"Armed with the glowing reference from my professors, I was accepted into the PhD program at the University of Virginia."

"Where you met Bertie," I said.

He smiled at my boss. "The light of my life."

"Don't give me that," Bertie snapped, obviously not quite ready to forgive Eddie yet. "And I'll remind you that if that's the case, I'm but the fifth light of your life."

"But most definitely the brightest." Eddie, I knew, had been married four times. Or was it three? He didn't seem entirely sure.

"Can we carry on?" Connor said. "What happened then?"

"I left that apartment one night when Wayne was staying over at a girlfriend's, leaving no forwarding address. This was in 1985, before you could find just about anyone on Facebook. I went home to Asheville, took a summer job in a landscaping company, and debated my options. I decided I had to prove myself, if only to myself, that I could do it. That I didn't need to cheat. So I went to Virginia, and I earned my PhD through nothing but my own work."

"It ended well, then," I said. "I can understand why seeing Wayne would have upset you, but that happened a long time ago."

"I don't know if Wayne still has Rose's paper, but he might. My master's thesis is part of my academic record. A provable accusation of plagiarism would ruin my career, never mind my reputation, even all these years later." He turned to Bertie, his eyes full of tears. "For what it's worth, what I did back then has haunted me ever since."

She gave him a soft, sad smile and gripped his hand tighter.

"You said you spoke to Wayne at our reception," Connor said. "What happened then?"

"He asked to be introduced to my friends. I told him no. He and I were not friends and we had nothing to discuss. He said he disagreed, and he persuaded me to come with him and have a private chat."

"In the hallway off the ballroom," I said. "Where it takes a turn past the restrooms."

Eddie turned to me. "How did you know that?"

"Never mind. What happened then?"

"He said he remembered me well, that he often wondered what I was doing these days. He said something about the good old days when we'd been young and foolish. Those were the words he used. Foolish. He reminded me that I . . . owed him money. My stomach had been a ball of knots since the moment I recognized him. I wanted to get out of there, so I told Bertie I was unwell."

"Just so we're sure what we're talking about," Connor said, "the guy was alive and well when you last saw him?"

"He was. He made a parting comment about us catching up sometime, and he walked away. I stayed where I was for a few minutes, trying to catch my breath and control my panic, and then I went in search of Bertie. We left. In the taxi to Bertie's place, I changed my mind. Fortune favors the bold, and I'd be bold. I'd go back and tell Wayne to leave me alone. *Publish and be damned*, in the immortal words of Sir Winston Churchill."

"Wellington," Bertie said.

"What?" Connor said.

"*Publish and be damned.* Arthur Wellesley, the Duke of Wellington, said that, not Churchill, when a lady of his acquaintance threatened to reveal their exploits to the papers."

"I stand corrected," Eddie said.

"I'll forgive you this time, as Wellington is a good two thousand years after your period."

Connor and I rolled our eyes at each other.

Eddie continued with his story. "Instead, once I arrived at the hotel, I changed my mind once again. Fortune might sometimes favor the brave, but rash acts often do not. The cab that dropped me had left, so I grabbed another and asked the driver to take me to Rodanthe."

"Before you continue," I said, "did you go into the hotel? Did you see Wayne again?"

"No to both those questions. I stood on the steps of the hotel for a few minutes, debating. Wedding guests were starting to leave, taxis being called, so I grabbed one. Fortunately, I had my wallet on me, as he wanted a lot of money to come this far at that time of night and he wouldn't get a return fare to Nags Head."

"The police never found this taxi driver," I said.

"It was one of those gig economy things, not a regular taxi company. The guy told me it was a part-time job for him. With what I was offering to pay in cash, and because I hadn't gone through the company, they'd have no record, so he was going to tell them he was going out of service. Which reminds me. Why are the police looking for me?"

Connor and I exchanged another look. I gave him a slight nod and he said, "Wayne Fortunada was found dead the following morning. The woman he was with—"

"Who just happens to be my aunt Joyce," I said.

"—says she left him at the reception and he did not come back to their room. The police are assuming he died in the early hours of Sunday morning. He was found by a cleaner."

Behind the glasses, sorrow filled Eddie's expressive eyes. "I'm sorry to hear that. Despite our differences, we had been friends once. But I still don't know what that has to do with me."

"He was murdered, Eddie," Bertie said. "Don't you understand? The police think you killed him and skipped town. That you are, as they say in the old mystery novels, on the lam."

Eddie's face was such a picture of shock that in other circumstances I might have laughed. His mouth opened. It closed. It then opened again, and he said, "But . . . I didn't. Are you sure?"

"Sure he was murdered?" Connor said. "No doubt about it."

"Sure the police are looking for you?" I said. "They might not have a warrant out for your arrest. Not yet, but they consider your disappearance to be significant. A waiter saw you and Wayne in the hallway. He told the police you were arguing."

Eddie let out a long breath. "Goodness. I suppose I should turn myself in."

"Don't put it like that," I said. "But yes, you need to talk to them."

"I assume Detective Watson is in charge?"

"He is."

"Good." Eddie stood up. He adjusted the too-large sweatshirt. "Then we'll be off."

"Where did you get those clothes?" Bertie asked. "They don't fit you too well."

"Found them in a closet. Dan is a generously proportioned man. I'll change into my suit for my interview with the authorities." He picked the book off the side table. "I'm sure he won't mind if I borrow this."

Chapter Eight

Eddie didn't have any luggage, so it was no more than a couple of minutes before he'd changed and gathered his things and we all piled into Connor's car for the trip back to Nags Head. Before doing that, Eddie wrote a note for Dan, thanking him for the accommodation and mentioning he'd borrowed a book. "In case he drops in while I am . . . uh . . . detained in Nags Head." He slipped the book into the pocket of his crumbled suit jacket, and when his hand came out, it was holding a balled-up tie. "Oh, there it is," he said. Eddie then checked to make sure the stove was off, disconnected the water, unplugged the small appliances, and locked the door.

Waving off Connor's offer to do it for him, he crawled under the house in search of the hook on which to place the key. With much groaning and moaning, the occasional thump of head meeting board, and mutters about not being able to find the hook—all accompanied by Bertie telling him to get a move on—Eddie finally backed out from under the house. He stood up, dusted sand off the knees of his good, and probably only, suit, and announced that he was ready to go. Bertie affectionately reached up and brushed a tangle of cobwebs out of his hair.

Bertie and Eddie took seats in the back of the car. Eddie didn't say much, and Bertie simply stared out the window. As soon as we had cell phone reception, I called Sam Watson and told him I'd located Eddie and explained that there'd been a misunderstanding.

"A man can't be located in this day and age for three days and that's a misunderstanding?"

"That's Eddie," I said. "In fairness, he did try to contact Bertie, but something . . . uh . . . went wrong."

"Where are you now?"

"Leaving Rodanthe. We can be at the station in about twenty minutes."

"I'll be waiting."

I watched the blowing sand and the occasional flash of water over the dunes. What little I'd heard of the conversation between Wayne and Eddie in the hallway didn't entirely correspond with what Eddie had told us. Granted, I didn't know Wayne well—I didn't, in fact, know him at all—whereas he and Eddie had been young together. I hadn't heard any anger or hostility in Wayne's voice. More sadness and regret. He'd told Eddie he wanted to be repaid, but even that was said with more of a *Let bygones be bygones* tone than any outright suggestion of danger. When Wayne emerged into the hallway where I'd been listening, he hadn't seemed angry or full of aggression. Just thoughtful, maybe a touch sad.

Had Eddie overreacted? Eddie admitted that his one act of plagiarism had haunted him all his life. Coming across Wayne again all these years later had been an enormous shock. Had Eddie seen the threat in Wayne he'd expected to see? Rather than what was there?

I couldn't see that it mattered. I didn't for one minute believe Eddie had killed Wayne and then run off into the night. I didn't know Eddie all that well, but I did know Bertie. And if Bertie gave her friendship—even her love—to this man, then I believed him to be a good person.

If Wayne had blackmailed Eddie all those years ago, and I believed Eddie's story, then Wayne had not been a good person. If he'd blackmailed Eddie and then come back for more, it was entirely possible he'd made other enemies over the course of his life. Enemies who might not simply run off into the night the way Eddie had done.

Had one of those enemies been at my wedding? I had to admit that it would seem so. Plenty of people had been at my wedding. Connor and I had kept firm control over the guest list. We'd invited my closest friends, my coworkers, my family, Connor's family, friends, and coworkers. But people I didn't know had also come. People like Wayne himself. The plus-ones, such as Kristen's friend Ray. One of the hotel staff working at the event might have known Wayne in the past and recognized him. Wayne was a heavy smoker; perhaps he'd encountered someone he knew in the parking lot also out for a quick smoke.

I'd met Wayne for the first time at dinner Friday evening. He'd been friendly, charming, polite (except for the wine foofaraw). Quite different from the way he'd behaved at the wedding reception, where, by all accounts, he'd drunk too much, been short to Aunt Joyce, not mixed with the other guests, and been sullen when approached. Which was the "real" Wayne? Had Friday been a front, and then on Saturday something—or someone—shocked him into reverting to type? Had he started to drink too much when he was confronted by something he didn't want to deal with, rather than vice versa?

I twisted in my seat and spoke to Eddie. "Did you by any chance notice anyone else at the wedding you were surprised to see?"

"Other than Wayne, you mean? No. I didn't know anyone apart from Bertie's library crowd and those of your friends whom I'd met previously at your engagement party."

"Are you detecting, Lucy?" Connor asked.

"Just trying to place everyone leading up to the time Wayne died. We know Wayne was murdered. We know Eddie didn't do it."

"Thank you for the vote of confidence," Eddie said.

"But someone did. I hate to think that person was at my wedding, either as a guest or member of the hotel staff, but it looks like it."

As the black and white bands of the Bodie Island Lighthouse came into sight, rising above the marshes, Bertie said, "Lucy, I'll accompany Eddie to talk to the police. You can go in to work. Make my excuses, please."

"We'd better go straight to the station," Connor said. "Sam might not be waiting entirely patiently. I'll drop you off and then take Lucy home to get her car."

"And Charles," I said, "Can't forget Charles."

"One can never forget Charles," Connor said. "Bertie and Eddie, call me when you're finished, and I'll give you a lift to our house to get Bertie's car."

"Your uncle Amos is a lawyer, isn't he, Lucy?" Eddie asked.

"Criminal defense lawyer."

"Maybe you can ask him to be on standby."

"It won't come to that," Bertie said quickly.

I wasn't so sure. "I'll give him a heads-up."

* * *

I would have liked to accompany Bertie and Eddie into the police station to hear what Watson had to say and what Eddie had to say in return, but Connor held up one hand when I started to unfasten my seat belt. "Let them go alone, Lucy."

"As you may have noticed, Eddie doesn't always concentrate on what's the most important matter at hand at any given time."

"Bertie's with him. And Eddie, I suspect, is quite capable of concentrating on matters at hand when he has to."

I watched them walk up the steps together, holding hands. Bertie in her yoga gear, Eddie in his wedding guest suit, the borrowed paperback tucked under his arm.

"At least he has something to read if they have to wait long," I said.

Connor gave me a smile. "Always the librarian."

He put the car into gear, but I said. "Hold on a sec."

Bertie and Eddie had reached the top of the steps. Detective North held the door open for them as a man I knew walked out. North said something to him, and he nodded before running lightly down the stairs. North then spoke to Eddie, and they went inside.

The man spotted Connor's car and saw me watching. I gave him a wave, and he came over with a smile. "Hi. Lucy. Mr. Mayor."

I rolled down my window. "Louis, I never had the opportunity to thank you for doing such a lovely job at our wedding." Louis Rodgers was a waiter at the Ocean Side as well as a patron of the Lighthouse Library, where he regularly brought his children to story time.

"Easy to do a good job when you have such nice guests," he said. "I was sorry to hear about that guy who died."

"As were we," I said. "Although we didn't know him well. Tell me if it's none of my business." Connor stabbed me in the side with his elbow, but I ignored him. "I can't help wondering if you were talking to the police about that."

"Yeah, Lucy, I was. Dave Willshaw, that's the hotel manager, left messages for everyone who'd worked on Saturday evening to contact the police. I didn't come in earlier because I went to Raleigh Sunday morning to visit my mom and just got back."

"Did you have anything to tell them?"

"Don't you have to be getting to work, Lucy?" Connor said.

"Won't be a minute," I replied.

"They showed me a photo of the dead guy," Louis said. "I remembered him. He drank a heck of a lot but didn't cause any trouble that I was aware of. Other than with the woman he was with." He grimaced. "I overheard her telling him to cut down, and his reply wasn't all that polite. She left in a huff, and he stayed, but I don't know for how much longer. People were starting to leave, including you two, and I didn't notice when he'd gone. They'd been seated at one of the smaller tables with one other couple. The cops asked me how everyone at the table had gotten on." He shrugged. "Fine. No trouble there, far as I noticed. And I would have. You'd be surprised at some of the things people say in front of the waitstaff. I coulda told them the other woman at that table was not having the great time she was pretending to. Family trouble, I figured. She confined herself to throwing poisonous looks, between snuggling up to the guy she was with, at the other tables. One in particular, where everyone pretended to ignore her. Some of the things I've seen at weddings, you wouldn't believe."

"Thanks, Louis," I said. "Ronald has some great ideas for preschool programming later in the spring. I hope we'll see you and the kids there."

"You sure will. Bye. Bye, Connor." He trotted off.

Connor tutted. I gave him a smile and a *What can I do?* shrug. He ruffled my curls. "Learn anything?"

"Joyce and Wayne's tablemates were Kristen, my soon-to-be-ex-sister-in-law, and her new boyfriend, Ray something."

"Ray Croft, according to Gloria." Connor pulled onto the street and headed for our house.

"Right. Kristen shouldn't have even come to my wedding, as she's no longer with my brother and she and I are not friends, never mind that my mom made no attempt to pretend she was welcome. That lot were seated at what Aunt Joyce called the Richardson family outcast table, and the poisonous looks

Kristen was throwing were probably directed to my brother Kevin. With a couple of asides to Mom. Wayne behaved totally differently on Friday night than he did on Saturday. I'm wondering why and if that had anything to do with what happened to him."

Connor laughed. "Louis said Wayne and Ray Croft got on okay."

"Seemed to be getting on okay. When they were forced to sit together at the reception, Wayne might have decided to make the best of it. Maybe he pretended seeing the guy hadn't bothered him. Not if they were old friends." I mulled that over for a few seconds, and then I said, "But none of our business, right? Unless Sam decides to hold Eddie. You don't think they'll arrest Eddie, do you, Connor?"

"It doesn't look good that he couldn't be found for three days until we tracked him down. But if there's no other evidence . . ."

"Which there won't be. A waiter reported that Eddie and Wayne had been arguing, but Eddie explained what happened. I myself overheard some of that conversation, and I wouldn't call it an argument. Anything can happen, though, and Eddie wants a lawyer on standby, so I'll give Steph a quick call." Stephanie Stanton was a partner with Uncle Amos at his two-person law firm.

My friend answered the phone on the third ring. I could hear the buzz of conversation in the background and the *tap, tap* of her heels as she walked down a corridor. "Is that the blushing bride? What's up? Give me a sec, Lori. I'll be right there."

"It's Lucy, yes. And I'm sorry to report that my post-wedding glow has been temporarily suspended. You heard about the man who died in the hotel Saturday night into Sunday morning?"

"Yeah, I did. He was a guest at your wedding. I was asked if I knew anything about it."

"Did you?"

"No. I might have seen the guy, but I didn't speak to him. Why?"

"This is just a quick heads-up, but Eddie McClanahan is currently at the police station, being interviewed by Detectives Watson and North. He might know something about what happened. I said I'd call you on his behalf."

"Interviewed, as in arrested and cautioned or simply called in for a friendly chat?"

"The latter. So far."

"Okay. I'm on my way in to court. Shouldn't take long, and after that I'll be available for the rest of the day. Call me if this escalates and he needs me to come down. If you can't get me, call Amos, and he'll act until I'm free."

"Thanks, Steph."

"Take care." She hung up.

I put away my phone.

Connor said, "I need to go to the office. I have a noon meeting I'd prefer not to miss. Are you going straight to the library once you get your car?"

"Soon as I get Charles."

Connor pulled into our driveway. He came with me into the house for his briefcase and laptop, gave me a quick kiss as I was calling for Charles, and left.

"Soon as I get Charles," I said to myself once the door was closed, "and make some phone calls."

I'd learned that unexpected things can happen in a police investigation. In case the police did have some reason to hold Eddie, I wanted to be prepared.

First, I texted Bertie to tell her Steph was waiting for their call if she was needed. I then phoned Aunt Joyce. I could hear the sound of low conversation in the background when she answered.

"Hi, Aunt Joyce, it's Lucy. Hope I'm not bothering you?"

"You're not, dear. I'm having lunch at a charming little place by the pier, but I'm dining on my own. Your parents left this morning."

"I wanted to check in. Make sure you're okay."

"I'm perfectly fine. Why would I not be? Oh, you're worried that I might be grieving over the death of Wayne. I'm sorry he died; he did have his fun moments, but as I said, I'd decided to disinvest myself of his company."

"Uh . . . okay."

"You think me cold, Lucy. Perhaps I am. Emotional entanglements have never done me well in life. To assure you that I'm not entirely cold, I've been in touch with Wayne's family. His parents live in Florida, and they are not in good health. I volunteered to stay here until I can make arrangements to have him returned to them."

"That was nice of you."

"As I said, not entirely cold." I heard a smile in her voice. "It turns out his birth name is Fort. Wayne Fort. I assume Fortunada was an attempt to pick a lucky name for his acting career. In that he was not entirely successful. But that's of no matter anymore. I picked up from general conversation that you're on good terms with the local police. Do you have any idea as to when they will be releasing the body?"

"I'm not on that good terms with them, and no, I don't. Sorry."

"There are worse places to wait."

"Indeed there are. If you're wanting some suggestions as to where to go to see the sights, let me know."

"I will."

"You'd be welcome to come to the library book club on Thursday evening. We're discussing some of the works of Edgar Allan Poe."

"Is that so? I've always adored Poe. I intended to major in American literature in college. Never got my degree, though. I seem to remember something about a wild weekend in the Village that turned into far more than a weekend." She sighed—with regret or fond memories, I couldn't tell. "A story for another day. As for Poe, I used to reread his stories every few years, but it's been a while. Thank you, dear. If I'm still here, I'd enjoy coming." I heard a voice and the shuffling of plates and cutlery. "Here's my food arriving now. If there's nothing else?"

"One quick question, please. You sat with Kristen and her friend at the reception. Gloria said his name was Ray Croft."

"That's correct."

"How did he and Wayne seem to be getting on?"

"Perfectly fine. Coincidently, Ray's an actor. He's had some small parts on Broadway, and thus he and Wayne had something in common to discuss, although Ray's a good fifteen or twenty years younger than Wayne. Wayne didn't like to admit it, but he hasn't had a part in considerably longer than that. Still, they did have that background in common. Wayne was quieter than he would normally be when he encountered someone happy to hear about the good old days, but Ray talked enough for the both of them. He talked enough for all of us, truth be told."

"You didn't notice any animosity between them?"

"Not him in particular, no. I believe I've mentioned, more than once, that Wayne was in a foul mood. He was moderately polite to our table companions but nothing more than that. At the beginning of the evening, anyway. As time passed and he drank more, he got quieter, sullen even."

"What about Wayne and Kristen? How did they get on?"

"Why are you asking this, Lucy?"

"I'm just trying to put a picture together about what happened that night."

"Your mother warned me that you might want to do that. Kristen was also not in the best of moods. Anyone would have thought Wayne and Kristen were partners and had had a fight. I don't mean they were angry at each other; more like neither of them was having a good time. Wayne didn't try to pretend to be enjoying himself, but Kristen did. It was all so very fake, her attempting to show Kevin how delightfully happy she is without him. Ha-ha. She also pretended not to notice your mother throwing daggers at her from the head table. Now, if that's all, dear, my soup is getting cold."

"I'll let you go, then. Bye."

I hung up. So Ray was on Broadway. He and Wayne might well have had a far stronger connection than Aunt Joyce noticed. As for Kristen, had she been trying to show off to Kevin or pretending not to be upset at encountering Wayne?

I checked the time. My mom and dad would be in the air right about now. I sent Mom a text: *Can you call me when you have a minute. Question about the current situation.*

I wasn't investigating. I was simply asking questions. If I got any answers, I'd take what I knew straight to Detective Watson.

I looked up from my phone to see Charles sitting by the cat carrier, watching me. "Let's go to work," I said.

* * *

The library was busy for a Tuesday, and I tried to put thoughts of blackmail and murder most foul out of my mind as I went about my work. I tried, but I wasn't entirely successful.

Bertie called around three, as the toddlers' story time was getting out and hordes of cute little kids were spilling down the spiral stairs, clutching their books in one hand and their parents' hands or the banister in the other, calling good-bye to Ronald or hello to me.

"Eddie and I have arrived at my house. The police had a great many questions for him, but eventually they said he could go."

"That's good."

"I won't be coming in today. I have to admit, if only to you, Lucy, I'm finding all of this quite overwhelming."

"I understand. I'm glad Sam believed what Eddie had to tell him."

"He did. I think he did, at any rate. That other detective, the new one, I'm not so sure about him."

"What does that mean?"

"For all his absent-minded-professor manner, Eddie is an astute judge of character. He sensed a great deal of hostility from that Detective North. He admits North and Sam might have been playing good cop/bad cop—"

"That's not Sam's style. He doesn't play games."

"Which is what I told Eddie. He got the impression that if it was up to Detective North, he would have been held and charged. Eddie is, as you know, a linguist; the nuances of how we use language are something of which he is fully aware. At one point the detectives excused themselves from the room and Eddie heard them arguing in the hallway, although he couldn't make out the precise words. Sam came back into the room and told Eddie he was free to go. He didn't see Detective North again."

"I can't say I was all that impressed with North myself, but he's new and he's likely trying to prove himself."

"You're probably right. In any job, the young, green newcomer has one of two ways of making his mark: he either submits to the authority of the older person and learns from that, or he tries to immediately override what he sees as the old way of doing things. Detective North is doing the latter. That doesn't always work out to everyone's advantage."

"Right now, what matters is that Eddie's not been charged. What are his plans?"

"He has classes to give at Blacklock tomorrow, and Sam said he could go home as long as he can be reached if needed. He'll leave in the morning."

"Okay. Call me if you need anything."

"I will. Thank you, Lucy."

Cell phone reception inside the thick stone walls of the lighthouse is unreliable at best, so we never rely on our mobile phones. Bertie had called me on the landline, and I'd taken the call standing to one side of the circulation desk, where Louise Jane was helping the children and their parents check out their books. I hung up to see that the patrons had been dealt with and Louise Jane was making no attempt to hide that she'd been listening to my end of the conversation.

"Problem?" she asked.

"No. Something's come up, so Bertie won't be in for the rest of the day."

She gave me that smile that always put me in mind of a circling shark. "If you need my help, Lucy, please feel free to ask."

"Thanks. You can shelve the books on the returns cart, please." Charles had come down after his favorite part of the day—story time—and taken his post on top of the stack of books being returned to watch the children leave. When he shifted his weight, the pile wobbled dangerously.

"I meant," Louise Jane said, "I'll help with the investigation."

"No help needed," I said, "as there is no investigation. On my part, anyway."

"What reason, then, might you and Bertie have to discuss the delectable Detective North? You're a married woman, and although that's never stopped anyone before from admiring a good-looking man, you have been married for all of three days, and my intense knowledge of the human condition combined with my Sherlockian observational skills tell me you're over-the-moon happy in your marriage. So far, anyway. As for Bertie, she might have a wandering eye, but the man we're talking about is about twenty years her junior. Not that that means anything in this day and—"

"I'm simply asking questions, that's all."

"You've said that before. How's that worked out? I seem to remember a certain incident at the Settlers' Day Fair one year when yours truly—"

"Saved my life. I did say thank-you for that, didn't I?"

"As I recall," she admitted.

The timely arrival of a patron saved me from (1) an analysis of the time Louise Jane did save my life and (2) further explanation that I was not investigating, only asking questions.

"Louise Jane, I simply cannot get that computer to work. Good afternoon, Lucy. My congratulations on your marriage."

"Thank you, Mrs. Lancaster."

"*Not work* can mean a lot of things," Louise Jane said. "The computer was working fine a few minutes ago."

"It will not bring up the page I'm interested in reading."

Louise Jane stood up. "I'll have a look, but I have to remind you we have children's safety protocols installed."

Mrs. Lancaster was in her eighties, sharp eyed and sharp tongued. "I'll have none of your insolence, girl. Let me remind you I play bridge with your grandmother once a week. I am trying, not that it's any of your concern, to access the local newspaper, where, so I've been told, my great-granddaughter's exploits on the high school soccer team are prominently featured."

"Congratulations," I said. "You must be very proud."

"Thank you, dear. I am. Louise Jane, I don't know why you can't be more like Lucy. Lucy never makes snide comments."

Mrs. Lancaster headed across the room, back to the computers. Louise Jane meekly followed, but not before throwing me a look that might be considered lethal. I smothered a laugh.

Chapter Nine

Connor and I had finished dinner. He was getting some work done and I was reading 'The Tell-Tale Heart' in preparation for Thursday's book club meeting when my mom finally returned my text.

"Sorry I didn't call you earlier, dear, but our flight was delayed, and when we eventually landed, your father had to deal with some sort of an emergency at the office, which turned out to be no emergency at all. Then when I got home, it was to discover that the landscaping firm has quit on us. Imagine! Business, apparently, has picked up so much this spring they've decided to concentrate their efforts on another part of town, which means that, at the busiest time of the year, I am left scrambling to find a reliable firm to maintain our garden."

"My sympathies."

"Sarcasm does not become you. I only now remembered you wanted me to call you. Which I am doing."

"When we were at Aunt Ellen's, you said you thought you remembered Kristen's boyfriend from somewhere. I was wondering if you've given that any more thought."

"For once, Lucy, I'm ahead of you. Our flight was delayed, my new book turned out to be incredibly boring, so I had time to think."

"And?"

"And I remembered. Although, I must confess, I wasn't actually thinking about him. Or about Kristen and Kevin and their problems. I was remembering that I was supposed to confirm arrangements to go to a play with Andrea Myers and her husband when it popped into my head."

"The mind is a wonderful thing."

"It is indeed. This happened less than a year ago. Six months, perhaps. Kristen and I went to see a play. That man, Kristen's partner at your wedding, was one of the actors. Dreadful play, turgid dialogue, unimpressive acting, including his. It was an off-off-Broadway thing visiting Boston for one last gasp before being assigned to the dump heap of theatrical history."

"You're sure it was him, Ray Croft? Did you get a close look?"

"I'm positive. Almost positive. The theater was small, and we had front-row seats. He was in stage makeup but nothing over-the-top, dressed in modern street clothes, not anything I'd call a costume. I couldn't understand why Kristen had wanted to see that particular play." She chuckled. "Now I know. It was unusual, as in unprecedented, for Kristen and me to go to an event of any sort alone together. She suggested it as an early birthday treat. In retrospect, I thought she'd been trying to butter me up and get me onto her side for the impending divorce. What I particularly remember, now it's all coming back, is that she and I did not leave together at the end. We'd met for a drink before going to the theater and took separate cabs when the play was over." Mom chuckled again. "I now suspect she didn't go straight home, if you catch my meaning."

"I do, Mom. So it's possible Kristen was seeing this guy Ray while she was still living with Kevin."

"More than possible. Likely."

"Thanks."

"Lucy, dear, I know you have an inquisitive mind, something your father and I always encouraged, but I'm not entirely happy with this conversation. In the past, you've become involved when someone you cared about died or was implicated in the death. But Wayne meant nothing to you, and not even Joyce seems unduly upset at his passing. I'd like you to promise me you'll leave all this up to the police."

"I won't do anything dangerous, Mom," I said. "Satisfying that inquisitive mind is all." My mother's impressions of my childhood are different from mine. Rather than encourage inquisitiveness or curiosity, she did all she could to stifle my desire to escape the old-money, country-club, wife-of-law-partner lifestyle I believed she was trapped in. As for my dad—he pretty much didn't notice me for a substantial part of my life.

I'd fled Boston and come to the Outer Banks as much to escape my mother's influence as to start a new life. It was only later, when Mom came to visit and had issues of her own to deal with, that we connected on a personal level and found a new respect for each other's choices. An offshoot of that visit was my dad coming to realize he was on a dangerous path to losing what he valued most.

"It was a lovely weekend, dear," Mom said. "Truly a beautiful wedding. Your Connor is a marvelous man, and it's obvious he adores you totally. Which is nothing more than you deserve. I fully expect to see you two in Boston before too much longer."

"And you're welcome here anytime."

"I know that, dear. I know that."

We hung up. I put the phone on the counter and thought about what she'd said. Why was I asking questions about Wayne and his death? The Nags Head Police, in the person of Detective Sam Watson, were perfectly competent and very good at their jobs. Let them deal with it.

Mom had said I had no personal reason to be involved. But I did. Wayne died at my wedding. At a hotel packed with my family and friends. And I knew a murder investigation could get unpleasant, not only for the guilty party but for everyone who was even partially involved. Such as Eddie and Bertie.

If I could smooth things over a bit, why not?

Let that inquisitive mind loose.

The next thing my inquisitive mind had to consider was whether or not Kristen's relationship with Ray Croft had any relevance to the death of Wayne. If not, I'd declare it none of my business and back away.

According to Eddie, Wayne had not been above resorting to blackmail in his youth. He'd gotten three thousand dollars out of Eddie, money Eddie could ill afford. He'd come back for more and hadn't gotten it, but had Wayne then decided blackmail could provide him with a welcome bit of extra income? It was possible Eddie wasn't his first victim and Wayne had simply been doing what he did best.

Had he continued along that line up until his death? It was definitely an angle worth considering.

Kristen and Kevin were heading for divorce court. Kevin was angry and felt betrayed and probably humiliated. He was prepared to fight to the last penny. And that probably wasn't an exaggeration. Kristen would be determined to get the best settlement she could. I knew very little about matrimonial law—nor did I want to ever find out—but I had to consider that if Kevin knew, and could prove in court, that Kristen and Ray had been having an affair while Kristen was still living under the same roof as her husband in apparent matrimonial stability, it might strengthen Kevin's hand in the divorce case.

Kristen would, obviously, not want that to happen.

Had Wayne known about that? Aunt Joyce assumed Wayne and Ray met for the first time at the wedding, but it was possible they already knew each other. Wayne might have met Kristen previously, in Ray's company. When he understood the situation between Kristen and her husband and in-laws, did he decide to turn his hand to a touch of blackmail?

Ray might not care too much what happened to Kristen's divorce petition, but Kristen certainly would.

Kristen, I concluded, was a prime candidate for blackmail.

I'd had a marvelous time at my wedding. Currents had been flowing around me all evening of which I'd been blissfully unaware. I'd love nothing more than to continue to be blissfully unaware, but Wayne had died, and thus the whereabouts and personal relationships of everyone at the hotel that evening was of interest to the police. And, ergo, of interest to me as well.

I put the kettle on to make myself a cup of tea. "I'm in the kitchen," I called through to the dining room. "Can I get you anything?"

"A beer would be nice, thanks," Connor called back. "I'm about to call it a night."

We didn't yet have a proper study in the house. Our plan was to turn the ocean-facing room on the second floor into a library/den. Work on the house had slowed to a crawl over the last few months as wedding planning took precedence, on top of which Connor's dad hurt his back and had been laid up for a couple of weeks. He typically was ready to leap back into the renovations after a healthy dose of painkillers and a day or two of rest, but Marie, Connor's mom, told their doctor what was up, and Fred received a stern lecture on age-related injury and long-term effects of neglect. Connor's own work schedule had been brutal over the winter. He was in his second term as the mayor of our town, but he's also a dentist. He doesn't intend to run for office again and has firmly declared his political career is over, so to keep his hand in and his dental office functioning, he does pro bono work and sees some favored patients one day a week.

While the kettle came to a boil, I went into the pantry for the tea bags. When we first moved in, this enclosed little room had contained a lot of secrets, but now it was nothing but a convenient space off the kitchen in which to store food jars and cans and packages of dried goods.

Secrets. Everyone has their secrets. Well, almost everyone. I didn't have any secrets from Connor. Did that mean I'd had a boring life before meeting him again as an adult? Probably. A boring life can be a good thing.

Then again, I didn't always share with him what I was doing about investigating murders. Not because I was keeping secrets, mind, but to keep him from worrying.

Not the same thing at all.

I found the tea bags and popped one into my mug as the kettle whistled. I poured the boiling water over the bag and added a splash of milk. Before returning to my book, I changed the music on my iPad. I'd been playing contemporary rock, but I needed to listen to something softer and calmer as the end of the day approached.

Once again, my subconscious took control, and I was reminded of someone else who'd been out of sorts at my wedding. I checked the time. Not yet ten. I should be able to make a quick call.

I love the open design of the main area of our house, but sometimes it can be a disadvantage. I was uncomfortably conscious of Connor working at the dining room table. Because I didn't want to disturb him, I took the phone into the bedroom to place my call. Not that I didn't want him listening to my conversation. It wasn't that at all.

"Good evening. TK Rare Books. Theodore Kowalski speaking," answered a voice in a deep, rich English accent. As part of his attempt to present himself as a serious literary scholar and an important book collector, Theodore, a thirtysomething native of

North Carolina, put on what he considered to be an upper-class English accent, along with tweed jackets drenched in the scent of tobacco (although he didn't smoke) and rimless glasses with clear lenses (because he had perfect vision).

"Hi, Theodore. I hope it's not too late to chat."

"Not at all, Lucy." The accent slipped slightly. "I'm negotiating a deal on the West Coast and just got off the phone with them."

"Buying or selling?"

"I'm buying. This person lives in Vancouver, but their late father lived in Kill Devil Hills, and the heirs want to get rid of his lifetime collection of classic mystery novels. I've been told it includes some promising early editions of Poe."

I wasn't surprised to hear my friend was buying and not selling. Theodore's a book collector and dealer. He does far more collecting than dealing, meaning he often buys items he then can't bear to part with or no one else wants. He barely makes a living from the few books and other collectables he does manage to sell, but he's content, and I believe that's all that counts.

"Be sure and stay out of bricked-up wine cellars," I said.

"You've been doing your reading for book club."

"I have. How's *Monte Cristo* coming?"

"Slowly."

I chuckled. "As for why I'm calling. I assume you heard that a body was found in the hotel on Sunday morning."

"I did. The man was a guest at your wedding. No one you're close to, I hope?"

"I'd never met him before last week. He came as my aunt Joyce's date, and even they weren't close."

"I was interviewed by the police about it. They asked if I'd observed anything about the man or if he'd been seen arguing with anyone. In all honesty, I could say I'd never seen him before, and I didn't pay any attention to him at the reception.

I was no help to the police at all." He cleared his throat. "The simple fact that you've asked me this question leads me to conclude that you, Lucy, are trying to be of help."

"I'm curious about one thing."

"I'll help if I can."

"The fiddle player in the band that played at the reception. Lorraine. You said she seemed off. Can you explain what you meant by that?"

"I can't see what that has to do with the man who died, but yes, she wasn't on form that night. She appeared to be ill or distracted. Lucy, you don't think—"

"I don't think anything. All I'm doing is gathering information."

A long pause came down the line. I let Theodore think, and eventually he said, "Distracted, yes. That might be the word. Lorraine's an enthusiastic, bouncy performer. Even when she's not required to be playing, she gives her all to the other players in terms of encouraging the audience to dance, mock conducting the rest of the band, playing the ham behind their backs, that sort of thing. Saturday she was stiff. She played her notes okay, but her personality, her enthusiasm, simply wasn't there. I don't think she even smiled unless the spotlight turned directly on her. Her bandmates noticed, and I saw them giving her worried looks."

"You said Lorraine's mom's a friend of your mom's and you know her personally. Do you think she'd agree to talk to me?"

"Lucy, she might have been having a bad night because her boyfriend dumped her or she was fired from her job that morning."

"In that case, I'll thank her for her time and leave."

"I can call her. I suppose it wouldn't hurt to ask."

"Thanks, Teddy."

"Anything for you, Lucy. Anything for you."

"Who are you talking to at this time of night?" Connor asked as he came into the bedroom.

"No one!"

"No one? With your phone in your hand and a guilty look on your face."

"I do not have a guilty look on my face. Do I?"

"Lucy."

"Okay. I'm gathering information about what various people might have been up to on Saturday night. That's all."

"If I didn't love you so much and know you as well as I do, I'd be angry at you for getting yourself involved in something that's none of your business."

"Unfortunately, Connor, it is my business." I threw the phone onto the nightstand and dropped onto the bed. "Eddie was interviewed by the police and they let him go. That doesn't mean he's in the clear. It might only mean they're gathering more evidence against him. He must have told them he had a supposed argument with Wayne not long before the man died. He would then have had to tell the detectives about his and Wayne's history. The blackmail in the past, the possible hint of further blackmail in the present. And then he comes back to the hotel alone and disappears for three days—yes, I can see that looks suspicious to those of a suspicious mind. Now, we know Eddie didn't do it."

"Do we?"

"Do we what?"

Connor sat next to me. Charles strolled into the room and jumped into my lap. I stroked his long, soft fur, and he purred.

"Do we know Eddie didn't do it?" Connor said. "You don't know him, Lucy, other than as Bertie's friend."

"I like to think I'm a good judge of character."

"Everyone thinks they're a good judge of character." He put his hand on top of mine, and together we stroked Charles.

"Don't get me wrong, Lucy, I don't think Eddie did it either. I believed everything he told us in Rodanthe. But what I think, or you think, doesn't matter."

I sighed and rested my head on his shoulder. "My mom says I have an inquisitive mind. She also says she and Dad encouraged that, which couldn't be further from the truth, but I'm happy if she believes it. Maybe my inquisitive mind gets the better of me sometimes."

"You do what you have to do, Lucy. But please, please, don't put yourself in danger."

I smiled at him. "I promise."

The sound Charles made sounded suspiciously like a laugh.

Chapter Ten

Wednesday was my day off. I'd planned to spend a good part of it writing letters of thanks to people who'd kindly sent us wedding presents.

Over a bowl of cereal and blueberries, I decided I could still do that. Later.

"Any plans for today?" Connor asked as he poured his own cereal.

"Write thank-you cards. If I don't get those done soon, they'll hang over my head forever. And end up never getting done."

"Be sure and thank my great-aunt Alice for the toast rack. It's a souvenir of her 1973 visit to London."

I laughed. "Top of my list. Her heart was in the right place, and that's all that counts."

"Don't forget, I told you I have that dinner meeting with the other area mayors tonight. I'll try not to be too late. Have you told Charles you're not going to the library today?"

I looked down to see the cat sitting by his carrier, his intense blue eyes fixed on me as though he were saying, *Get a move on*. When Charles lived in the library, he went to work every day except Sunday. He was still having trouble getting used to the new schedule.

"I love my job," I said, "and I know you love yours, but as much as I love it, I need some time off now and again. Must be nice to love it so much you can't bear to take a day off."

Connor put his breakfast dishes into the dishwasher. "If I had a job where I could take a nap whenever I wanted and people fussed over me constantly, I might not want to miss a day either."

"Sounds like your job when you're at home," I said with a smile.

"Love you," he said, as he went to get his things.

"Love you more," I called after him.

Once Connor had left, I tidied up the kitchen and then showered and dressed. I wanted to have a chat with someone, but I decided not to phone ahead. Better, I thought, to catch my prey unawares.

I arrived at the Ocean Side Hotel at nine o'clock, hoping a person on vacation would not yet have gone out for the day. One woman stood behind the reception desk, dealing with a guest, while a family of four, surrounded by a mountain of luggage, waited not terribly patiently to be seen to.

"Tyler," the man said, "if you do that to Madison one more time, I'm going to leave you behind."

"Yeah!" six-year-old Tyler shouted. "More vacation!"

"Have you no sense?" the woman snapped at her husband. "All you're doing is encouraging him."

"Pardon me for trying to be a responsible father," he replied.

While the parents glared at each other, Madison, all of five years old, stuck her tongue out at her brother.

"Mom!" he wailed.

I decided to have a quick look around for the person I was after before asking the receptionist to make a call to the room. I headed for the restaurant.

"Good morning," the hostess said. "Table for one?"

"No, thank you. I'm looking for someone. Okay if I have a peek?"

"Certainly, Mrs. McNeil."

I was glad I hadn't asked for a table for one. If I had, word would be all over town by lunchtime that the mayor's new bride was breakfasting alone.

I found my sister-in-law Kristen sitting by herself at a table for two next to the windows overlooking the pool area and beyond it to the boardwalk leading over the dunes and through the sea oats to the beach. She had a plate piled high with offerings from the buffet, along with a glass of orange juice and a carafe of coffee. Her iPad was propped against a salt cellar, and she was idly scrolling through it with one hand while she drank coffee with the other.

"Good morning." I put on my warmest smile.

She looked up and blinked in surprise. "Lucy. I'm surprised to see you here."

"I had some final details to settle with the hotel and thought I'd pop in and see who was up bright and early."

She nodded, her smile stiff. "Lovely wedding, by the way. I had such a marvelous time. You don't happen to know if Kevin's still in town, do you?"

"No."

I stood next to her table, smiling inanely, not moving. Finally, as expected, she gestured to the spare chair and said, "Won't you join me?"

Thank heavens for good manners. I plopped myself down. "Thanks. I've had breakfast, but a cup of coffee wouldn't go amiss." The extra place was already set, and I shoved the cup toward her. Kristen poured the dregs out of the carafe.

"I didn't get a chance to talk to your friend the other night," I said. "Ray, is it? How long have you known him?"

Her eyes narrowed. "Not long."

"Where did you two meet? Does he live in Boston?"

"He's from New York. We met when he was doing some work in Boston. That was . . . quite recently. Very recently, if you must know."

I hadn't asked, but I didn't push the point. "I'm sorry you and Kevin are having difficulties."

"Difficulties is putting it mildly. Kevin is not being reasonable. And, I might add, your mother isn't helping the situation any."

"My mother, like all mothers, wants her children to be happy, no matter how old they are. How are your kids, by the way?"

"They're fine. They're with my mom this week. I didn't bring them to the wedding because, well, because I didn't know how they'd react to seeing me with a new man. Ray's a dear, and we're so very happy together." She looked at me through eyes that didn't appear at all happy, more like wary. She thought I was acting as a spy for my brother.

"Not a breakfast eater?" I asked.

"What?"

"Ray? Not wanting breakfast?"

"He's sleeping in. As one is allowed to do on vacation."

I sipped my coffee. Cold and far too strong. "Have the police spoken to you about the man who died on Saturday?"

She shoveled eggs into her mouth. "They did, but I couldn't help them. Ray and I sat with him and Joyce at dinner, but I'd never met him before."

"Did you notice him behaving at all oddly?"

"What's *oddly* mean, Lucy? As I said, I didn't know him."

"Did you notice anyone paying particular attention to him that evening?"

"Other than Joyce? Who was, by the way, absolutely furious all night. She accused him of deliberately embarrassing her."

"Had he?"

"He didn't dance on the tables or assault any of the waitresses, if that's what you're asking. It's not comfortable attending the wedding of people you don't know. Joyce should have cut him some slack. Instead, she overreacted and got mad. She stalked out and told him he could find his own way back to New York. Sounds exactly like the behavior of a member of the Richardson family to me." She looked directly at me. "Present company excluded."

"Thanks. You hadn't met Wayne before. What about Ray?"

"You mean did Ray know him?" She shrugged. "Their paths had crossed on occasion. Ray's a stage actor. He's been in some major Broadway productions. You might have seen him once or twice, Lucy."

"Unlikely. I haven't been to a play on Broadway since I was in college. Not since Mom dragged me to New York for what she called my 'cultural edification.' " What other people call shopping.

"Your loss." Kristen spread butter on a slice of toast and added a huge dollop of strawberry jam. Her eyes wandered to her iPad, still open in front of her.

I didn't take the hint. "Did Ray tell the police he knew Wayne?"

Toast hovered in the air, halfway to her mouth. "I don't know what he told them. We were interviewed separately, and I didn't ask."

That was a lie. She and Ray would have discussed what each of them had to say to the police.

"I'm sorry, Lucy, but I have some things to attend to this morning. I'm very active in the PTA at the kids' school, and an issue has arisen." She indicated her iPad.

"Nice talking to you," I said. "Maybe I'll see you again before you leave."

"That would be nice," she lied again. The relief on her face when I made indications of leaving was palatable.

"What are your plans going forward?" I asked. "Are you planning to stay in Boston? You'll probably have to sell the house, right?"

"Kevin's being difficult about the sale of the house. Kevin is being difficult about everything. When the divorce is finalized, the kids and I will be moving to New York."

"Kevin won't like that. He wants to be close to the kids."

"I don't intend to allow Kevin to have anything to say about it." She took a huge bite out of her helpless piece of toast. "Kevin isn't quite the innocent little dear your mother thinks he is."

I didn't ask what that meant, and I left her to her breakfast and the demands of the PTA.

I didn't ask Kristen if she'd killed Wayne because he'd threatened to tell Kevin she and Ray had been fooling around when she and my brother were still together. I didn't tell her that if she'd killed Wayne to silence him, she needn't have bothered. My mother knew the situation, and my mother would not be keeping it a secret from her son and his lawyer.

My phone rang as I was crossing the lobby. The display said *Theodore*, and I answered.

"Good morning, Lucy. I talked to Lorraine, and we've arranged to meet for lunch today. I hope that will work for you?"

"Yes, thanks."

"Twelve o'clock at Josie's?"

"I'll be there. Did you tell her why?"

"No, and I have to admit, Lucy, I'm feeling extremely guilty about that. I didn't tell her you'd be joining us, and I didn't quite know how to come straight out and say we want to question her as to if she'd killed a man, so I mumbled something about enjoying her music at the wedding and wanting a chance to reconnect." His clear discomfort in this conversation caused his fake accent to slip to the point of disappearing.

"I'll make it look like happenchance I ran into you," I said.

"I might have mentioned that her mother's a longtime friend of my mother."

"You did."

"Our mothers had some notion when we were younger that maybe Lorraine and I could be . . . more than childhood friends."

"And . . . ?"

"That . . . didn't transpire. I wouldn't want her to think I'm . . . reconsidering."

"Lunch at Josie's is the perfect setting for a causal chat for old times' sake. It's not as if you've invited her to drinks and dinner."

"I suppose not. You're always so wise about these things, Lucy. I'll see you at Josie's, then."

I hung up before he could change his mind.

Now it was my turn to feel guilty. When it came to other people's personal entanglements, I wasn't wise in the least. Apart from that, it's one thing for me to ask questions—because I believe when a murder is committed at my wedding, that makes it my business—but quite another to drag my friends into doing something they're uncomfortable with.

I checked the time. Coming up to ten. I had two hours before my meeting with Lorraine. Enough time to run home and get a good start on those thank-you cards.

Chapter Eleven

My cousin Josie might well be the hardest-working person I know. The woman doesn't seem to need sleep, and even when she's not working, she's always on the lookout for something to do, such as helping out in the kitchen at her husband's restaurant. I'm nothing but delighted that all her hard work has paid off and she's made her place the hippest, hottest, most popular coffee shop in Nags Head. Josie's Cozy Bakery is now regarded as *the* spot for running in to grab a takeout coffee and baked good or to enjoy a casual light lunch.

As I drove into the strip mall where the bakery's located, I wondered how that no-sleep thing was working out now that she and Jake had Ellie.

The parking lot was almost full but not crammed to the point of illegal parking, as it would be at the height of the season. Locals know not to even try to have breakfast or lunch at Josie's at a reasonable time in the summer.

It was ten after twelve. I didn't want to arrive right on time and find that Theodore and his friend were late. If this was supposed to be a casual, unexpected encounter, I couldn't hang around waiting for them to come in.

Trying to be circumspect, I peeked into the bakery windows. I couldn't spot my quarry, but as several tables are tucked out of sight of the windows, that didn't mean they weren't here. A small line in front of the counter waited patiently to be served.

"Afternoon, Lucy," a man said as he emerged, clutching a takeout cup and a paper bag.

"Hi," I said, forgetting his name. I couldn't stand here peeking in the windows forever, so I grabbed the closing door and went inside, to be instantly enveloped in a cloud of warm steam and the marvelous scents of sugar and cinnamon, hot pastries, and bread straight out of the oven. People chatted and laughed and drank coffee, the espresso machines steamed and gurgled, and the barista called, "Extra-large chia latte and low-fat chocolate cinnamon latte with whipped cream." What, I wondered, was the point of ordering a low-fat drink if you asked for whipped cream on the top? A group of teenage girls on their school lunch break, all long shiny hair and toothy white smiles, grabbed their drinks and sandwiches and headed for the door, laughing.

Josie had decorated her place in a mixture of Seattle coffee culture and Outer Banks fishing community, and it worked surprisingly well. Behind the serving counter it was chrome and subway tiles, giant steel machines emitting clouds of steam, open cupboards displaying stacks of white cups and side plates. Another shelf held baskets of Josie-made bread, and mouthwatering pastries filled the glass-fronted display counter. In the seating area, the tables were made of reclaimed and restored ships' barrels and wooden tea chests, and the chairs and stools were upholstered in a nautical-blue fabric trimmed with rope. Photographs and paintings of Cape Cod scenes hung on the sea-blue walls.

I spotted Theodore and Lorraine as soon as I came in. They were seated at a high-topped table for two tucked into a corner beneath a photo of the Bodie Island Lighthouse taken on a winter night, the light from the lamp high above shining on the ice-covered marsh. Teddy was dressed as though he'd recently returned from a stroll around his country estate in pressed trousers, blue shirt, thin blue tie, and a Harris tweed jacket with elbow patches. Lorraine's hair was gathered in a clip at the back of her head, her only makeup a touch of pale-pink lipstick. She wore a belted brown dress under an oatmeal sweater. Judging by her appearance, she split her two worlds neatly in two—high school English teacher by day and punk rock musician by night.

I approached their table with a smile. "Hi. Nice to see you." Thick sandwiches had been unwrapped from butcher paper, and mugs of coffee sat on the table in front of each of them. Theodore had added a giant-sized chocolate chip cookie to his lunch, and Lorraine had selected one of Josie's justifiably famous pecan squares.

Theodore leapt to his feet, almost knocking his stool over. "Lucy! This is a surprise! I wouldn't have expected to see you here!"

Lorraine gave him a curious look. Considering Josie's my cousin and I come here at least once a week, usually more, Theodore was laying it on a mite thick.

"You remember Lorraine, of course. Who played at your wedding? Wasn't she great? She and her band, of course. They were great too!"

"Of course I remember. Connor and I met with Lorraine to make the arrangements."

"It was a marvelous wedding," she said. "We had an enormous amount of fun, and it was obvious your guests did too."

"Except for that man dying." Theodore's voice was so loud, people at neighboring tables lifted their heads. "Why don't you join us, Lucy? You're not in a hurry, I hope." He glanced around, seeking an extra stool. He looked almost desperate when he realized one wasn't at hand.

"I'm glad I ran into you," I said to Lorraine, while Theodore dashed off in search of a seat for me. "A great many people told me how much they enjoyed your music on Saturday. Perfect dance music for a variety of ages and energy levels."

She smiled. "Thanks. That's always good to hear."

I staggered as something was shoved up against my legs. I collapsed onto a stool.

"Why don't I get you a coffee, Lucy?" Theodore said, "Something to eat? Muffin? Danish? Maybe a sandwich?"

"A latte would be nice, thanks."

Lorraine watched him go, a soft smile on her face. "Dear Teddy. Truly an original." She took a bite of her sandwich.

"You and he were friends when you were young, he told me."

"We were. We spent a lot of time together, as we're around the same age and our mothers were great friends. Still are great friends. Our mothers, that is. I hadn't seen Teddy for ages before Saturday."

I should have prepared myself better. Now that I was here, I couldn't think of a way of approaching what I wanted to talk to this woman about. It would be somewhat insulting to come straight out and say, "I noticed you weren't playing very well. Any reason for that?"

Fortunately, Lorraine herself broached the topic. "I heard about what happened. After the reception, I mean. That man dying. I'm sorry. Were you close?"

"I didn't know him at all. He came as my aunt Joyce's plus-one. We'd never met. I've been told the circumstances of his death are suspicious. Did the police talk to you?"

"They did. To all of us in the band, I mean. Asked if we'd seen him arguing with anyone or anyone acting suspiciously around him. They never say what *suspiciously* means, do they?"

"No. What did you say to that?"

She put her sandwich on the table and studied my face. "Teddy's a dear. I'd forgotten that about him. Part of what makes him such a dear, and sadly an original, is that he's truly a nice man. And nice means honest, in my book anyway. He was talking about you before you suddenly appeared. *What a coincidence.* Not. He said you've been of help to the police before. I didn't ask what that meant. Should I have?"

"Here you go, here you go." Not the latte I'd asked for but a mug of coffee dropped onto the table in front of me, and Theodore settled himself into his seat. He gave us both huge smiles. "Isn't this nice?"

To my considerable surprise, Lorraine laughed. "Oh, Teddy. Please don't ever change. Okay, Lucy, only because it's important to Teddy, I'll answer the questions you're too polite to come straight out and ask. The man who died at or shortly after your wedding reception was named Wayne Fortunada, and I had met him before, I'm sorry to say. After college, I spent a few years in New York City, trying to make it as a musician. You can judge the success of my musical career by the fact that I teach English at a high school in North Carolina and give private violin lessons to kids whose lack of talent is matched only by their lack of interest."

"Nothing wrong—" Theodore began.

"I know, Teddy, I know. And believe it or not, I'm perfectly happy with the way things turned out. I'm a good enough musician but nowhere near good enough to make it to the top. I play classical violin." She cocked her head, lifted her hands to one side, and moved her fingers across an imaginary instrument. Her fingers were long and her nails cut short. "As a child I took piano lessons, but it never truly grabbed me, so I switched to violin and totally fell in love with strings. I thought that would be enough. It isn't. Not in the rarified air of symphony orchestras in New York City or even small local orchestras. I thought classical music would rise above all the petty jealousies and minor resentments of more commercial theatre. Was I ever wrong. It's worse in classical music because opportunities are so much more limited. I . . . I didn't like myself in New York. I was becoming someone I didn't want to be. I eventually realized it, and I left. I have Wayne Fortunada to thank for that."

"Why?" I asked.

"I was acquainted with him, but only peripherally. At the time—this was about ten years ago, give or take—he was going out with a woman who was a major donor for a small orchestra in SoHo. Very cutting-edge, risqué, experimental interpretations of the music, lots of buzz around them. By going out with, I mean he was her temporary paid companion."

Lorraine picked up her coffee cup. She cradled it in her hands and gazed into the middle distance. Remembering. "I had an audition with that orchestra. I was excited about it, and I believed I had a good shot at landing it. They presented the sort of music I wanted to play." She gave Theodore a soft smile. "At the time I considered myself to also be risqué and cutting-edge, capable of generating lots of buzz. How we fool ourselves. Anyway, this other woman, who doesn't need to be named, was my main competition. She wasn't a better musician than me, but she was tall and leggy and pretty and knew how to play it up."

"That shouldn't matter—" Theodore began, but Lorraine interrupted him.

"Shouldn't. But it does. I did something I'm not proud of, and I justified myself, to myself, by saying all I was doing was trying to even the odds out a bit."

I sipped my coffee and said nothing. Teddy was watching Lorraine closely, his eyes wide with such admiration it might verge on adoration.

That a relationship between Lorraine and Teddy had come to naught, despite their mothers' conspiring, clearly had not been Theodore's intention.

"The orchestra put on a fund-raising reception the night before the auditions," Lorraine continued. "The bill was footed, as it usually was, by Wayne Fortunada's lady friend. Wayne was there, of course, front and center, being shown off and showing off. He was one of those people who has no talent and never had any success but's able to convince everyone that doesn't matter. The other thing about Wayne was that he was not only being observed but always observing. He watched everything and everyone. When I first met him, I liked him. I thought he was naturally curious about people, and I like that. Again, more fool me. What he was doing was searching for opportunities to exploit people. I handed one to him on a silver platter."

"What did you do?" Theodore asked.

She reached across the table and put her hand on his. "First, I need to you know that wasn't me, Teddy. Yes, it was me then. But it's not the me I am now. I was young, I was ambitious, and I found myself surrounded by people who'd do just about anything to make it."

"What did you do?" he repeated.

I felt as though I were no longer at the table. That I'd slowly dissolved into the warm coffee-and-pastry-scented air.

"One of my friends at the time was, believe it or not, dating a low-level drug dealer. She was quite open about that, thought it was a great lark. I asked her to get me something I could slip into my rival's drink."

"That's dangerous," Theodore said.

"You think? Dangerous. Stupid. But I did it. My intention was to get my rival too sick to be able to perform at the audition in the morning. In that, I was completely successful. She missed the audition." Lorraine shook her head. "She didn't get that job, so a month later she applied for, and got, a position with the American Symphony. Last I heard of her, she was touring in Europe. If you look at it that way, I did her a huge favor. I didn't get the job either. I made a mess of the audition, the result of guilt probably. The job went to a guy I'd never even heard of before. I'd like to say that was the end of that, but it wasn't. Wayne Fortunada, who'd been watching everyone that night, had seen me fiddling with the other woman's drink when she looked away. Not only seen me, but he took a picture of his lady friend surrounded by her circle of hangers-on. And there I am, in the background, my hand hovering over the glass."

"He blackmailed you," I said.

"Yup. Pay up or he'd show the picture to his friend under the pretext of being shocked, shocked that people would reduce themselves to that level, and I'd be blackballed forever."

"Did you?"

"Pay? Yes. He didn't even want a lot of money. Good thing, as I didn't have a lot of money to give. He did it, I think, more for the feeling of having power over someone than the money. Then again, maybe he needed even small amounts of money. His lady friend kicked him out not long after, I heard. I paid up, I reconsidered my life choices, and I came back to Nags Head. In a way, I can say Wayne Fortunada did me a favor. Who knows what I might have done next if I hadn't had a wake-up call. Not a lot of demand for classical violinists at Nags Head weddings, so I now play fiddle in a girl band and I love it."

"Did you tell the police this?" I asked.

"No. In all honestly, I told them I might have seen Wayne some ten years or so ago but we hadn't been friends then, or even acquaintances, and I haven't seen him since. Which is true. I didn't lie." She began wrapping up her barely touched sandwich. "I'm sorry to run, Teddy, but I have to be getting back."

He threw me a questioning look.

"I think you should tell the police what you've told us," I said.

"Why would I do that?" Lorraine asked.

"It helps to paint a picture of Wayne. If he was the sort to blackmail you, it's entirely possible he had enemies."

She stood up. "It was a long time ago. What's past is past. His death had nothing to do with me."

"I'm afraid it doesn't work like that. Everything can be relevant in a murder case, and we don't get to pick and choose what we want the police to know."

She studied my face once again. I tried to look supportive. "It's aways bothered me," she said eventually, "what I did. What I learned about myself. Seeing Wayne again reminded me that I haven't forgiven myself. It turned out okay for her, the other musician, but it might not have. I didn't even know what I was giving her. I told Teddy the story because I like him and trust him, but maybe I shouldn't have talked to him with you sitting there."

"You knew this meeting was arranged," I said.

She grinned. "Yeah. I guessed. Okay, for what it's worth, I didn't talk to Wayne on Saturday. I told the cops that, and they seemed okay with it and had no more questions for me. I don't think he even recognized me. Guys like Wayne don't. They don't notice people unless they're beautiful or rich women, or both, or men with influence he can take advantage of. People he can blackmail. A girl behind the fiddle in a small-town band? He didn't so much as glance in my direction. I thought he looked miserable all night and the woman he was with wasn't putting up with it. I told the cops that too. You can tell them what you want, Lucy." She picked up her purse. "Thanks for the lunch, Teddy. It was nice seeing you again."

He scrambled to his feet. "Would you like to come to book club with me tomorrow night?"

"Book club?"

"At the library. You teach English now. You did English at college, right?"

"I did a double major in music and nineteenth-century literature."

"I don't suppose you've read *The Count of Monte Cristo*?"

"Of course I have, but it's been a while."

"Better than the rest of the group. Dumas was too ambitious for them, so they're reading Poe."

"I love Poe."

He smiled at her, clearly willing her to say yes.

"I'd love to come," she said.

"Great! It's at the library. Seven o'clock."

"I'll see you there." She walked away.

Theodore dropped back onto his stool. Underneath his clear glass lenses, his eyes were shining.

Okay then. "Thanks," I said.

"Oh, sorry, Lucy. What was that?"

"I said thank-you. I'll see you tomorrow."

"Yes. Tomorrow. Too bad Lorraine couldn't be of any help, but it did her some good, I think, to talk about what's been bothering her." He stood up, and we walked out of the bakery together. He headed for his car, waving an absent-minded good-bye to me.

I watched him go. Had Lorraine been of no help? I wasn't so sure. Just because she said Wayne hadn't recognized her and she hadn't spoken to him didn't mean that hadn't happened.

Eddie believed Wayne had been threatening him with exposure of his youthful indiscretion. Had Wayne done the same to Lorraine?

Lorraine was a schoolteacher as well as a private music instructor. If word got out that she'd once drugged another woman's drink, no matter how long ago, she'd be fired and her source of music students would dry up instantly.

I liked Lorraine. Theodore obviously liked her a great deal. Could I, in all fairness, rat her out to the police? I reminded myself that I had nothing to rat about. She'd not asked me to keep her confidence, but she had told me things that would help Sam Watson paint a picture of the dead man.

I had the good detective's personal number in my contact list, and I placed the call. When he answered, I could hear the sound of a busy office in the background. "Lucy. What's up?"

"I hope I'm not bothering you, but—"

"But you've learned something you think I might want to know." His voice became muffled, but I could hear him say, "It's Lucy Richardson. Give me a minute."

"Lucy McNeil," I said.

He chuckled. "How could I forget. What's up, Lucy?"

"A couple of people at my wedding, apart from Eddie, had had previous contact with Wayne Fortunada. Did you know that?"

"Why don't you tell me what you know?"

"I know he wasn't a nice man, and it's likely he made enemies everywhere he went."

"Which is becoming my impression, but I'd like to hear your specifics. Where are you now?"

"I'm at Josie's."

"Perfect. I'm about ready for lunch as it is. Can you give me fifteen minutes? I've a couple of things to talk over with Detective North first."

"I'll be here."

I put my phone away and went back inside. I ordered a latte for me and a large black coffee for Watson and took a seat at the table recently vacated by Theodore and Lorraine. While I waited, my cousin's head popped around the kitchen door. When she spotted me, she came over, wiping her hands on her apron.

"Hi, sweetie. Alison told me you were here." She nodded to the two drinks. "Meeting Connor?"

"Sam Watson."

"To talk about that guy who died on Saturday night?"

"Yes."

She gave me a big grin. "Mom was looking after Ellie yesterday afternoon because Jake's mom had a doctor's appointment. Jake dropped her off on his way to the restaurant, and Grandma Gloria told him you're investigating."

"I'm not investigating. Just . . . pondering the situation."

"Don't tell Grandma that. She's wanting to help with your noninvestigating."

"Perish the thought. As long as we're talking about it . . . did you notice anything amiss at the wedding?"

"Not a single thing. I was in blissful ignorance, as I hope you were at the time, Lucy."

"I was."

"Good. It was so great to be out with adults again, sitting down to a good meal, having interesting conversations, dancing with my darling husband. Between all of that and constantly wondering if Ellie was okay without me on what was our first night apart, I wouldn't have noticed if an elephant had charged through the room. Sam called me on Sunday, and I told him that. Maybe not in such graphic terms." She laughed. "As for all the high drama swirling around the family—oblivious once again."

"You're lucky about that."

The door opened and Detective Watson came in. I half rose in my seat and waved.

"I'll leave you two to solve the problems of the world," Josie said. "Detective, can I get you anything? Lucy ordered you a coffee, but I can have one of the baristas bring you a sandwich or pastry if you'd like. Personalized service. Not everyone gets that."

"Thanks, Josie. A roast beef sandwich would be great. And whatever dessert you have to spare. I'll pay at the cash on my way out."

Josie waved and headed back to her sugar-and-cinnamon-scented domain.

Watson didn't have time to waste on chitchat, so I got straight to the point as he sat down. "You spent most of your career in New York, right?"

"Yeah, I did. I was a young and green patrol officer with the NYPD, eventually made detective working missing-persons cases and then homicide." He took a sip of the waiting coffee—black, no sugar, the way he liked it. "Thanks for this. CeeCee, who's an Outer Banks girl to the tips of her toes, never much liked the Big Apple, and that's an understatement, but she put up with it for my sake. When I'd gone about as far in my career as I wanted to go, she convinced me to come back to my roots. And here I am, thinking retirement might not be a bad option."

"Is that why the department hired Detective North? To take over from you?"

"Not specifically. We needed someone, staff's always turning over, and we've been shorthanded for a while. But I can't say it wasn't in the back of the chief's mind. As for me, don't tell CeeCee this, but I'm not entirely sure I'm ready to hang up my hat. I hope I've got a few years still left in me. It's always nice to have options, though. Enough of that; you didn't call me to ask about my career plans. Why the question about New York?"

"The origins of this case, I believe, lie in New York City. Specifically in the entertainment world."

Watson nodded. "Fortunada was a two-bit singer and dancer in his youth and more recently a hanger-on to the moderately rich and only peripherally famous. He was, in my personal opinion, a loser."

"Is that an official police term?"

"Might as well be. He was born in the Bronx, always lived in and around New York City. I've run his record, of course. Some minor embezzlement. A jail sentence for petty theft. Another more serious theft charge from a woman he was"—he made quotation marks in the air with his fingers—"'friends with.' The case never went to court, almost certainly because he gave the item back and she didn't want the sordid details splashed across the papers. All that plus Eddie McClanahan's story of blackmail tells me the guy wasn't exactly a respectable citizen."

"You think what Eddie told you is a story? As in made up?"

"No, I think it happened the way he says. I have to tell you, Lucy, Eddie's not in the clear. A witness reported that he overheard Eddie and Fortunada engaged in an intense discussion in the hotel hallway. Eddie left the hotel almost immediately after. Left, and then returned to the hotel, prior to disappearing for three days."

"You can't think—"

He lifted one hand. "What I think is not under discussion here. The idea of arresting him has been mentioned, but I squelched that. His behavior that night was suspicious, yes, highly suspicious, but Eddie's getting on in years and he has no history of violence. That's come to police attention, at any rate. It's been pointed out I might be closer to some of the people in this case than I should be. My response is that in a small town, it's hard, if not impossible, for the local police to be completely detached." He gave me a wry grin. "Never in all my years with the NYPD did I ever come across a personal friend even peripherally involved in a case. I didn't come here to tell you what I've learned, Lucy, but for you to talk to me. What else do you know about these New York connections?"

"Roast beef on a baguette and a lemon tart," the server said.

Watson leaned back to allow her to put the food in front of him. "Thanks."

I wished I'd asked for a sandwich too. It looked wonderful. As for the lemon tart—golden pastry, shimmering yellow lemon filling, crown of whipped cream—it might have been calling out my name. I tore my eyes off it and said, "Before I tell you, I should remind you I overheard Wayne's end of that conversation too, the one between him and Eddie. At the time I hadn't known Eddie was the person Wayne was talking to. I still don't know for sure he was. Wayne might have been talking to someone else. Although the timing is right, according to what the waiter said."

"Go on."

"My interpretation, for what it's worth, considering I had other things on my mind at the time . . ."

Watson smiled at me around a bite of his sandwich.

"Is that it wasn't an argument." I hesitated, suddenly aware that Eddie might not have told Watson as much as he told Bertie, Connor, and me. Eddie had interpreted Wayne's words as a threat to continue the blackmail. Stopping that threat might be considered grounds for murder.

"What was it then?" Watson asked.

"A discussion. A conversation. I didn't hear any hostility in Wayne's voice, and when I saw him moments later, he didn't look angry. More . . . sad. I don't believe he and Eddie argued." My voice trailed off. If it ever came to court and I was called as a witness, my interpretation of a snatch of half-heard conversation when, in my own words, "I had other things on my mind" would count for nothing. "You've said Wayne has a record as a minor thief, and we know he wasn't above blackmail. It's possible someone followed him to Nags Head, right? Killed him and went straight back to New York. Either to avoid another blackmail attempt or for simple revenge."

"Anything's possible."

"It's also possible this person didn't specifically follow him here but spotted him in town or at the hotel and . . . decided to take action."

"Again, possible. A hotel's a busy place, particularly on a Saturday night. As well as your wedding, plenty of hotel guests coming and going. Staff going about their jobs. Customers in and out of the restaurant and the bar. A couple of business meetings had been held there earlier in the day. Fortunada was a heavy smoker, and your aunt told me he excused himself a couple of times during the evening to go out for a smoke. We've tried to speak to everyone we can find, but there are always people we can't find, and not necessarily because they don't want to talk to us. They don't listen to the local radio or check local news online, or they left town first thing in the morning before word got around. Gathering all that information from all those people is part of the job. I'm assuming, Lucy, you know this. So what do you want to tell me?"

"Two things. First, my sister-in-law Kristen came to the wedding with a date. She and my brother are separated."

"I spoke to them. Kristen Richardson and Ray Croft."

"Ray's from New York City, and he's an actor."

Watson nodded.

"He knew Wayne from that world."

Watson's face remained expressionless, but something in his eyes told me this came as news to him. "How do you know?"

"Kristen told me. She said she doesn't know if Ray told you he was previously acquainted with Wayne or not, but I'm pretty sure she was lying. They would have talked it over at great length."

"When interviewed, people often leave out details they think are irrelevant or not necessary. They aren't always trying to be deceitful."

"Kristen's a prime candidate for blackmail." I went on to tell him what I knew about Kristen and Ray's relationship. "Someone told me Wayne was highly observant in that he was always searching for people's weakness and a way to exploit them. It wouldn't have been difficult to realize that Kevin and Kristen's divorce threatens to be down and dirty and each of them will be looking to gain an advantage over the other. My parents quite obviously have money; easy to assume Kristen and Kevin do as well, even though they don't."

As I spoke, Watson ate his sandwich and drank his coffee. All the while he kept those intense gray eyes fixed on me. "Okay. I'll consider that. I might have another chat with this Ray Croft. Ask if there's something he forgot to tell me. In the meantime, you can tell me about this person who told you Wayne was always looking for a blackmail opportunity."

"That's my second point. Lorraine Kittleman, the fiddle player in the band that played at the wedding."

Watson nodded. "They were all interviewed."

"She might not have told you she herself was once blackmailed by Wayne Fortunada. Again, when she lived in New York City, about ten years ago."

Watson shook his head sadly. "She neglected to mention that minor detail. Anything more?"

"No. Sorry."

"Don't be sorry. That's a lot of info, and it's info I didn't have. Did she speak to Fortunada on Saturday?"

"According to what she told me, not only did she not speak to him, she doesn't think he even noticed her."

"Does she know you're telling me this?"

"She does."

"Someone else I need to have another word with. As for you, Lucy. Think back for a moment to the conversation you overheard in the hallway. Has anything come to you about who the other person might have been?"

"No. Sorry. Is it official, then? That Wayne was murdered, I mean?"

"No doubt about it. Strangled by a length of cloth. Most likely a tie. The tie, unfortunately, is gone. We're searching for it, and that hotel generates a heck of a lot of trash in a day, but it's mighty easy to hide or dispose of a common necktie. Wear it out of the hotel and toss it in the trash a couple of miles away."

"Does a tie mean a man did it?"

"Not necessarily, and I said likely a tie. Could have been a woman's scarf. They only found a couple of fibers on the body and no way of telling exactly what sort of garment they were from."

"Every male guest at my wedding wore a tie," I said. "And I can think of several scarves and wraps the women had."

"Yup."

"Do you know the time of death?"

"Sometime between twelve thirty, when he can be positively placed for the final time, and around four AM." He sighed. "The scene's clean, more's the pity. We're still looking, but it's going to be difficult to determine if Fortunada was lured into the storage room and killed or moved there immediately after death. Unfortunately, the Sunday morning cleaners did an excellent job on the hallway. The carpet was thoroughly vacuumed and the walls dusted. The doorknob to that closet was covered in prints, but considering several people tried to get in, I'm not hopeful of finding anything. The inside knob was wiped down, almost certainly by whoever was in there when they shouldn't have been, and they would have wiped the outer as well. Not much to go on. Not yet." He gave me a wry smile. "But we'll get him, Lucy. Him or her. You can count on that."

He wrapped the last of his sandwich in the paper it had come in and folded his tart into a napkin. "I have to be going. I'll finish this later. I have some new lines of inquiry to explore. It's been a busy week. We haven't made any arrests in Saturday's jewelry store robbery, but I'm confident we're getting close."

"I sometimes forget you have more than one case to work on at a time."

"Murder always takes precedence, but yeah, other things have to be seen to. I've got North doing most of the robbery angle so I can concentrate on Fortunada, but he's helping on that too."

"Is it him who's pushing for you to charge Eddie?" I was being bold in asking the question, but for a moment Watson seemed almost chatty.

"No comment." He started to stand up, but at that moment his phone rang. He checked it and answered. "What's up? Yeah, I'm leaving here now. Five minutes."

The people at the surrounding tables had left, the line at the counter was down to two people, and at the moment no one was coming in or out. The sound of the busy bakery fell away, and I could hear the tinny voice on the other end of the line as it said, "Don't know why you're wasting your time with her."

"My time to waste," Watson said. "Five minutes."

He put his phone away, gave me a nod, and left, clutching his unfinished sandwich and the luscious-looking tart.

On my way out, I detoured via the serving counter and ordered a lemon tart to go.

* * *

Connor had told me he wouldn't be home for dinner tonight, so I made myself a bowl of soup and a sandwich. Later, I was sitting at the island in the kitchen, enjoying a cup of tea, and making last-minute notes for tomorrow's book club meeting when the doorbell rang.

I found Detective Kyle North on the doorstep.

"Good evening, Detective," I said with a smile. "How can I help you?"

He didn't return the smile. "I took a chance you'd be home, Mrs. McNeil. I've a couple more questions about the events of Saturday night, if you don't mind."

I glanced behind him but could see no one else. He'd come alone. "Come in, please. I'm having a cup of tea. Can I make you one? Or if you'd prefer a cold drink, I've a jug in the fridge."

"Nothing, thank you." He stepped into my home and looked around with interest. "Nice place you have. You've done it up nicely."

"Thank you. My husband and his father did most of the work themselves, and we're very happy with it."

Charles emerged from the kitchen to see who was calling. He took one look at the visitor and hissed. North ignored him.

I led the way to the kitchen. I took a seat on a stool at the island and indicated to Kyle North he could do the same. He didn't; he leaned against the doorframe, looking around. Charles returned to the multilevel cat tree next to the window, but he didn't settle down. Instead he stood there, watching us through narrowed eyes.

I sipped my tea. "How can I help you, Detective?"

"You and your husband found Edward McClanahan hiding out in Rodanthe. Did he have much to say to you on the way back to Nags Head about events of Saturday night?"

"I wouldn't call it hiding out."

"What would you call it?"

"He'd taken the opportunity to get away for a few days and was unaware the police wanted to talk to him."

"So he says."

North watched me. I shifted uncomfortably.

"I compared your statement to his and both of them to another witness. You said you heard Fortunada arguing with someone shortly before he died. The other witness identified McClanahan, and McClanahan himself confessed that he and Fortunada argued."

"I never said it was an argument, Detective. I said I heard two people talking, and then Wayne came around the corner."

"Think back, Mrs. McNeil, to this argument."

"It wasn't an argument."

"Whatever you want to call it."

I let out a long breath. I didn't like the way this conversation was going, but I wanted to be helpful. "I heard Wayne ask the other person if they liked his suit. He said his lady friend had bought it for him."

"What else?"

"He . . . said the other person owed him money."

"Did he say how much or what for?"

"No."

"Did he say he expected to be paid what he was owed?"

"No."

"He was angry. Threatening to this other person." North didn't make it sound like a question.

"No. Not at all."

"You're sure of that?"

"Well, no. I mean, I can't be entirely sure. All I'm saying is that's not the impression I had."

"Your impression. Of overheard snatches of a conversation you were not party to. So much not party to it, you don't even know who the second person was."

"Yes, but . . ." My voice trailed off.

"According to Professor McClanahan, he and Fortunada had a history. Did he tell you about that?"

"He told me a bit about it. They were roommates at college. That obviously had been a long time ago."

"A long time, yes. But memories can last a long time, wouldn't you agree?"

"I . . . guess so."

"Bad memories in particular. Is McClanahan a wealthy man?"

"I have absolutely no idea. I wouldn't think so. He's a university professor."

"Comfortable, then."

"Like I said, I don't know anything about that."

"Comfortable in his lifestyle. Comfortable in his job. A professorship, the respect of his peers, the admiration of his students. He wouldn't want anything to upset that comfort, would he? The thing about blackmail, Mrs. McNeil, is that the stench can linger for a long time. A very long time."

"I told you all I know about this. I'm not going to speculate or try to guess at anyone's meaning."

"Speculate? I wouldn't want you to do that." He stepped away from the doorframe. "I've been told you've been of help to Detective Watson in the past when people you know have been involved. I'd advise you to remember that I'm not Watson. I'll also advise you to think things over. If you're not telling us everything in some desire to protect your friend . . ." He let the sentence trail away. "Thanks for your time. I'll see myself out." He turned and walked out of the kitchen.

I finally gathered my wits, jumped off my stool, and hurried after him. "Have a nice evening," I called to the closing door.

I looked down to see Charles standing at my feet, his eyes fixed on the door. "There's a new sheriff in town," I said.

Chapter Twelve

One of the highlights of my working month is the meeting of the Bodie Island Lighthouse Library Classic Novel Reading Club. We usually get a good turnout from the core group of members who come to regular meetings as well as those who have a specific interest in the book of the month. Everyone's welcome to bring guests.

Josie's a member of the club, and she used to provide the evening's treats. Once she had Ellie and her schedule got even more frantic than normal, I insisted we could do without her contributions. Several people, Butch Greenblatt most of all, were disappointed, but no one dared object when I brought out boxes of cookies bought at the supermarket.

Thursday evening, Louise Jane and I set up chairs in the third-floor meeting room and laid the small table with napkins and glasses, pitchers of lemonade and tea, and the cookies arranged on a plate.

"Any more developments in the murder, Lucy?" Louise Jane asked.

"No."

"Would you tell me if there were?"

"No."

"Bertie's been on edge this week."

"Yeah, she has." I said no more. Bertie was on edge. She'd told me Detective North had been talking to Eddie's coworkers and acquaintances as well as combing through his past. Eddie had never been in any trouble with the law, and apart from a couple of tickets for distracted driving, he had no police record.

"Eddie knows he didn't kill Wayne," Bertie confided in me, "but he's still worried that the police seem to be focusing their attentions on him. Some of his colleagues, and you know of whom I speak, are whispering about no smoke without fire."

I knew full well. We'd had encounters with two history professors from Blacklock College in the past, McArthur and Hoskins, and they were not inclined to be friendly to the library or anyone associated with it. Never mind that the always-blunt Professor McClanahan never failed to take every opportunity to let them know what he thought of them and their department. I hadn't told Bertie that North had called on me last night or that his questions had been specifically focused on Eddie, but I had told Connor when he got home.

"If you think he's concentrating on Eddie unfairly, say something, honey," Connor said. "But it sounds more to me like he's crossing his *t*'s and dotting his *i*'s. New job, high-profile case. His chance to make an impression straight off the bat, and he's working hard at it. That's a good thing, right?"

"I suppose," I'd admitted. "As you said, we can't be positive Eddie didn't do it, as much as we don't believe he did."

"I can try to help however I can," Louise Jane said now, "but as the killing didn't happen here in the library and had nothing to do, as far as we know, with the history of the lighthouse, my usual sources can't be of much use."

Louise Jane's "usual sources" were the paranormal inhabitants of the lighthouse and the surrounding marsh. As far as I was concerned, those individuals didn't exist, and so I didn't give their insights a whole lot of credit.

"Awful shame about all those renovations at the Ocean Side," she said. "They totally ripped up the back staircase where the betrayed chambermaid used to hang out, and she up and left. Otherwise, I would have tried to make contact with her to ask if she observed anything on Saturday."

"What a pity," I said.

"Although . . . the guy was locked in a closet, wasn't he? Sort of like in 'The Cask of Amontillado.' I wonder if he's going to be the new resident ghost of the Ocean Side."

"You start saying that, Louise Jane, and you'll be banned from the hotel. As you were when you went around asking guests if they'd spotted the ghostly chambermaid."

"You can't hide the truth," she said. "Are we ready?"

"We are."

We went downstairs to greet the members of our book club. As soon as I stepped outside the thick stone walls of the lighthouse, my phone beeped to tell me I had a message. Aunt Joyce, saying she'd decided to pass on book club in favor of a quiet night in front of the TV.

The last of the daylight was fading in the west, and the first of the stars were coming out over the ocean. High above us the powerful light flashed in the rhythm I've always found so steady and comforting. As the first headlights broke the gloom between the row of red pines lining the laneway, Louise Jane cleared her throat. "I invited a guest tonight."

"That's nice. Anyone I know?"

"Uh, yeah. Kyle."

I glanced at her. The color was high in her cheeks, and her eyes sparkled. "You mean Kyle North? The new detective? Did he accept?"

"He said if he could make it, he would. He . . . uh . . . likes classic novels."

That came as a surprise to me, but I said nothing. People have hidden depths. "When were you talking to him?"

"I popped into the police station this morning, just trying to be helpful. I thought he might have more questions for me about what I might have seen on Saturday. He thanked me for being such a conscientious citizen."

I hid a grin.

"He said he'd like to see this library he's heard so much about. He's new to town, and it would be nice for him to start to get to know people, don't you agree?"

"How thoughtful of you," I said.

Cars pulled into the parking lot, and people began walking up the path. Theodore was one of the first to arrive, and he stood with us, shifting nervously from foot to foot as he watched for the arrival of the car he was particularly interested in.

Between Louise Jane and Theodore, I thought, we might have to change the name of our group to the Bodie Island Lighthouse Library Classic Novel Dating Club.

Turnout was good tonight, and I greeted people as they arrived and invited them to go on upstairs. To Theodore's obvious joy, Lorraine was among them. He greeted her profusely and offered to escort her to the meeting room personally. She gave him a broad smile and accepted. Before they went inside, she said to me, "I had a visit from the police first thing this morning. I assume you put them up to that?"

"I told Detective Watson you'd met Wayne previously, yes. You knew I was going to."

"That's okay. I told him what I told you. He tried to get me to confess that I'd taken my chance to get revenge, but his heart wasn't really in it. I was with my bandmates all that night, either performing or taking a break with the rest of them."

"Who interviewed you?" Louise Jane asked.

"Detective North."

"Come along," Theodore said. "We want to get good seats. I'm so pleased you were able to make it, Lorraine. I know you'll enjoy the group." He hustled her inside.

"Teddy's gotta be careful he doesn't come on too strong," Louise Jane said. "Women don't like that. Oh, gosh. Here comes a car I don't recognize." Her arm shot out and gripped mine. "Do you think . . . yes, it's him. He came."

She waved. "Yoo-hoo, Kyle! Here we are."

The new detective sauntered up the path. "Evenin', ladies."

"I'm so glad you made it." At that moment the lighthouse light flashed; Louise Jane's smile was so bright it competed with the thousand-watt bulb shining far above us. "I was afraid you wouldn't be able to find it."

He gave her a quizzical look. "You can see the light from miles away."

"Which," I muttered under my breath, "is the entire purpose of a lighthouse light."

"Yes, yes," Louise Jane gushed, "but people sometimes miss it. You might have had a development in the case and gotten tied up. Did you?"

"Nothing worth mentioning." He spoke to Louise Jane but gave me a sideways glance.

"Why don't I show you to the meeting room. We're about to start, right, Lucy?"

"You go on ahead," I said. "I'll give it another five minutes, and then I'll lock the door and come up."

"After the meeting, if you'd like a private tour of the lighthouse," Louise Jane said, "I'd be happy to give you one." She giggled in a very un–Louise Jane–like way. "I myself am not only knowledgeable about the history of the building, I actually live right here."

"You live on the grounds?" North said. "I didn't see a house."

"Better than that. I have a charming little apartment on the fourth floor. It was a bit of a dump when I moved in, but I fixed it up nicely."

The door slammed shut behind them. The Lighthouse Aerie had not been a bit of a dump when Louise Jane moved in. I'd cleaned it thoroughly before moving out, and she'd passed me on the stairs as I carried the last of my things to my car.

Talk about coming on too strong . . .

I chuckled to myself.

The next people up the path were my friends Steph and Grace, who'd come together.

"No Butch tonight?" I asked.

"He pulled some overtime," Steph said. "They're canvassing the area near where that jewelry store robbery happened again. A robbery in broad daylight and they can't find anyone who saw anything. Before we go in, I should mention that I spoke to your friend Eddie McClanahan. He hasn't retained my services. Not yet, but he knows he can call our office if needed."

"Bertie told me he'd been summoned back to town and questioned again."

Steph pulled a face. "I didn't know that. He should have told me or Amos. He needs representation if that happens again."

"I'll have a word with Bertie. Oh, one thing. You won't believe who's come to book club."

"Who?" Grace asked.

"Detective North."

Steph shook her head. "Small towns, gotta love them. Don't worry about me, Lucy. I'll make nice to the new boy." She bared her teeth, and Grace and I laughed.

"Go on up," I said. "Meeting's about to start, and I'll be right there."

A car I didn't recognize pulled in at the top of the path. A woman got out, waved good-bye, and the car drove away.

"Hi, Lucy." CeeCee Watson hurried down the path. "I'm glad I'm not late. My blasted car wouldn't start, but while I was standing in the driveway yelling at it, my neighbor came out. She was going into town so offered me a lift, even though the library isn't exactly on her way."

"I'm glad it worked out."

"Sam's finishing a few things at work, and he'll pick me up when we're done. I loved the reading you assigned us, and I'm eager to hear what everyone else thought."

"Go on in. We'll be starting soon."

I waited another few minutes, but no one else arrived and no more lights broke through the trees lining the lane. I locked the door behind me and climbed the stairs. If anyone came late, they'd ring the bell and someone would go down to admit them.

Most of the chairs in the meeting room had been taken, as was the lap of Mrs. Fitzgerald, our library board chair. Charles had assumed his customary place.

Theodore sat next to Lorraine, and they were already deep in a discussion of *The Count of Monte Cristo*. Louise Jane was bustling about, ensuring Kyle North had an adequate supply of refreshments and introducing him to everyone.

He didn't look like a man who was interested in getting to know a woman, I thought. More like he was annoyed at her attention and trying to hide it. I read nothing into that. As a new resident of Nags Head, he was welcome here. Sam Watson must have mentioned that the library community is often involved in things of concern to the Nags Head Police, so North might have taken advantage of Louise Jane's invitation to check the place—and us—out.

"Kyle's the new detective with the NHPD," Louise Jane said.

"Pleased to meet y'all," he said, his hands full of cookies and tea.

Charles half rose from the comfort of Mrs. Fitzgerald's lap, arched his back, focused his intense blue eyes on North, and hissed.

"Shush, you." Mrs. Fitzgerald tapped the cat's nose. "Never mind him, young man."

North shrugged and popped an entire cookie into his mouth. "Not a cat person myself."

"He's a lovely cat," Lorraine said, leaning over to give Charles a pat on his head. He preened and accepted the compliment.

"You're an Outer Banks boy is my guess," Mrs. Fitzgerald said. "Judging by that accent." Charles hissed once again, but then he settled down under Lorraine and Mrs. Fitzgerald's calm, gentle strokes.

"Yes, ma'am," North said. "Born and raised in Duck, but I've been away in the big city for a few years. It's nice to be back."

"Outer Banks boys never stray far from home." She gave me a wink. "Nor do newly inaugurated Outer Banks girls. Before we begin our meeting, I'd like to propose a toast to the new bride."

I blushed as everyone lifted their glasses and said, "To Lucy and Connor."

North watched me. He didn't join the toast, and his look, I thought, wasn't entirely friendly.

Congratulations over, everyone supplied with refreshments, I took my seat. "Some background for our visitors, Lorraine and Kyle. The book originally proposed for this month was *The Count of Monte Cristo*, which most of us agreed is far too long, so as an alternate we settled on three of the best-known stories from Edgar Allan Poe: 'The Murders in the Rue Morgue,' 'The Tell-Tale Heart,' and 'The Cask of Amontillado.'

In particular, 'The Cask of Amontillado,' like *Monte Cristo,* is a tale of revenge, so I thought we could kick off the discussion tonight talking about revenge and the lengths people will go to get it."

"Kyle," Louise Jane said, "you might be able to provide some examples of that. Real-life cases you've seen centering on revenge."

"I don't—"

"Old cases, I mean. Nothing current or that's still to be settled in court."

"I've only just made detective," he said.

"As the old Klingon proverb says, *Revenge is a dish best served cold,*" Cee-Cee Watson said. "But in real life, except for a few obsessed people, folks generally get on with things, and that early desire for revenge, which burns red-hot, soon fades. Detective North, we haven't met. I'm CeeCee Watson. Sam's wife."

"Pleased to meet you, ma'am."

"What CeeCee says may be true," I said, "but revenge is a powerful driver of plot in novels and short stories."

The discussion began. In 'The Cask of Amontillado,' in contrast to *The Count of Monte Cristo*, the reader doesn't ever find out why the protagonist wants revenge, so we spent a great deal of time speculating.

"My favorite of all of Poe's stories," Louise Jane said, "is 'The Tell-Tale Heart.' Soooo creepy!"

"Truly the stuff of nightmares," Mrs. Fitzgerald agreed.

"You could argue it's a revenge tale as well," Steph said. "The heart itself is calling out, trying to get revenge."

"Did everyone read 'The Murders in the Rue Morgue'?" CeeCee asked. "I hadn't read it before, and I was struck by how much the amateur detective in that story is like Sherlock

Holmes. As you all know, Sam's a great fan of Sherlock." She turned to North with a smile. "If you don't know now, you'll find out soon enough."

North didn't return the smile.

"That's an interesting line to pursue," Theodore said. "Auguste Dupin is often considered to be the prototype for Holmes. He only appears in that one story, whereas Holmes was in sixty stories and novels. If Poe had continued writing about Dupin, would that character be as popular as Holmes is today and Sherlock Holmes largely forgotten?"

"I loved the way he was able to follow his friend's meandering thought process simply by observing what the friend was looking at," I said.

"Okay for fiction," North said. "Try taking that to a judge and saying, 'Your Honor, the accused must have done it because he blinked twice when I said hi.' "

"It's not about proof," Lorraine said, "but about leading the detective to the realization of what happened. Then the detective can get the proof."

"Yeah, right," North said.

She lifted one hand. "I'm not saying, Detective, that's the way it works in the real world. But you have to admit it makes a great story."

"Maybe not my sort of story," he said.

"At this book club," Louise Jane added quickly, "we read all sorts of things. Right, everyone? Not only detective fiction or even primarily detective fiction. Do you like adventure stories? I'm going to suggest *Treasure Island* for next month. A rip-roaring tale of pirates and buried treasure." The pleading look she gave him was almost painful to behold.

"I don't have a whole lot of time for reading." He glanced at CeeCee. "What with settling into the new job and all. It's been busy."

"And we're so glad you were able to find the time to come out tonight," Louise Jane gushed.

Everyone shifted uncomfortably—everyone except Theodore, who was gazing openly at Lorraine, and Lorraine, who was smiling back at him. I cleared my throat and hurried the discussion along. "Poe's considered a master of horror. As Mrs. Fitzgerald said, 'The Tell-Tale Heart' is genuinely creepy. Do you think his horror stands up in the modern age?"

And the discussion continued.

Even without Butch's help, the cookies were eventually decimated and the jugs of tea and lemonade emptied of all but melting ice. Charles was snoring lightly on Mrs. Fitzgerald's lap when people began to make ready-to-leave gestures. Steph and Grace gathered up their bags. "Sorry to run, Lucy, but I've an early morning appointment," Steph said.

Seconds after Grace and Steph left, the buzzer rang to tell us someone was at the door.

"That's probably Sam now." CeeCee collected her purse and got to her feet. "Thank you for an interesting meeting, Lucy. Detective North, it was nice to meet you at last. My husband's spoken a great deal about you."

"Thank you, ma'am." North nodded politely. Perhaps only I noticed that CeeCee pointedly failed to mention that her husband had spoken *favorably* about the new detective.

Charles and I escorted the last of our guests downstairs and through the main room of the library. I couldn't help but overhear Theodore saying something to Lorraine about going for a coffee to continue the discussion about Poe and her replying that that would be nice.

Louise Jane prattled happily to Detective North about the history of the lighthouse and the important research work she was doing for the library. He couldn't have appeared less interested if he'd tried.

Steph and Grace must have found Sam Watson waiting outside, as he'd come into the library to wait. He appeared startled to see North descending the stairs with us. "Is something happening here I should know about, Detective?"

"Nothing in particular," North said. "I came to these people's book club. I wanted to get to know some of the folks in the community better." He looked at me as he spoke. Now it was my turn to feel uncomfortable.

"That's always good," Watson said.

"CeeCee, if you have a quick minute," Mrs. Fitzgerald said, "I need to talk to you about the fund-raising dinner for the hospital foundation."

CeeCee threw a look at her husband. "Go ahead," he said with a smile. The women went to the magazine nook so Mrs. Fitzgerald could have a seat. Charles followed.

"Thanks for coming, Kyle," Louise Jane said. "I hope you enjoyed yourself."

"It was okay."

"Uh . . . great. The evening's still young. How about—"

"Louise Jane," a book club member called. "Can you help me, please? As long as I'm here, I'd like to check out this book."

"Lucy can help you," Louise Jane said.

"You help the lady," North said. "I can find my own way back to my car."

"Okay. Uh . . . give me a call sometime. I know all the great places to see in Nags Head."

"Like I said: born and raised in Duck."

I decided I didn't like Detective North much. He might be a good detective, and he might be wanting to make a favorable impression at his new job, but on a personal level, he was shockingly rude. Louise Jane could be a mite pushy, but that was Louise Jane's natural personality, and she was trying to be friendly. As for the way he looked at me, I didn't think the detective liked me either, although I couldn't think what I'd done to offend him.

"Can I have a word, Detective?" North said to Watson. "As long as we're waiting."

"Sure." They stepped to one side and stood next to the shelves marked MORRISON–PROULX.

I didn't intend to eavesdrop. Honestly, I didn't. A single book remained on the returns cart. I picked it up and took it to be shelved. It just happened to be Harper Lee's great work, which belonged on the other side of the shelf next to where the detectives were standing.

"That woman's leading you down the garden path." North's voice came through the double row of books perfectly clearly.

"What's that supposed to mean?" Watson asked.

"She thinks she's some sort of hot-shot amateur detective. She was prattling on upstairs about some character named Auguste Dupin, who solves cases instead of the police. Him and Sherlock Holmes. Who you, your wife says, are a big admirer of."

"I like Holmes, sure. Lots of people do. I don't know what you're getting at, North."

"At first, I couldn't understand why you were giving that library chick"—I assumed that meant me—"so much of your time. Listening to whatever amateur-detective rubbish she's spouting and sending me off to question people because she told you to. Now I get it: she thinks she's Sherlock Holmes, and you're swallowing it."

I let out a small gasp as Charles's bulk flew past me to land on the top of the shelf. I held my breath, prepared to slip away if the police parted the rows of books to see what was going on here. But they were too involved in their conversation. Charles's tail moved slowly back and forth in front of my face as he peered over the shelf.

"There's that blasted cat," North said. "I hate cats."

"Careful, Detective," Watson said. They were keeping their voices low, but I could hear the anger creeping into his, and not because of the new detective's aversity to cats. "You're new here, so I'll cut you some slack. Lucy's been a great help to me in the past. She's smart, she's highly observant, she remembers things, and she's got a particularly good read on people."

I preened under the praise. It's said no one hears anything good about themselves when they're eavesdropping, but I appeared to have smashed that rule.

"Unlike some," Watson continued, "I don't believe the police should shut out help when they're offered it."

"She's been of help to you in the past, you say. That guy, Fortunada, was killed at her wedding. You don't think that's a heck of a coincidence?"

"No, I don't. I was at Lucy and Connor's wedding. Many of the people here tonight were at that wedding, including my wife. We've interviewed most of them. That's what small-town policing's all about. People."

"You can't tell me it's never occurred to you that she's arranging things so she can then rush forward to offer her help to the police?"

"What are you saying, North?"

"She was on-site when the body was found. She was on the scene when the police arrived, all ready and eager to help. She just happened to be the one to find that McClanahan guy where he was hiding out. What I'm asking is, how much does this supposed friend of yours want everyone to think she's a modern-day Sherlock Holmes? In this case, as well as the others you say she's helped you with, how involved is she in not just poking her nose into things that are none of her business but instigating events in the first place?"

I was no longer hearing only good things about me. I was saved from bursting through the shelves, grabbing Detective

North around the throat, and throttling him by the arrival of CeeCee Watson. “There you are, Sam. I’m ready to go.”

“I’m coming, honey. I heard what you said, North, and you’re way off base.”

“We’ll see,” North said. “If she’s been playing you all this time, you have to think what that will mean for your career. What’s left of it.”

Chapter Thirteen

"Good book club?" Connor asked when I stormed into the kitchen, slamming the door behind me. I kicked off my shoes, threw my purse and the car keys onto the island, dropped the cat carrier on the floor, and opened the door. Charles flew out and disappeared down the hallway.

"Yes!" I growled.

"Okay." Connor held a door stopper of a sandwich in his hand. "Want to tell me what made it so good?"

"No." I marched out of the kitchen. I made it as far as the bedroom, where I threw my jacket on the bed, and then I returned to the kitchen.

Connor hadn't moved.

"What's your take on Detective North?" I asked.

"I have no take. The department's been wanting to hire a new detective for a while. It's no secret Sam's thinking of retiring. He's more than earned it. North's qualified; he has good references from his last job; he said he wanted to return to his Outer Banks roots." Connor chuckled. "We Bankers always like to hear that."

"Why didn't they hire from within?"

"No one ready yet. Between you and me, Lucy, and strictly confidential, Butch is almost there, but not quite yet. The chief says give him another year or two and a detective job will be his, if he wants it. If and when there's an opening. Obviously something happened tonight that's upset you. Did North call you again? What did he want?"

"He didn't call me. He came to book club, at Louise Jane's invitation. I . . . don't think I like him."

"Does that matter?"

"No." I should have told Connor what I'd overheard, but I kept quiet. Maybe I was embarrassed to have been eavesdropping. I told myself it didn't matter what Detective North thought of me. No one in Nags Head, beginning with Sam Watson, would believe I'd killed Wayne Fortunada so I could make myself seem important in a police investigation.

Would they?

* * *

Whether because of North's insinuations or not, I decided I would do no more detecting in this matter. I'd learned a couple of relevant things, and I'd reported them directly to Sam Watson, as any good citizen should.

The library was busy all day on Friday, as is normal. Ronald had a program for toddlers in the morning, one for preschoolers at two, and then an after-school book club for grades one to three. Patrons were stocking up on reading for what promised to be a pleasant early-summer weekend, and teenagers were desperate to get that research book they should have read two weeks ago for the essay due on Monday.

Several times during the day, when I'd had a minute to myself, my hand had hovered over the phone. I wanted to call Theodore, and ask—oh so subtly—how his coffee date with Lorraine had gone and by the way, had she confessed to having killed Wayne because he'd blackmailed her ten years ago.

I reminded myself I was no longer involved and never made the call.

I wasn't quite so circumspect as regards Kristen and Ray Croft, but considering she wasn't favorably inclined toward any members of the Richardson family at the moment, there'd be no point in trying to—oh so subtly—question her again.

Today was Aunt Ellen's day to volunteer at the library, and she arrived shortly after opening with Gloria in tow. Gloria had dressed for the day in a pale-pink Chanel suit with pearls.

"I insisted," Gloria told me, as she brushed my cheek with her lips, "on coming along. I so love spending time in libraries."

"I didn't know that," Aunt Ellen said with a smile. "What library in New Orleans are you a patron of?"

"Time is such a rare commodity, and at my age, a lady must portion it carefully. As you'll find out, Ellen dear. Between all my service clubs and volunteer committee responsibilities, I don't always have the leisure time I'd like." She eyed her daughter-in-law. "Which is why I so much enjoy having a break and spending some of my precious time with you and Amos."

Score one for Gloria.

"Now, you pretend I'm not here and go about your duties. I'll take a seat, why don't I?" Gloria looked around. Our library is small, and although it seems to be able to stretch at the seams when needed, there isn't much room for seating. Other than office chairs at the computer tables and a couple of upright chairs for parents waiting for children, there's only one comfortable chair, a well-worn wingback. It was currently taken by its regular occupant, Tim Snyder. A childless widow in his eighties and a retired high school teacher, Mr. Snyder enjoyed the company to be found at the library, and he came to relax in the magazine nook and catch up on his reading. Since making friends with Ralph and Jo Harper, he visited the library less often these days, but he was still a regular, and much loved, fixture.

"Yes. Same questions about what happened Saturday evening. I suspect he's trying to trip me up about the time Eddie and I parted and Eddie returned to the hotel. I can't be tripped up, as I'm positive about the time because I checked it when we got into the cab. North tried to get me to say Eddie was angry when we separated rather than thoughtful, as he was."

"You know that's normal police routine, Bertie. Maybe not putting words in people's mouths, but they need witnesses to go over their statements again and again. People forget things, and they often misinterpret what they've seen."

"I know. It's just . . . hard."

"What time was this?"

"Late. Around nine thirty." North must have gone to Bertie's immediately after leaving book club. "He didn't bother to call before coming over, so I'm lucky he didn't find me in my night attire. In any other situation, I'd admire the new detective for his tenacity. This is his first big case in a new job, and he's wanting to make his mark. That's a good thing." She gave me a weak smile. "Except when he's bothering my peace of mind."

I smiled back.

"He did have a question about you, Lucy, one I didn't know how to interpret."

My smile died. "What sort of question?"

"He was interested in how you found out where Eddie was staying for those few days. I told him what happened, that you remembered an overheard conversation and tracked down Daniel Estevez, but I'm not sure he was convinced. He said something about no one has that good a memory."

"I do," I said. "We all do. Scraps of random detail stick in our minds for years, gathering cobwebs but not entirely forgotten, and then the sunlight breaks through and it's remembered. Which is rather an awkward metaphor, but you know what I mean. Our engagement party was an important event in my life, and unlike my wedding, I didn't do any of the work or have any of the worry about it, so I was free to relax and enjoy and take it all in."

"You don't have to convince me, Lucy. I know how that mind of yours works."

"If you're getting uncomfortable at the direction the police's questions are going, it might be time to hire a lawyer. Steph came to book club last night, and she told me she hasn't heard from Eddie again after she initially spoke with him."

"Dear Eddie. I suggested he retain her and Amos, just as a precaution, but he insists that as he didn't do anything wrong, he doesn't need a lawyer. It doesn't always work that way. I told him that, but you know Eddie. I wonder sometimes how that man manages to get by in the modern world. He would have been perfectly suited to a medieval university. A life of quiet study and contemplation. Growing his own vegetables and making beer. Oh well, as that's not likely to happen, he's coming for the weekend, and we're going away for a few days to try and forget about this nonsense."

"That's good. If you need anything, we're all here for you."

"I know, Lucy. I know."

A weekend break, I thought as I walked down the hallway back to the main room of the library, would do Bertie and Eddie a lot of good. An air of stress and worry hung over my boss. I knew from past cases that a murder investigation could be hard on everyone involved. The innocent, the guilty, the family and friends of the innocent and the guilty.

Mr. Snyder, who'd spent the past hour shifting in his chair and muttering about how uncomfortable it was, had left. Gloria had fallen asleep, her head bobbing over her chest. Charles was still in hiding.

Two people I never expected to see in my library were standing in front of the circulation desk, chatting to Aunt Ellen. "Kristen. Ray. Hi. What brings you here?"

Kristen turned to face me. Her eyes blazed so much fire, I hesitated. I glanced at Ray, who had suddenly taken an intense interest in the arrangement of the floor tiles beneath his feet.

"You." Kristen put her hands on her hips.

"Me?"

"You set the cops on us."

"I didn't set anyone on you. I told Detective Watson what I'd learned."

"You told him what I told you in confidence."

I extended my arms and held my palms out. "I'm sorry, Kristen, but there's no such thing as confidence in a murder investigation."

The buzz of chatter filling the room earlier had stopped. People were frozen in the act of taking books off the shelves or putting them back. Fingers hesitated above the keyboards of the public computers. The sound of children's voices drifted down from the second floor, and Charles's little face popped between the railings on the stairs.

"What! What!" Gloria awoke with a start.

"Do you have any idea how embarrassing it is to have the police poking their noses into your private life?" Kristen snapped.

"Actually, I do," I said.

"Questions about my marital and dating relationships? About my pending divorce?"

Aunt Ellen stood up. "Kristen, this is not the time nor the place."

Kristen ignored her. She took a step toward me. I took a step back. "You think you can trick me into giving up my rightful claim for all I deserve after putting up with Kevin Richardson for twenty miserable years."

"Stop this, Kristen. I'm not trying to trick you, and I'm not interfering in your divorce proceedings."

"Do you know what he said to me when I told him it was none of his business?"

"What who said?" Aunt Ellen asked.

"That nosy detective. He said he'd arrest me if I didn't answer his questions. Arrest me! Wouldn't Kevin love to take that to court."

"What's going on here?" Bertie stepped into the room.

"A personal matter," Aunt Ellen said. "Unfortunately, these people don't seem inclined to take their grievances elsewhere."

"In that case," Bertie said, "I have to ask you to leave."

"I'm not going anywhere, not until I get a retraction from Lucy," Kristen said. "Tell the police you made it up."

"I'm not going to do that," I said.

"Speaking of police, do I need to give them a call?" Bertie asked calmly. "I have asked you to leave."

Kristen stabbed a finger in my direction. "Wouldn't you love that. Another nail in my coffin."

"Rather than putting nails in any coffins," I said, "I didn't invite you here, so whatever happens from this point on is up to you."

Bertie stepped forward. "I'm the library director, and I'm telling you to go. If you do not leave immediately, I will have no choice but to call the police."

Louise Jane and Denise hovered on the stairs, watching. Aunt Ellen had picked up the desk phone and was waiting for Bertie to issue instructions. Gloria had a firm grip on her cane.

"Ray," I said.

He lifted his head. "Yeah?"

"Why don't you take Kristen to the car? She came here to speak to me, and we've spoken. Nothing more can be gained by staying."

"I don't like being threatened by the cops either," he said.

"I doubt very much they threatened you."

"Call it what you like."

Louise Jane stepped off the staircase and came to stand beside me. Charles ran to the circulation desk, also offering us his support. He hissed at Kristen and bared his teeth at Ray. From overhead, I could hear the excited voices of small children as story time came to an end. I didn't want the kids coming down here and seeing this scene.

But Kristen was not in the mood to go quietly. "Even worse," she said, "you told your mother."

"I wouldn't say that's worse than being accused of murder by the cops," Ray said.

"Shut up," Kristen said.

"To the contrary," I said, "my mother told me where she'd seen you and Ray before."

"Ellen," Bertie said. "Make that call. This cannot continue."

"I've got your back, Lucy," Louise Jane whispered in my ear. "Too bad I don't have my parasol to hand." She was referring to a previous incident where, in full southern belle costume, she'd wielded the accessory to great effect. I didn't reply.

"Let's go." Ray took Kristen's arm. "I told you this was a bad idea."

Kristen yanked her arm away. She threw me one last angry glare, and then all the aggression melted out of her. Tears welled up in her eyes, and her upper lip quivered. "I . . . only want Kevin to be fair."

Aunt Ellen walked around the desk. "Surely you don't want me calling the police. Why don't I walk you to your car, dear? We haven't had a chance to talk. How are the children doing? I was sorry not to see them this past weekend. They must be growing up so fast." She put her arm around Kristen's shoulders and began guiding her to the door.

Ray looked around him. "Nice library. Is this a real lighthouse?"

I decided Ray Croft wasn't too terribly bright. Or overly sensitive to the mood of a room. The patrons were still watching us. Bertie's stance indicated she was prepared to defend her library to the death, and Charles would be the first to die at her side. Gloria had risen to her feet and gripped her cane as though girding for battle.

"Yes," Louise Jane said. "The current building is the third on this spot. It was built in 1872 and converted into a library in . . ."

As Ellen and Kristen moved toward the door, everyone, including me, relaxed.

That had been premature.

The door opened, and absolutely the last person I wanted to see at this moment walked in. My brother Kevin. Kristen's estranged husband.

He started when he saw Kristen and glanced in confusion at Aunt Ellen. Then he looked beyond the two women and caught sight of me. His eyes quickly roamed around the room, and finally he recognized Ray. He grimaced, and his attention returned to Kristen. "What are you doing here?" he said.

"Are you following me?" she bellowed. "Spying on me? Trying to dig up dirt you can use in court?"

"Following you? No. I came to see Lucy. I'm leaving soon and wanted to say bye. Why would I care what you and your overweight, overage boy toy get up to?"

Ray had turned away from Louise Jane when he heard Kevin come in. "Hey, who you calling overweight?"

"I'm calling you overweight, buddy. And that's the least of the words I could use." Kevin pushed past Aunt Ellen and Kristen and marched into the library. "I didn't come here looking for you, but as long as I have you, both of you, let me tell you, pal, that if you're hanging around with Kristen because you think she's about to come into money, my family's money, that's not happening."

"Please, Kevin," I said. "Let's not do this."

"As good a time as any," he said.

"Better than a night at the movies," one of the patrons said.

"Got any popcorn on hand, Lucy?" someone added.

"Will you people get out of here!" Bertie yelled. "I'm closing the library. Now. Everyone go!"

"But the kids are still upstairs," a parent pointed out.

"Got anything to say, fat boy?" Kevin said.

With a scream of pure rage, Kristen leapt on his back. Kevin spun around, knocking her off. She fell hard, landing solidly on her rear end. She screeched in shock.

Ray roared and charged Kevin. He took a wild swing at my brother's face. Kevin danced out of the way, but he didn't retreat, and he aimed a return punch at the other man.

Patrons screamed. Charles screeched. Louise Jane jumped up and down. Phones were whipped out of purses and pockets. Bertie and Ellen both stepped toward the fighting men, and then, realizing that discretion was the better part of valor, they retreated. Gloria scurried behind her chair and waved her cane in the air. "Ellen! Do something," she ordered.

"I'm calling the police." Denise dashed up the stairs, heading for the phone in her office. Someone threw a book at Ray. It missed.

In real life when two men fight, it's nothing like you see in the movies. No fancy footwork, no straight-legged kicks, no flipping the opponent over your back or leaping nimbly to your feet after being knocked down. No ducking and weaving and bobbing.

Just a lot of grunting and grappling. And total and complete chaos.

Kevin delivered a punch to Ray's jaw, and Ray fell backward, crashing into the returns cart. The cart swayed and toppled over. Books flew in all directions. Ray bounced back and flew at Kevin. Both men collided with the wall.

Ronald came running down the stairs, a pack of excited four-year-olds at his heels.

"Go back, go back," Bertie yelled. "We've got this."

Ronald tried to herd his little charges back up the stairs, but they were having none of it, and curious faces with wide eyes and pert noses peered through the railings. A couple of parents ran to help with the kids.

Louise Jane swept a thousand-page reference book off a desk and wielded it like a cudgel as she prepared to wade into the fray.

"Louise Jane," Bertie yelled. "Stay out of it."

Aunt Ellen was yelling into the phone, "Police, police. Tell them to hurry."

Kevin took a punch to the face, and blood streamed out of his nose. He gave as good as he got to Ray's stomach, and Ray grunted in pain and doubled over.

Kristen egged them both on, yelling insults at Kevin and encouragement to Ray.

Louise Jane, holding the reference book high overhead, couldn't decide which target to hit. Instead, she dropped the book, grabbed Kristen, and shoved my soon-to-be-ex-sister-in-law out the door.

I heard sirens, heading our way.

Ray straightened up and swung at Kevin again. Kevin pulled himself out of the way and shoved his opponent full in the chest. Ray staggered backward and began falling in the direction of the computer monitor on the circulation desk. I ran for it and snatched it out of the way in the nick of time. He collapsed against the desk; keyboard and books and papers flew in all directions. I shoved the monitor at Aunt Ellen and grabbed the returns cart. I wrestled the empty cart upright and pushed it directly toward the grunting, panting, struggling men, who were once again grappling with each other. Neither of them was in particularly good physical shape, and neither, probably, had been in a fight since their teenage years. I rammed the cart directly into them. They separated and fell backward.

And there they remained, glaring at each other over the cart, hands on knees, fighting for breath, with bloody noses, cut lips, and torn clothes.

One patron clapped, and the others joined in. The kids on the stairs cheered. Charles spat.

"That," I said, still firmly gripping the handle of the cart, "was the most disgraceful episode of childish behavior I have ever seen."

The men avoided looking at me.

"I suggest you leave. Now," Bertie said. "If not, it sounds as though a ride will be provided for you."

The sirens pulled into our parking lot, and seconds later Butch Greenblatt ran in. He stood in the doorway, looking around. At the books scattered across the floor, Aunt Ellen clutching the computer monitor to her chest, the wide-eyed patrons, the red-faced Bertie, the children on the stairs, Ronald fruitlessly trying to encourage the kids to return to the children's library, Gloria waving her cane. Even Charles, still spitting and hissing. The two combatants, humiliated in their defeat.

Outside, Holly Rankin spoke to Louise Jane.

"Having some trouble here?" Butch asked calmly.

"Nothing we can't handle," Bertie said, equally calmly. "Thank you for coming so promptly, Officer Greenblatt."

"Always a pleasure, Ms. James. Mrs. McNeil, you got anything to say?"

"I don't know," I said. "Kevin, do I have anything to say to the police?"

My brother mumbled something that might have been "No" and wiped at his nose.

"What was that?" I said.

"No," Kevin said. "We're good here."

Denise stepped forward and handed him her handkerchief. "Keep it," she said.

"Ray?" I asked.

"What?"

"Do you have anything to say to the nice policeman, or shall I talk to him?"

"He started it," Ray said.

"Are you nuts as well as fat?" Kevin said.

The two men glared at each other across the returns cart.

Butch stepped forward. "You two want to talk it out, we'll take it downtown and let these people go about their business."

"No," Kevin said. "No need. I'm done."

"What about you?" Butch said to Ray.

"I'll get Kristen and we'll leave."

"I won't get another call about you two?"

"I only came in to say good-bye to Lucy," Kevin said. "I'm on my way out of town anyway."

"Good-bye," I said. "Don't hurry back."

"Sorry," he mumbled, and then he left.

Ray followed, and Butch followed him.

Bertie and I followed them, to make sure they actually did leave.

Kevin limped down the path, holding Denise's pink, lace-trimmed handkerchief to his nose. The police cars were parked half on the lawn, red and blue lights flashing.

"We're leaving," Ray said to Kristen. "I'm not going to jail because you have issues with your ex."

Kristen threw me a foul look before rushing to Ray's side and examining his face. "You poor darling. Are you okay?" She fumbled for her phone. "Let me take a picture in case we need to sue."

"Get a move on," Butch growled. "Now."

"Okay, okay." Kristen scurried off, and Ray followed.

Butch walked back to his car, keeping an eye on the combatants to ensure Ray and Kristen didn't try to accost Kevin. My brother got into his rental car and pulled away with a screech of brakes. He tore down the lane, going far too fast. I noticed Butch speaking into the radio at his shoulder. If Kevin kept going at that speed, he'd find a cop and a ticket waiting for him when he hit the highway.

"Are you going to be all right here now?" Officer Rankin asked Bertie and me.

"Yes," Bertie said. "Thank you for coming so promptly. They won't be back."

"If they are," Rankin said, "let us know."

I went back into the library. Everyone, from Gloria to the littlest child, was watching me.

Gloria settled herself comfortably in her chair. "If they had action like that at libraries in New Orleans, I might consider dropping in more."

"Never a dull moment at the Bodie Island Lighthouse Library," I said.

Chapter Fourteen

About the last thing I wanted to do on the first Friday evening of my married life was to have another dinner with my family.

Sadly, that seemed to be what was going to happen.

Aunt Joyce called me shortly after the Kristen/Kevin/Ray foofaraw on my personal phone. Reception in the library is poor to nonexistent, so I didn't get the call. After not hearing from me for about ten minutes, she phoned Connor. As Connor's the mayor, you don't have to be Sherlock Holmes or Auguste Dupin to track down his work number. She invited us to have dinner with her that evening, and before he could find a reason to decline, she mentioned that she wanted one last chance to congratulate us on our nuptials, and she expected Amos, Gloria, and Ellen would be joining us.

Connor said he'd have to check with me, to which Aunt Joyce said, "Excellent. I'll see you at Jake's at seven thirty."

"Sorry, Lucy," he said, when he called me on the library landline. "I think we're committed. Your aunt doesn't take maybe for an answer."

"I suppose we should be happy my family likes us," I said. "Ellen's here and she hasn't said anything about it."

"Joyce likely bypassed Ellen and Amos and went directly to Gloria." He laughed. "How's your day going?"

I glanced around the library. Louise Jane and Aunt Ellen were gathering books off the floor and returning them to the cart. Ronald had not been able to calm his little charges down, and a few of the boys—and some girls—were demonstrating their own fight moves to their concerned parents. Gloria was once again nodding off in the magazine nook, Charles was trying to find a new place to get comfortable, and most patrons had gone back to browsing the shelves. Bertie was smiling politely at two blue-rinsed, pastel-colored-blouse-wearing, sensibly shod ladies, regular library visitors despairing about the state of "young people these days."

A sharp-eared woman of a similar age popped her head out from the stacks. "If memory serves, Iris Mann, there was the time you and Masie Booth got into it over Bob Kincaid. Or was it Bob's brother Rob?"

One of the ladies chucked while her friend sniffed in disapproval. "Really, Betty. Where you get your notions, I never did understand."

"What I remember most," Betty said, "is torn hair and ripped dresses and a lot of tears. That plus words your mothers would have been shocked to hear that you even knew."

"It was"—Mrs. Mann threw a wink to Bertie—"not Rob or Bob but their cousin Rod. Dreadful flirt that Rod was. I wonder what happened to him?"

"Isn't he the one who went to Hollywood and was in the movies?" her friend asked.

"The cousins were named Rob and Bob and Rod?" Bertie said.

"Just a normal day at the Bodie Island Lighthouse Library," I repeated, this time in answer to Connor's question.

When I'd hung up, I went to tell Aunt Ellen she had dinner plans.

* * *

Aunt Joyce had made a reservation at Jake's Seafood Bar. It was a warm enough night we could be seated outside on the spacious deck, overlooking the calm waters of Roanoke Sound and the gently bobbing lights of boats at anchor off Roanoke Island. The fourth-order Fresnel lens of the Roanoke Marshes Lighthouse flashed in the distance.

We met Ellen, Amos, and Gloria as we were coming in. Gloria took Connor's arm and told him she'd had a delightful morning at the library. So delightful she was reconsidering her plans to return home next week. Behind her mother-in-law's back, Aunt Ellen made a gesture as though slitting her own throat.

Aunt Joyce was waiting for us at a table next to the deck railing. After initial greetings and once everyone was seated, she said, "I ran into Kristen and her . . . whatever he is in the lobby of the hotel as I was going out for lunch. At first, I thought they'd been in a car accident. The poor man looked positively dreadful. I tried to ask if he needed assistance, but Kristen snapped at me to mind my own business."

Aunt Ellen and I exchanged looks and ducked our heads to avoid breaking out laughing.

When I recovered, I looked up to see Uncle Amos and Connor eyeing us suspiciously.

"Why are Kristen and Ray still hanging around town?" I asked.

"Goodness knows," Aunt Joyce said. "I tried asking Kristen when they were leaving, and instead of replying, she said Kevin had gone home earlier today."

"That is a reply," I said. "She was only staying as long as he was, so she could keep an eye on him."

"Bad business," Uncle Amos said.

"You don't know the half of it," Aunt Ellen said. She then, with Gloria's active participation, entertained the table with a vivid description, complete with sounds and arm and fist actions, of the fight at the library. "Quick-witted Lucy here drove the cart directly between the two primary combatants and forced them apart. Heaven knows what might have transpired if she hadn't."

I dipped my head modestly.

"It was like being at the movies," Gloria said. "Better, as I had to move from my seat for fear of being trampled by the enraged fighters."

"The room was full of children and elderly patrons, some of whom might have abandoned all reason and decided to join the fray themselves," Aunt Ellen said.

"I always thought being a librarian was a safe, boring career," Connor said. "I've changed my mind since I met Lucy."

The waiter brought our drinks. When we'd all been served, Uncle Amos said, "As we were driving over, I heard on the radio they've made an arrest in the jewelry store robbery that happened last weekend."

"Good news," Connor said. "Any names?"

"Two people, but not anyone I recognized."

"The arrest will give Detective North something to be pleased about," I said. "Maybe now he won't have to try so hard to prove himself."

"If the arrested parties are guilty," said Uncle Amos, who'd spent his entire career as a criminal defense lawyer.

"Any reason to think they aren't?" Connor asked.

"None at all. I'm simply reminding all present that the operative word is allegedly. Lucy, I'm interested in hearing why you think North's trying, as you put it, so hard to prove himself."

"I get the feeling he's insecure, that's all. He's focusing his attentions in a direction I don't care for."

"What does that mean?" Connor asked.

I sipped my drink, gathering my thoughts. I was saved from having to answer when the waiter slipped a gigantic platter of hush puppies onto the table. "Compliments of Jake. A gift for the bride."

My cousin-in-law knows how much I adore these fried balls of dough. "Thank him profusely for me." I snatched one up and dipped it into the spicy sauce provided. "This getting-married thing is great. People keep being nice to us and giving us presents. We should do it again next year."

Connor gave me a smile so warm, my heart turned over.

"That's what I said three times," Aunt Joyce said. "I finally realized it was more bother than it was worth. Speaking of Wayne, not that we were, I've been in touch with his parents regularly over the last few days. I've got most of the paperwork required to have his remains sent to Florida when the police release them. They seem like a lovely couple, and I'm pretending their son and I were on the verge of announcing our engagement. Somehow that seems to make them feel better than the truth, which is I was finished with the dratted man."

"Had he ever been married?" Gloria asked.

"It would not appear so. A fortunate thing for the women of America."

"He attempted to charm me." Gloria took a hefty slug of her whiskey and soda. "A waste of his time. I took the measure of the man immediately."

Across the table from me, Aunt Ellen rolled her eyes.

"Have the police spoken to you again about events of Saturday night, Mother?" Uncle Amos asked.

"Only that once. When you and Ellen were there. It's been my experience that young policemen do not appreciate the observational skills of women of a certain age."

"You're right about that," Amos said.

"Have you been able to give them any more insights as to what might have happened, Joyce?" Connor asked. "Perhaps things are becoming clearer to you as time passes."

"I've been thinking about it. I can't think of much else. But no, nothing new. The police haven't contacted me again, not since we initially spoke to them on Sunday, and I've nothing to say if they do."

Something moved at the back of my brain. Before I could get a firm hold of it and examine it, Gloria said, "As for you, Lucy. I told you I wanted to be of assistance. I've been waiting for your call."

Connor said, "Assistance with what?"

"With the case, of course."

His face fell.

"Not only young policemen disregard the wisdom of women of a certain age, but some young women do so as well. Remember, Lucy, you can call upon me at any time."

"Lucy's not—" Aunt Ellen began.

"I'm not involved," I said. "Really, I'm not." I looked at the faces around the table. No one appeared to believe me. "I've told Sam Watson everything I know, and he's handling it. It's good that he has help from the new detective, don't you think, Uncle Amos?"

"What's the legal world saying about North?" Connor asked.

"He can be quick to jump to conclusions," Amos said. "Stephanie represented a man North arrested for stealing a car and taking it for a joy ride. Steph believed the man was innocent, and she thinks North was too hasty in arresting him. The guy got off. North wasn't happy about that. But, in all fairness, he came here with a good reputation from his last job, and general opinion is he's capable of taking over from Sam, if and when Sam retires."

"He says he took this job because he wanted to move back to the Outer Banks," I said. "Is that it, do you think? I'd assume there are less opportunities for promotion on a smaller force."

"I see no reason not to believe it. Big-city policing isn't for everyone, and living in a big city doesn't always suit someone who grew up in a smaller place." Uncle Amos turned to Aunt Ellen with a grin. "Sometimes there are other reasons. I would have set up my first practice in New Orleans had not my own bride wanted to come home to Nags Head. Best move I ever made. Other than marrying her."

"As I told you at the time, Amos." Gloria helped herself to a hush puppy. "You were far better suited to running your own small office than being part of a big corporate firm."

"As I recall," Aunt Ellen said, "you told him not to be a lovestruck fool and to take the money the big corporate firms were offering."

Gloria changed the subject smoothly. "Now, Lucy, when are you and Connor coming to visit me in New Orleans?"

"We'd love to," Connor said, "but it'll be a while. We're going to Paris in a couple of weeks for our honeymoon."

"Paris. Stuff and nonsense. What possible appeal could a foreign place like that have for a southern gentleman such as yourself? I insist you come to New Orleans instead. Now that is a romantic city."

"You could stay with Gloria," Aunt Ellen whispered to me. "How romantic would that be?"

I wasn't sure which would be worse: Gloria helping me with my "investigations" or Connor and I honeymooning under her supervision.

Fortunately, the conversation moved on, and I didn't have to consider either of those ideas further.

Chapter Fifteen

Whether it was the prospect of spending my honeymoon at Gloria O'Malley's house or residual shock from the fight at the library, I couldn't get to sleep that night.

I took a peek at Connor. He was sleeping peacefully, a gentle smile on his face. I hoped he was having nice dreams. I slipped out of bed, padded down the hall into the living room, opened the sliding door, and stepped onto the deck. The surf caressed the shore, and a full moon shone in a cloudless sky, shining a beam of white light across the black water. The beach was empty, and the lights were off in the neighboring houses. The soft, salty wind ruffled my curls. On the road, a single car drove by.

My mind was full not only of Gloria, who never took no for an answer, and Kevin and Ray's ridiculous fight, but of everything I'd observed and been told over the past week. I needed to gather my thoughts about this matter if I was ever to sleep again.

Sam Watson had told Kyle North I was observant. Observant and curious. That could be a curse. *Curiosity killed the cat*, as is often said. Maybe the reason I found myself involved, more than common sense would dictate, in these things was that I couldn't let a problem go. Perhaps I should take up jigsaw puzzles or buy a book of brain teasers.

As I didn't have any puzzles or brain teasers at hand, I went back inside and took a seat at the dining room table. I found a pen and a piece of scrap paper amid Connor's work pile. Charles knows he's not allowed on the table, so he took his place on the back of the sofa in the living room and studied me through narrow blue eyes.

"You know," I said to him. "I know you know; you always do. You didn't like Detective North when he came here and then to book club, and that's okay. I'm not entirely sure I like him either, but I'm hoping he just needs to settle into the new job and learn his way around. You weren't friendly to Kristen or Ray, but they didn't exactly make themselves welcome today. You seemed to like Lorraine okay. Unfortunately, you haven't met all the suspects in this business." I considered parading them through the library, forming a lineup in front of Charles.

As that wouldn't work, I wrote BLACKMAIL across the top of the paper in big black letters. I had to believe Wayne Fortunada's penchant for blackmail had gotten him killed eventually. At one time he'd blackmailed, or attempted to, Eddie McClanahan and Lorraine Kittleman. Kristen had said nothing about him doing the same to her, but she was susceptible to being blackmailed because of her affair with Ray, and she'd been in Wayne's company for much of the reception. By proximity, Ray would be affected if Kristen's secret came out—she would find herself in a difficult position in her divorce action. I added Ray's name to the list.

Including Eddie, I had four names: Lorraine, Kristen, Ray. Far too short of a list.

Why did people murder a blackmailer? To stop future blackmail, or in revenge for previous acts. As we'd discussed at book club on Thursday, people generally get over the desire for revenge quickly. Life goes on and other problems arise. But not always. Grievances can be nurtured for a long time and spring to the forefront when the object of the grievance suddenly makes an appearance or something reminds them of it.

There could, of course, be a myriad of other reasons for the murder.

What about Aunt Joyce? She prided herself on being an independent soul, a free-wheeling rebel. She told us she'd decided to cut Wayne adrift, but was that true? Had she been so humiliated by his actions that night she wanted to take her revenge? And cut him adrift in a more permanent manner?

I had to admit I didn't know my father's sister at all well. She'd had almost no contact with the family when I'd been growing up, descending upon us once every couple of years in a cloud of perfume, hair spray, and short skirts, bearing elaborate and totally unsuitable gifts.

I added Joyce's name to the list, and then I studied my notes.

Absolutely nothing leapt out at me.

Plenty of people had been in the hotel that night, apart from those at our wedding. Might one of them have spotted Wayne and decided to act on old grievances? The hallway with the restrooms and the small storage room were part of the general layout of the hotel, not used exclusively by people in the ballroom.

I looked at Charles. "Any bright ideas?"

He washed his whiskers.

Now that I was thinking of Joyce, I remembered that she'd said something at dinner that bothered me. I struggled to bring the thought into focus, but it stubbornly wouldn't come.

Probably nothing.

I started to stand up, and then I dropped back into my chair.

Aunt Joyce had said Wayne seemed to be having a good time when they first arrived in Nags Head, but his mood changed abruptly the moment they walked into the church shortly before three o'clock on Saturday. Did that mean Wayne had seen, or been reminded of, the person who eventually killed him in the church? It would be too much of a coincidence for the two situations to be unrelated. Yes, coincidences can happen, but for now I'd assume the change in Wayne's mood was directly related to what happened to him hours later.

If Wayne had seen someone in the church with whom he had an unpleasant history, that meant his killer was unlikely to have been a random hotel guest or member of the hotel staff.

That person had to be a close acquaintance of mine. Or of my or Connor's family. But not close enough to have been at the Friday night dinner, at which, apparently, Wayne behaved like his normal self.

Of the people on my list, the only one who'd been at the Friday dinner was Aunt Joyce.

I wasn't ready to scratch her name out yet. Something could have happened between her and Wayne after the dinner, but it made her, in my mind, less likely. I put a small X next to her name and went on to consider what Wayne might have seen or heard in the church.

I tried to mentally draw up the scene. The church had been full. The building was newly built, very modern, with straight lines and little adornment. Steph and Grace had been in charge of the flowers, and they'd done a magnificent job. Garlands and sprays of peach and white roses and lush greenery, matching my bouquet and the smaller ones the bridesmaids carried, were draped around the ends of the pews and replicated in two huge arrangements gracing the altar steps. The minister wore a long black robe with a cream-and-silver stole.

As for the people, aside from my bridesmaids, Josie, Steph, and Grace; Jake cradling sweet little Ellie; my parents, who escorted me up the aisle; and Connor (obviously) and his parents, I could bring nothing to my mind but a sea of smiling faces.

I didn't know for sure if Kristen, Kevin, Ray, or even Eddie had been there. It was possible Lorraine Kittleman had been, although not as a guest. I'd walked up the aisle, and then down again, accompanied by live organ music. Musicians took all sorts of small jobs, such as playing the organ at weddings. Connor and I hadn't met the musician; the minister told us she'd hired the person they regularly used for special occasions, and that was fine with us.

I put down my pen and rubbed my eyes. I was going in circles.

"Lucy, what are you doing?"

I lifted my head to see Connor watching me. His hair was tousled from sleep, his right cheek creased by his pillow. His pajama pants hung low on his slim hips, held up only by a loosely tied string.

"I don't know," I replied.

He came to stand behind me and rubbed at the back of my neck. I settled into the strength and warmth of his hands.

"Oh no," he said. "You're making a list."

"To no avail, I fear. I'm getting nowhere."

"The problems of the world are not always yours to solve, Lucy. You did your bit to help Sam by finding Eddie and help Eddie by letting him know what was going on. Isn't that enough?"

"I've been thinking I need a hobby. Sherlock Holmes brain puzzles, perhaps."

"Excellent idea." He kissed the top of my head and guided me to my feet. "Is Eddie in the clear?"

"Bertie's not entirely sure what the police are thinking, but he's not under arrest or any sort of caution. Steph and Amos are on standby in case a lawyer is needed. They're going away for the weekend. I mean, Eddie and Bertie are going away for the weekend. Not Steph and Amos."

"That's good, then."

"It's just . . . if the police never find out who did it, and that's entirely possible, the specter of the accusation will hang over Eddie for a long time."

"Eddie's a big boy. He can handle it. Besides, Fortunada was an outsider; no one will remember him in another month."

"That's true enough."

"A man like Wayne Fortunada makes enemies as he goes through life. Let the police take care of it, Lucy."

"I will," I said, meaning it. I scooped up the piece of paper, crumpled it up, and threw it into a corner.

Charles leapt off the back of the sofa, flew across the room, and began playing ball.

Chapter Sixteen

Saturday is always the busiest day of the week at the library, and today was no exception. Bertie and Denise don't normally work on Saturdays, and Ronald has a day packed with children's programming. Today he had a national parks ranger coming in and they were taking the kids into the marsh to study the vegetation and wildlife. By ten o'clock the main room of the library was packed, not only with the children but also parents in rubber boots, binoculars around necks and hats on heads. The unpleasant scent of excessively applied insect repellent filled the air.

Aunt Ellen would be accompanying them on their expedition; at the moment she was helping herd the children (and the parents). Gloria was ensconced in the wingback chair in the magazine nook. Fortunately, Mr. Snyder didn't usually come in on Saturdays, so there shouldn't be a battle of wills for possession of the prime seat.

The moment Gloria settled herself into the chair, Charles disappeared in a streak of tan fur.

"So nice to see children eager to learn, isn't it, Lucy?" she called to me.

"It is."

"I'm glad I had my children young, when I could truly enjoy them. Unlike this modern habit of waiting until late middle age."

One of the mothers, easily approaching fifty, gave Gloria a furious look.

"Yes," Gloria said, making no attempt to keep her voice down, "motherhood is a young woman's job. So much more difficult as age begins to slow you down."

That comment was clearly aimed at midthirties—and still childless—me. I ignored her and waved at the children as Ronald tried to get to get them to form an orderly procession to head out the door.

"Have fun!" I called.

Eventually the last straggling parent left, and the library was calm before the next storm descended.

An orderly procession . . . I mentally slapped my forehead. Last night, I'd struggled to bring up a mental picture of the audience in the church, but it had all been a blur. I'd forgotten that someone had been there with the express purpose of taking it all in.

The wedding photographer.

I took advantage of the momentary break when no one appeared to be in need of my assistance and gave him a quick phone call. "Hi. It's Lucy McNeil calling."

"Lucy. I'm sorry I haven't gotten back to you yet, but I was hoping to in the next couple of days. It's wedding season, and I did tell you it would be a week or more before I have the pictures ready to show you."

"Not a problem, Greg. I'm anxious to see them, but I can control my impatience. If I must."

"Thanks," he said. "I wish every bride would say the same."

"Having said that, I'm hoping I can have a sneak peek, but not of the finished product," I added quickly. "And not of most of them. I don't want to say why, but I'd like to see whatever you have of the audience in the church. Is audience the right word?"

"Congregation? Guests? Witnesses?"

"Them."

"I don't have many shots like that. A few of you and your parents entering, and then you and Connor leaving, but Reverend Bradly doesn't want us to stand by the altar, so I don't get a lot of pictures of the background in the church. I have plenty taken outside when everyone was mingling about after; will that do?"

"Those aren't exactly I'm looking for." Wayne had experienced his change of mood when he and Aunt Joyce first entered the church; if someone arrived late and slipped into the crowd, that person wouldn't have been the cause of his behavior. "Can you send me what you do have? In whatever form they are?"

"Sure, I can do that."

"One more thing. Did you hear that one of our guests was found dead the following morning?"

"Yeah, I did. My condolences. The police spoke to me, but I couldn't help. I left soon after the cake was cut and the dancing started."

"Did you see him doing anything that stood out to you? Like arguing with someone, maybe?"

"The cops asked me that too. I noticed the guy; judging by the look on his face, I thought he'd had a fight with his wife, but that was none of my business. The cops asked me to go through my photos, and I did, but it doesn't look like I got him in any of them."

"Thanks. You have my email address; can you send me the pictures I'm interested in that way?"

"As there's only a handful, email will work. I'm in the studio now, so you'll have them in five to ten minutes."

Louise Jane was working in the rare books room on the second level, and I phoned her. "I'm going on my break early. Can you keep an eye on the desk for a couple of minutes? It'll be quiet down here until the kids get back from their walk."

"Sure."

When she'd come down and was chatting to Gloria about some obscure part of Outer Banks history, I slipped outside. A wooden boardwalk winds through the marsh, leading to a pier and observation deck overlooking a small body of water. Ronald and his group were heading there, in search of what wetland life they might find. The sounds of excited children—and parents trying, with little success, to control them—drifted toward me. A group of Canada geese flew overhead, honking to stragglers to keep up. Frogs called to one another, the long grasses swayed in the light breeze, and the wind blew through my hair and stroked my cheek. I breathed in the fresh salty air. I love everything about working at this library; one of the main reasons is that I can simply step out the door to find myself surrounded by the peace and quiet of nature.

A woman screamed that something was moving in the grass. Children rushed to see what it was. Most of the mothers ran in the opposite direction.

Sometimes, it's peaceful and quiet in nature, but not always.

Outside the thick stone walls of the lighthouse, cell reception is good, and I accessed the email on my phone. Greg had sent me five files, each containing three photographs. They all showed either my parents and me following my bridesmaids up the aisle or Connor and me beaming at each other as we left the church. I used my fingers to expand the photos and slowly passed my eyes across them, studying the smiling faces in the background. All the smiling faces, that is, except that of Wayne Fortunada, standing next to Aunt Joyce. She was watching us, smiling, but he wasn't. His face was drawn, his eyes far away, as though he was remembering something he'd rather not.

I saw the familiar faces of my friends and family. Kevin stood between Mom and Luke in the first row of pews. Kristen and Ray were at the back, tucked into a far corner like the unwelcome guests they were. Kristen's smile was huge, as though she knew the camera was on her. Ray simply looked bored. Bertie and Eddie were there, with Ronald and Nan, Denise and Louise Jane. I smiled to see the trace of tears in not only Bertie's eyes but Louise Jane's also. Gloria was between Aunt Ellen and Uncle Amos. Jake and Ellie were with them, and the baby was fast asleep in his father's arms.

There were a handful of faces I didn't recognize, but not many. Out-of-town relatives of Connor's probably or people he worked with. I no doubt had been introduced to them at some point, but their names and faces had flown straight over my head. Everyone in the pictures wore suits and nice dresses; some of the women even had hats. That meant they were invited wedding guests, likely not someone who'd seen Wayne and followed him inside the church on the spur of the moment.

Everyone had been where I'd expected them to be, so I'd learned nothing. I closed my email, but I didn't put the phone away. Instead, I made another call.

"TK Rare Books," said Theodore in his fake English accent.

"Hi. It's Lucy."

"Lucy," he said in his normal North Carolina accent. "How may I be of service on this fine day?"

"I have a quick question."

"Shoot."

"Do you by any chance know if Lorraine Kittleman was at my wedding? I mean in the church, not at the reception. I . . . enjoyed the organ music and wondered if it was her playing. She told us she took piano as a child."

"It was. I saw her there, but we didn't speak, as she was obviously busy. We went for coffee after book club on Thursday, and she mentioned she keeps up her music not only in the band but by playing organ at some of the churches around town."

"Okay. Thanks."

"I should be thanking you, Lucy. I've enjoyed getting reacquainted with Lorraine. I . . . like her company. I'd like to . . ." He hesitated, and I waited it out. "Take things further. What do you think?"

I decided not to think like a woman who suspected the lady in question of being a killer and told Teddy what I'd tell anyone else in this situation. "You don't need to ask me, but for what it's worth, I say you should go for it."

"Excellent. Uh . . . how do I go about going for it?"

"You ask her out again. Up to you how serious you want to make it sound. Coffee is super casual, lunch slightly more formal. Dinner's the big deal datewise. If you invite her to dinner, she'll know it's a date, not just getting together with an old friend."

"I can do that. I think. Yes, yes, that's what I'll do."

"Good luck with it. Not that you'll need luck."

We hung up, and I smiled to myself at the childish enthusiasm I'd heard in my friend's voice. I desperately hoped Lorraine had not killed Wayne Fortunada or anyone else. Theodore was a good man, and he truly deserved to be happy.

The library was quiet with all the children and their parents and the volunteers gone exploring. Charles perched on a high shelf, watching Gloria. Clearly he, like Mr. Snyder, wanted his chair back, but Charles was far too frightened of the formidable old woman to approach her.

I remembered what Gloria had said about young people not paying attention to the wisdom of their elders. With a pang, I realized that included me. I approached her with a smile. "Can I get you anything, Gloria? A glass of water? We have a jug of tea in the staff room."

"I'm fine, dear, thank you. I enjoy coming to your lovely library, but I've changed my travel plans once again."

"Is that so?"

"Time for me to go home. I've booked my flight for Monday. If you have children of your own one day, you'll need to understand that they need their space. I fear I'm on the verge of overstaying my welcome. I'd never want that." Her face was drawn today, I thought. Some of the mischievous spark gone from her eyes.

"Did . . . something happen?" I asked.

"Oh, no, dear." She smiled at me. "Nothing at all."

"Good. That's good. I have something I'd like to ask you. You're an observant woman."

"I like to think so," she said.

"Saturday afternoon, you were at the church for our wedding."

"And a marvelous wedding it was, Lucy."

"I thought so too. Did you speak to Wayne Fortunada before going into the church?"

"No one has asked me that. When the police interviewed me, their questions were all about what I might have observed at the reception. I observed nothing significant, as I told them." She settled back in her chair and thought. "Let us step back a moment. I chatted briefly with him at dinner on Friday. I thought him charming and friendly, although at the same time I also thought him somewhat of a fake. He was the sort of man who likes to make a great show of fussing over elderly ladies, but if we ever asked him for a favor more than extending an arm, he'd run for the hills. Having said that, I'll take being charmed whenever I can find it."

I laughed.

"Ellen and Amos were chatting with friends outside the church prior to going in and taking our seats. Joyce and Wayne arrived in a taxi, and I greeted them. Joyce was polite enough, but him . . ."

"Him what? Was he not polite?"

"Stiffly polite might be the word, nothing but the bare minimum of what might be considered acceptable in proper society. The fake charm was gone, and he made no attempt to be friendly. He brushed me aside, verbally speaking, and snapped at Joyce to hurry up."

"How did Joyce react to that?"

"She didn't. I don't know if she even heard him. He went into the church, and she followed."

"That is interesting. Thanks."

Gloria studied my face. "Do you think it's significant?"

"I don't know what's significant and what isn't. I'm just asking questions, trying to put together a puzzle. Which police officer interviewed you?"

"Not Detective Watson, whom I met when I was here previously. The younger one. I forget his name. I liked him better than the late Mr. Fortunada. He made no attempt to patronize me or to charm me. He asked his questions and left. Perhaps he should have asked me more questions."

"Perhaps," I said.

* * *

I'd told Connor I was finished with trying to figure out who'd killed Wayne. That might not have been entirely true, but my subconscious appeared to have received the message. I enjoyed a proper night's sleep Saturday and didn't wake until the first warm rays of sunlight streamed through the bedroom windows. Connor told me that even though it was a Sunday, he'd set up some pro bono appointments at the dental office today, so I said, "How about breakfast on the deck before you have to go in?"

"That sounds like a good idea to me."

I kissed him and rolled out of bed. I'm not much of a cook, but I am learning. First things first, I fed Charles before starting the coffee. I then took sausages, eggs, and vegetables out of the fridge. While Connor showered and dressed, I put the sausages into one pan, and while they cooked, I chopped herbs, tomatoes, onions, and mushrooms prior to sautéing the vegetables in another pan. I melted butter in a third pan, to which I'd add beaten eggs.

I laid a tray with cutlery, mugs and plates, napkins, condiments, cream and sugar, and the coffeepot, and set the table on the deck. Our deck had been restored, like so much in our house, by Connor and his father. When we bought the place, the original covered porch, rotting under the force of the elements, badly needed to be replaced. The men ripped out most of the structure and rebuilt it while doing all they could to maintain the integrity of the unique exterior of the historic old house. As is customary in the design of the unpainted aristocracy, the porch wraps around three sides. Traditionally, the entire porch would be roofed, but we decided to keep the section facing the water open to the sea air and sunshine. The roof over the two wings running the length of the house was replaced with a replication of the original sloping roof extending directly out from the base of the second level. At the southern side of the house, the plan is to eventually screen it in to provide a sleeping porch—so beloved of children on hot, humid summer nights.

We'd bought a patio table and chairs and two lounge chairs with bright, colorful cushions, but the deck desperately needed some plants. The soil on our property is mostly sand, so we wouldn't be able to have much of a garden, but terra-cotta pots on the deck floor and steps, with smaller ones lining the railings, overflowing with brilliantly colored annuals, would look marvelous.

Back in the kitchen, I eyed Charles. "If you want to come outside, you know what that means." He didn't look pleased, but he grudgingly allowed me to put the harness on him and attach the cat leash.

Charles is an indoor cat, and he cannot be trusted not to forget that and chase after seabirds the moment my back's turned.

Connor came into the kitchen, his hair damp, smelling of good soap.

"Coffee's on the deck," I said. "I'll be right out with breakfast. Can you take Charles?"

I warmed two tortillas, laid them on a plate, put the sausages, vegetables, and eggs into bowls, and carried the lot out.

Connor had attached Charles to a post. The big cat pretended that wasn't an afront to his dignity and perched on the railing, calmly watching the activity on the beach.

Connor and I assembled our breakfast tortillas and ate in comfortable silence, watching the beach come to life. The forecast called for temperatures in the midseventies, and the first handful of brave (or foolish) tourists were venturing into the still-too-chilly-for-me water. Others had set up their towels and beach chairs and opened books and coolers. Bathing suit–clad children dug in the wet sand with their plastic shovels while others ran back and forth, fetching water in pails to help fortify the battlements. One dad was letting his two toddlers cover his legs in wet sand. Farther down the beach, colorful kites dipped and soared as they caught the thermals. A sea gull spotted our food and swooped low to have a closer look. Charles leapt to attention, and the bird wisely flew away.

"I have a full schedule all day, but I shouldn't be too late," Connor said. "How about I pick up some steaks on my way home and we can put them on the grill?"

"That would be nice."

He put down his napkin and leaned back with a satisfied grunt. His plate had been scraped clean. "That was good, Lucy."

"Thanks," I said. "Before you go, I forgot to tell you the good news."

He lifted one eyebrow. "Good news?"

"For Aunt Ellen, anyway. Gloria has finally booked her flight home. She leaves tomorrow. She was at the library yesterday, and when she left, she tried to get me to commit to a date for us to come to New Orleans. I managed to avoid that when one of the kids who'd been on the marsh excursion took a frog out of his pocket and set it free. It was last seen disappearing between numbers 500 and 599—the natural history section—closely pursued by Charles, most of the other kids, and one or two screaming mothers."

Connor laughed.

"I might not mind visiting her one day," I said. "I've never been to New Orleans, and I know she'd love nothing more than to show us around. With much added commentary on the history of her family in that city. Gloria can be overbearing sometimes, but she does mean well, and I think she has a good heart." I read the look on Connor's face and added quickly, "I don't mean we should go there for our honeymoon."

"That I'm glad to hear. You got anything on today?"

"A slow and lazy day, exactly what I want. I'll get caught up on the laundry, and after that I might go to the garden center. It's time to get some plants out on the deck. Later this afternoon, I've been invited to pop around to Josie's. She's not going to the bakery today, so she invited me to come over and enjoy some baby time."

"Sounds like a nice day."

While Connor freed Charles and carried him into the house, I cleared the table and took the dishes into the kitchen. Connor headed for work, and I surveyed the mess.

I'd made breakfast for two, not prepared a state dinner, but you wouldn't know that by the condition of my kitchen. Four frying pans, several mixing bowls, two cutting boards, almost every knife I owned. Eggshells and vegetable scraps covered the counter, and more than a few had fallen on the floor.

I loaded the dishwasher, tidied up after myself, tossed a load of laundry into the washing machine, and headed to the garden center.

I indulged myself buying terra-cotta and ceramic pots, flats of impatiens, and more than enough tall grasses, begonias, and geraniums to landscape the entire stretch of beach outside our house, never mind my deck.

Back home, I wrestled bags of potting soil, plants, and pots out of the car and lugged them around to the front. Then, while Charles supervised from the railing, I spent a happy few hours preparing my little garden.

Finally, I sat back on my heels and admired my work. My hands were covered in soil and my pants were filthy, but I was very pleased with myself. My phone rang and I checked it: Josie. Probably with a reminder that I was due at her place shortly. I answered, saying, "Believe it or not, I've been gardening. Let me clean myself up and I'll be over."

"I'm sorry, sweetie, but do you mind taking a rain check?"

"I don't mind, but what's up?"

"We had a rough night followed by an early morning, and Ellie's been restless ever since. She's finally fallen asleep, and I'm hoping she'll be out for a couple of hours."

"And you want to grab some sleep too. I totally get it. I can come anytime."

"Thanks, sweetie."

"Sweet dreams," I said.

I was disappointed not to get the promised baby time, but there would be plenty of other opportunities. I admired my garden once more before going inside to clean myself up.

I spent the rest of the afternoon deep in a good book. At six o'clock I was rummaging in the fridge, searching for things to throw together for a salad to accompany those steaks Connor promised me, when my phone rang once again. Connor's dental office this time.

"Hi, Lucy. It's Irene. Connor asked me to call you. One of his patients had an unexpected encounter between his mouth and a baseball bat at his son's team practice, and he's in need of an urgent consultation. Connor agreed to see what he can do, and the patient is on his way in. We can't say what time we'll be finished until we've had a look at the damage."

I cringed at the thought of taking a bat to the mouth. "Thanks for letting me know. I hope the patient's going to be okay."

I put the vegetables back in the fridge. No steaks on the grill tonight. Probably no relaxing evening on the deck watching the sun go down with a glass of wine and each other either.

Such was life. I took the lasagna Aunt Ellen had given me out of the freezer and placed it on top of the stove. I'd heat it up later, and it would do for whenever Connor got in.

While I was waiting for him, I decided to treat myself to a nice long walk on the beach after all my hard work. I changed out of my dirt-encrusted gardening clothes into capri-length jeans and a light sweater, told Charles I'd be back soon, and let myself out of the house. I kicked my flip-flops off at the bottom of the stairs leading to the beach and carried them in my hand.

It was after six, and only a handful of people remained on the beach, catching the dying rays or setting up their fishing poles. I crossed the warm sand until I reached the edge of the incoming tide line, then turned and headed north. Our house is one of the last in Nags Head, almost at the town's southern border. North of us lie other houses and eventually the hotels, restaurants, and shops of town. To the south are the wild beaches and low dunes of the Cape Hatteras National Seashore.

The beach—any beach—has to be the perfect place for contemplation. I started by thinking, as I usually did in times like this, about Connor, and how lucky I was to have found him. My mind wandered to our wedding and how marvelous it had been. Aside from Kevin and Kristen and their problems, which had nothing to do with me, my family were all in a good place. My parents' marriage was repaired, my mom was happy with my life choices, my dad was proud of me. I'd made a new life for myself in the Outer Banks and at the Lighthouse Library, and I was so very glad I'd made the decision to leave the big city.

The big city. Unfortunately, that took my meandering thoughts to New York City and what had happened to both Eddie and Lorraine there at the hands of Wayne Fortunada. We had plenty of crime in small towns, but I guess it's easier to hide in the cities.

Sam Watson had come from the NYPD. I'd never talked to him about his experiences there. Maybe I would one day. He'd be sure to have some interesting stories to tell.

Thinking about crime in New York City brought my wandering thoughts back to Wayne and what might have contributed to his demise in Nags Head. I tried to shove them away. I'd let those pesky thoughts destroy a good night's sleep the other night. I wouldn't let them spoil my walk.

But you can't stop thinking about something just because you want to, and once an idea is in your head—it's in your head.

A beach ball flew past my face, and two screaming children ran after it. The man watching them lifted a hand and said, "Sorry." I gave him a wave of acknowledgment.

Wayne Fortunada, so I'd been told, had never been to Nags Head previously. It was beyond feasible that he'd been murdered by a random killer who happened to be wandering the hallways of the Ocean Side Hotel that night. He'd come all this way, to a place he'd never been, to attend a wedding of people he didn't know, and found himself confronted by a specter from his past. That specter had killed him.

Sam Watson told me Wayne had a record for embezzlement and theft, but nothing for the blackmail I knew he'd engaged in. He must have chosen his victims carefully. People like Eddie and Lorraine—young people with reputations to lose. Either that or they were the only people he could get the dirt on because people like them didn't expect to be blackmailed.

My mind wandered freely as I walked on, watching my bare feet make depressions in the sand, seawater rushing over my toes, sandpipers scattering at my approach.

My trail of meandering thoughts ended in a mental explosion. I stopped dead.

Was it possible I'd missed something lying right under my nose? Had I made a simple assumption that prevented me from asking the right question?

I pulled my phone out of my pocket. I called Stephanie Stanton first. We exchanged greetings, some minor news, and then I asked the question that had so suddenly come to me.

She gave me an answer that had my head spinning in all directions and my thoughts tumbling all over each other.

My next call was to Aunt Joyce.

"Good evening, dear," she said, over the sounds of a restaurant in the background. "I was going to call you shortly. The police will be releasing Wayne's body sometime tomorrow. His parents have asked me to escort it to Florida, and I will do so."

"That's kind of you," I said.

"I'm doing it for them. Not for him. Well, perhaps a little bit for him. I was angry at him at the end and prepared to be done with him, but we did enjoy some good times together. Wayne never pretended to be anything he wasn't, and I have to remember I never asked him to do so." Her voice was tinged with sadness and what might have been a trace of regret. "Such a waste."

"Speaking of Wayne . . . I have a question about Saturday. The day of the wedding. You told us you had breakfast at the hotel together, you spent time at the pool, and then you arrived at the church in time for the wedding. Did he do anything else that day? On his own, I mean?"

"Nothing. We were together all day, as well as the day before. Why are you asking this, Lucy?"

"Indulge me. You took a taxi to the church, is that right?"

"Yes. Your mother was at your house with you and your bridesmaids. I have to say, my dear, if I didn't at the time, that you were simply the most beautiful bride I've seen in a long time."

"Thank you."

"As for your new husband . . . if I were thirty years younger, I might tell you to watch out." She laughed heartily. I didn't join in.

She coughed lightly and said, "To continue. Millar went with Kevin, Luke, and Barbara. Lloyd and his wife, whose name I never can remember, also took a taxi, although they pointedly did not invite Wayne and me to join them."

"Did anything out of the ordinary happen on the way to the church?"

Aunt Joyce thought. I heard the tinkle of her wine glass as she put it down. I held my breath, and all the sounds of a Sunday evening at the beach fell away.

"Now that you mention it," she said.

Chapter Seventeen

My walk ended abruptly, and I hurried home as quickly as I could. At the bottom of the stairs, I jumped up and down trying to stuff my feet into my flip-flops. I took a deep breath—my excitement was making me clumsy—and slipped my feet into the shoes.

I let myself into the house. "Careful, Lucy," I said out loud. "Take your time. Your enthusiasm has gotten the better of you before."

Charles eyed me from the top of the cat tree. "I'm onto something," I said to him as I called Sam Watson's personal number. I got voice mail politely telling me to leave a message. "Hi. It's Lucy. I've had an idea, and I'd like to talk it over with you. Bye." I hung up, and then I wondered if I should have been more forceful and told him it was urgent. I considered leaving another message but decided not to. It was a Sunday, and the good detective should be allowed some time off. I also thought about calling the police station and asking them to have Watson get in touch with me, but instead I swept up my purse, grabbed my keys off the hook by the door, and called to Charles, "Won't be long."

I locked the kitchen door behind me, jumped into my car, and backed out of the driveway. Sam Watson wasn't working, but I knew other police officers. Not only Butch and Holly Rankin; most of them had been called to the library at one time or another. Our library could be, unfortunately, a hotbed of police activity.

Traffic heading into town was heavy as people returned from their day's outing to Rodanthe and points south. An accident at Whalebone Junction didn't help. As my car edged forward, I could see that two cars had met in the middle of the intersection. No one seemed to be hurt, but Butch stood between two men who were gesturing wildly and screaming at each other. Their body language made it clear they were on the point of coming to blows. Holly Rankin was talking to a tow truck driver while another officer directed traffic around the scene.

Finally I was clear, the traffic sped up, and I could carry on. I'd briefly considered stopping and talking to Butch. To tell my friend what I was thinking. What I knew. What I thought I knew. But I hadn't cared for the look on those men's faces, and I doubted Butch would have appreciated the interruption.

The police station shares the parking lot with town hall. The lot was almost empty on a Sunday night. As I drove up, the first of the streetlamps came on.

I parked out front and ran up the steps to the police station. I hesitated at the doorway. I took a deep breath and wiped my hands on the seat of my pants. Then I opened the door and walked into the small lobby.

The officer behind the partition looked up as I entered and said, "Hey, Lucy. What brings you here at this time of day?"

"I need to talk to Sam Watson. I called him, but he isn't answering, so I hoped—"

"He's not on duty tonight. But Detective North's in." He picked up the phone. "Let me call him."

"No! I—"

"No bother."

"I'd rather not . . . disturb him. Is anyone else around?"

"Most everyone's out. First, a bar brawl broke out near the pier, and then reports of an accident at the Junction started coming in. Detective North, Lucy McNeil's here to see you. Yeah. Mayor's wife." He put down the phone and gave me a big friendly grin. "He'll be right with you."

"Never mind. I've gotta go. I just remembered an appointment."

"Congratulations on your marriage, by the way. Do you have any plans for a honeymoon?" He smiled at me. The officer was an older guy, on the verge of retirement. Sunday nights were normally pretty slow in the police station, and he was glad of the chance for a friendly chat.

Good manners prevented my escape. "We're going to Paris next month."

"Paris. Don't you be telling my wife, now." He waved a finger at me. "She has Paris smack-dab at the top of her bucket list. Maybe when I retire, we can find the time to go there. Do you know that—"

The door to the inner areas of the building opened, and Kyle North came into the lobby. He gave me a smile that didn't quite reach his eyes. "Mrs. McNeil. This is a surprise. How can I help you?"

I glanced at the officer behind the desk. I opened my mouth to tell him I needed to speak to someone else. Anyone else. Before I could say anything, the phone rang, and he turned from me to answer it.

"Mrs. McNeil?" North said.

"I . . . uh . . . I remembered an appointment. Yes, that's right, I have an appointment. It's not important. I mean what I have to say isn't important, not my appointment. My appointment is important. I'll . . . write a letter. Gotta run."

His hand shot out, and he grabbed my arm. I sucked in a breath. My heart pounded.

"You don't seem okay. Can I give you a lift home?"

I pulled my arm free. "No. Thank you. I'm fine."

"Is your husband at home?"

"No, he's working late at his dental office. I mean . . . yes, he's home. Now. At home. Our house."

I ran out the door, galloped down the steps, and dashed for my car. I fumbled in my purse for my keys, finally found the fob and flicked it. I jumped into the car and switched on the engine. As I tore out of the parking lot, I glanced out the side window. North stood at the top of the steps, watching me.

Could I have made any more of a mess of that?

As I headed toward home, I used Bluetooth to call Connor. His cell phone didn't answer, so I called the office and got the answering machine. If he was with his patient, his dental assistant, Irene, would be helping him. No one would be at reception at this time of night to pick up the phone.

The situation at Whalebone Junction had been resolved. The police and one of the damaged cars were gone; the other pulled to the side of the road.

I drove through. As I turned off the main road onto South Old Oregon Inlet Road, the lights of the cars behind me fell away. To the west, the sky was streaks of pink, purple, and dark gray. To the east, beyond the scattered lights of the houses lining the oceanfront, all was dark.

My eyes kept flicking to my rearview mirror. One car followed me out of the Junction, but it soon slowed and turned into a driveway. I reached my house and pulled into my own driveway. I parked the car, switched it off, and let out a long sigh of relief. Home. I'd lock myself inside and give Butch a call and then try Sam Watson again. This time I'd tell him exactly why I needed to speak to him. Then I'd sit tight and wait for Butch to arrive, Connor to get home, or Watson to return my call.

I got out of the car.

"You left in a hurry, Mrs. McNeil," came a voice out of the darkness. "Want to tell me what had you in such a panic all of a sudden?"

Chapter Eighteen

The light above my kitchen door shone on Detective Kyle North's face. Behind him, I could see an unmarked police car, painted black. He'd followed me, keeping the headlights off as we came down the street.

I let out a frightened squeak. "Nothing." I cleared my throat. "I mean, nothing. No panic. I'm sorry, but it's late and I'm tired. We can talk in the morning. My husband called and said he's home now."

"I don't see his car. He drives a BMW, right? Nice wheels."

"It's . . . in the garage."

"Y'all moved all that construction equipment out of there?"

"How'd you know . . . ?"

"I just happened to drive by the other day when he was getting something out of the garage, and I noticed it's packed to the rafters. You yourself told me the mayor and his father did most of the work renovating this house themselves. They did a good job."

"You've been watching us?"

"I figure you need watching, Mrs. McNeil. Nothing good comes of thinking you're some sort of hotshot private detective with all that Sherlock Holmes and Auguste Dupin nonsense."

I edged backward, gripping my keys. If I could get to the door . . .

I hadn't been entirely sure the new detective had murdered Wayne Fortunada, but I had no doubts about that now. The look on his face, the mean smile curling around his mouth, the trace of amusement in his dark eyes, told me as much.

I kept my eyes on his face and backed slowly away, one cautious step at a time. I tried to remember if I'd locked the kitchen door behind me. I normally do, but my mind had been preoccupied with my errand. If I had locked it, by the time I got my key into the lock and the door open, he'd be on me.

"I kept hoping you'd drop it," he said. "But it doesn't look like that's going to happen. Watson told me you're stubborn that way, and once you get an idea in your head you won't let it go."

"If you hurt me," I said, "You'll never get away with it."

"Hurt you? Why would I hurt you, little Lucy? You came to talk to me at the station, clearly distressed. Officer Forrest will testify to that. He'll say he has no idea why you left so abruptly. Naturally, I followed you, strictly out of concern for your welfare. I got here, but I was, tragically, too late to be able to save you."

The back of my foot hit the steps leading to the kitchen door. I took the first step up.

"Why don't we go inside and have a nice chat." North's voice was calm, his posture relaxed and comfortable. A spark of pure malice burned in his eyes.

"I'd . . . rather not. The house is a mess."

"I don't mind. Your professor friend Eddie. *Tsk*, *tsk*. Turns out he's not much of a friend."

I took the next step. "What does that mean?"

"He realized you were getting close to finding out what he'd done, with all your questions and interference, so he decided he had to get rid of you. Unfortunately, he ran off before I got here. But he won't get far."

Another step. For every step I took, North took one. He'd reached the bottom of the steps now. The motion light over the kitchen door had come on when I drove up. It shone on the madness in his eyes. My hands shook so much I was afraid I'd drop the keys.

"Wayne Fortunada," I said. "What was he to you?"

"I made a stupid, stupid mistake. A moment of weakness. It had been a one-time thing. It got me out of a financial jam, and I wouldn't have needed to do anything like that again, but him . . . Fortunada. Stupid name. I paid him off, but then he followed me all the way here, to Nags Head. I should have dealt with him in the city, but I didn't. I guess that was my second mistake."

It sounded as though Wayne had been blackmailing Detective North. I didn't much care about that at the moment, but as long as he was talking to me, he wasn't killing me.

Another step for me. He was below me now, looking up. If I lashed out with my foot, I had a chance of kicking him in the face. But he was a strong, quick young man, a trained police officer. I was a librarian wearing flip-flops. If he grabbed my leg and I lost my balance, it would all be over for me. I would be fighting for my life, but he was propelled by a sort of calm indifference. I didn't think my chances were good. All I could do was try to keep him talking until . . . something happened. Connor came home. Sam Watson got my message and rather than call decided to pop around.

It wasn't terribly late, but the street was quiet. No one out catching the night air or walking the dog. The neighbors to the north, the side next to our driveway, didn't live here full-time, and their house was wrapped in darkness. A couple of cars drove slowly past, but North stood firmly between me and the road, blocking any chance of escape.

"Eddie and Bertie have gone away for a few days," I said. "Out of town. You won't be able to frame my . . . what happens to me . . . on him."

"They got back this afternoon. We haven't limited his movements, but we did ask him to check in to the station regularly."

"Bertie's with him. She'll tell them that."

He shrugged, not much caring. "She's not exactly a trustworthy source, now, is she, not when it comes to her gentleman friend. We, the forces of law and order, will have to sort it all out. Too bad he left a pen behind at the police station the other day. A nice pen, too. From his university. His prints are all over it. Your grieving husband will testify that pen wasn't in your house earlier."

"What did Wayne have on you?" I'd made it to the top step. My shaking hands fumbled behind me for the doorknob. I turned it.

Locked.

"That's none of your business, little Lucy. Suffice to say, I had to make sure, once and for all, he wouldn't come back for more. And so I did. This conversation is getting boring. Open that door."

"It's locked."

"Then unlock it, Mrs. McNeil."

He didn't attempt to climb the steps, no doubt because my intentions were written all across my face: the only chance I'd have to fight him off would be when he had one leg raised and was momentarily unbalanced.

"I said unlock the door, Lucy."

I half turned and, keeping one eye on him, put the key in the lock. "You won't get away with this," I said.

"I always do. Not that you'll ever know."

The lock turned. I shoved at the door, hoping to get inside and slam and lock it before North could make it up the steps.

But he was fast, and he'd been waiting for the moment. He leapt up the stairs and shoved me hard, pushing me into the opening door. I fell against it and staggered into the kitchen. I had to keep to my feet; if I fell, I was finished. I grabbed the back of one of the stools and held on. By the time I'd regained my balance and turned around, North was in my kitchen. He kicked the door shut behind him. He smiled at me.

"Poor little Lucy. Got in way over her foolish head."

He took a step forward. I glanced around, desperately seeking something, anything, I could use to defend myself. The block of knives, which ironically had been a wedding gift from Aunt Joyce, was on the counter, on the far side of North. I cursed my tidiness. The breakfast dishes and the cast iron frying pans had been washed and put away. Tea towels were folded neatly over the handle of the oven, and Aunt Ellen's frozen lasagna rested on the top of the stove. Charles's cat tree next to the window was empty.

I tried to slow my breathing, to say calm. But it wasn't easy. My hand sought my phone, deep in my pocket. I had no chance of getting it out in time to make the emergency call. My heart pounded in my chest, and Connor filled my thoughts. North continued smiling as he approached me. It was all so quiet.

A screech of pure rage broke the silence as a ball of tan-and-white fur burst into the kitchen. Charles leapt onto the top level of the cat tree, propelled himself across the kitchen, hit the counter next to the sink, and from there he was once again airborne. Sharp teeth and extended claws landed on the back of North's neck and clung on. The man screamed in shock and pain. He spun around, not quite sure what was happening, his arms windmilling in an attempt to get rid of whatever was attacking him. Charles dug in harder, hissing and spitting.

For the briefest of moments, I was frozen in shock. Then I moved. I dodged past North, yelling and swatting and trying to turn around to see what was happening behind him. Charles howled. Drops of blood began dripping down North's neck. The man made a grab for the cat's swinging tail, but Charles whipped it away in time.

Charles might be fast and he might be tough, and he knew he was fighting for my life, but he weighted ten pounds at the most. It wouldn't be long before North got control of him.

Aunt Ellen's lasagna awaited heating on top of the stove. I grabbed it. She'd packed it into a glass casserole dish and it was still frozen, the contents as hard and solid as a brick.

"Charles!" I bellowed. "Go, now!"

The cat leapt off North and landed nimbly on the kitchen island on all four feet. Suddenly free of the weight attacking him, North was thrown off-balance, and he pitched forward, toward me, his neck extended. As he struggled to regain his footing, I lifted the casserole dish high and brought it down on the back of his head with all the strength I could muster. The dish shattered. The man screamed.

He collapsed, falling to the floor in a swearing heap. He hadn't been knocked out, and he gave his head a shake as he lay between me and the door to the outside.

"Charles, run!" I ran out of the kitchen, across the dining room and the living room to the sliding door leading to the deck. I threw the latch and pulled the door open. Fresh sea air rushed to greet me as my feet hit the new boards. Across the deck, past my lovely new plants, the white of the geraniums glowing in the last rays of the day's light. Down the steps to the beach. Charles caught up and he flew past me, a ball of fast-moving fur and feline rage.

As I ran, I pulled my phone out. I swiped it to make the emergency call to 911. "Help, help. He's after me."

I kept running, but I dared to throw a look over my shoulder. North staggered out of the house, his right hand pressed against the back of his neck. He saw me, and to my dismay, he stumbled down the steps and broke into a run in my direction. I kicked my flip-flops off and continued in my bare feet. He was in street shoes. Hopefully that would slow him down.

"I'm here, madam," said a calm voice from the depths of my phone. "I'm sending the police now. Where are you?"

I shouted my address. "I've made it to the beach. I'm running . . . south." In my panic and desperate need to get away from the man intent on killing me, I'd turned right, which took me in the wrong direction. Instead of north, to the houses, where people were relaxing on decks and balconies and other people were strolling along the shore, I'd gone south. Toward the empty, desolate stretches of the Cape Hatteras National Seashore. Night had fallen, and the sand dunes to my right were nothing but an outline of shadows against the darkening sky.

"Stay on the line please, madam. What's your name?"

"Lucy Richardson. I mean, Lucy McNeil." I dared to throw another look over my shoulder. North had recovered from the cat attack and was running flat out. I could no longer see Charles. He could do nothing more for me now. Hopefully he'd sought a place of safety.

"Mrs. McNeil?"

"Yes, yes. I'm here. Call Sam. Tell him it's North."

"North? You said you're going south."

"I am going south. It's North. North's after me. Please call Sam Watson. Call Butch. Call Connor." I gripped the phone tighter as I ran blindly across the sand. Soft seawater brushed against my feet; grains of sand few into my eyes and into my panting mouth. Not a single person was within shouting distance.

No one except North, relentlessly following me. To my relief, he wasn't gaining. If anything—I hoped—the distance between us seemed to be increasing.

I half turned and dared to slow slightly. I yelled into the wind. "I've called 911. The police are coming. I told them it's you. You can't get away, North."

He didn't seem to have heard me. He kept coming, feet pounding the sand, arms pumping, eyes fixed straight ahead. The madness was full on him now, and he'd abandoned all reason and any sense of self-preservation. I turned inland: I needed to get as near to the road as I could so the police could find me in time. The sand was softer away from the water's edge, and that made running difficult. If it was difficult for me, in my bare feet, it would be all that much more difficult for North in his street shoes. I chanced another glance over my shoulder. Seeing the direction I was heading in, he'd swerved to intercept me, trying to cut me off.

I put on what I knew would be a final burst of speed. The soft sand gripped my feet, pain stabbed through my side, my legs trembled, my lungs struggled, and my breathing labored.

"Help's almost there, Mrs. McNeil," said the voice in my phone. "Are you still on the line?"

"Yes," I gasped.

"Can you get to the road?"

"Trying."

"It's dark out now. Do you have a light?"

"Light, no." I stepped in a hole and tripped. I cried out, but managed to regain my footing without falling. Luckily, I'd kept my grip on the phone.

"What's happened? Are you all right there?" she asked.

"Tired. Fell."

Light. I needed light. I fumbled for the flashlight app on the phone and flicked it on. The soft white beam lit up the ground in front of me, and I could see a small dune lying directly in my path. I struggled up it, the sand holding me back, my lungs burning, my heart threatening to burst out of my chest.

I heard the blessed sound of sirens, far away but getting closer, and moments later the first of the flashing red and blue lights broke the dark.

I fell and, rather than trying to get up, scrambled on my hands and knees to reach the top of the dune.

North was gaining. I could hear his deep breathing getting closer and the sound of sand slipping beneath him.

I staggered to my feet, but I could run no farther. I turned around.

He was about twenty yards behind me, also struggling to make it up the dune.

I lifted my phone, and the light shone on the rage in his eyes. I snapped a picture, and then another and another, as he got closer and his face came into focus. The last phone call I'd made, before 911, had been to Sam Watson, so his number was at the top of my recent calls list. I sent him the pictures.

If I died, here, at the top of this sand dune, I'd ensure everyone knew who'd been responsible.

Seeing that I'd stopped, North stopped also. He stared at me. He started to yell, but then he looked past me. Something dawned in his eyes, and he spun on his heels and scrambled down the dune, heading back the way he'd come.

Then sirens and flashing lights were all around me, and men and women were shouting and running toward me.

I dropped to the soft sand and knelt there, gasping for breath.

"Lucy! Are you all right? What's going on?"

I pointed in the direction North had gone.

"Holly," Butch shouted. "You're with me. Paul, stay with Mrs. McNeil."

A hand touched my shoulder, and a voice said, "You're safe now."

My phone said, "I'll leave you to it, Mrs. McNeil. Good night."

Chapter Nineteen

I cradled a mug of hot chocolate between my hands and snuggled deeper into the blanket over my legs and the cushion behind my back.

"Who," Connor said, "is Auguste Dupin, and why do I care?"

"A Sherlock Holmes prototype," Sam Watson said. "From a story by Poe. About all North had to say when Holly and Butch caught up to him was that he wouldn't be brought down by any slip of a woman thinking she's Auguste Dupin."

Connor groaned.

Back on the sand dunes, when I'd finally recovered my breath and some of my wits and been helped to my feet on quivery legs that could barely hold me upright, I'd refused the offer of a ride to the hospital. Instead, the police had driven me home, where I found not only Charles, snoozing contentedly on the highest level of the cat tree, but Connor and Sam Watson waiting for me. Connor was still in his scrubs, and he explained that he'd been washing up after the emergency patient left when the 911 operator called to tell him his wife was fleeing down an empty beach at night, pursued by a police officer gone mad.

"You were lucky, Lucy," Watson said.

I stroked Charles, who'd moved from the kitchen to my lap after Connor made the hot chocolate, to which he'd added a hefty splash of brandy, and tucked me onto the living room sofa.

"Luck," I said. "Had nothing to do with it."

"North's cooling his heels in a cell," Watson said. "Claiming it's all a misunderstanding. He followed you from the police station because he was worried about your mental state. You attacked him and ran away. He chased after you, fearing you might harm yourself or someone else. What do you have to say to that?"

"He was intent on killing me," I said calmly. "No doubt about it."

"If nothing else, those pictures you sent me should clinch it. The man looks totally out of control. Before I talk to him, can you take me through what happened tonight?"

I sipped my drink and gathered my thoughts. "Connor was delayed, so I went for a walk on the beach. I thought about all that had happened, and all of a sudden everything came together with the realization that North had killed Wayne. I called you, Detective." I filled the men in on what happened from that point on.

"Go back a step," Connor said. "Lots of steps. What made you decide North had to be the killer?"

"He's from the Outer Banks. Duck, I think he said. Everyone said he'd come back from 'the city.' " I made quotation marks in the air with my fingers. "I simply assumed the city was Raleigh or maybe Durham. Someplace in North Carolina, anyway. The origins of this case lie in New York. Wayne was from New York; all his blackmail attempts, the ones we know of anyway, were made in New York. He met Aunt Joyce in New York. He'd never even been to North Carolina before. It was only this evening, when one thought led to another and then to another, as Auguste Dupin explained, that I understood my assumptions about North were incorrect. You worked in New York, Sam, and then you came back to the Outer Banks. No reason North hadn't done the same. I called Steph, and she confirmed it. He'd spent most of his career with the NYPD."

"Still seems like a stretch to me," Connor said. "Lots of people live in New York City, and they're not all killers, far as I know."

"That's true, but it made me wonder what else I'd been missing. And once again, it was right in front of me, but I hadn't seen it. The jewelry store robbery."

Connor shook his head. "I don't get it, honey. The robbery happened Saturday afternoon, shortly before our wedding began. Wayne was with your aunt Joyce on the way to the church, wasn't he? Surely he didn't stop to hold up a jeweler on the way? Joyce might have remembered that."

"North was the lead detective on the robbery," Watson said. "I appreciated having him to take that on."

"I'm not saying Wayne committed the robbery," I said. "Only that he was there, on the scene. I called Aunt Joyce to ask her if anything out of the ordinary happened on their way to the church. She told me Wayne had run out of cigarettes, and he asked the cab driver to make a stop. Which is why the cab didn't take the direct route down the Croatan Highway from the Ocean Side to the church. He detoured to a convenience store in a strip mall. The store he chose just happened to be located in the same mall as the jeweler that had been robbed moments before. The thief escaped in a car. The police were, of course, everywhere in that mall parking lot. The cab was stopped and the cabby asked if he'd seen anything. The officer who stuck his head in the cab window was Kyle North."

"I never made the connection," Watson said.

"North asked the cabby where they were going, and Aunt Joyce piped up and gave him the name of the church. She also told him they were staying at the Ocean Side Hotel. The cabby said he hadn't seen anyone fleeing the scene, and North said,

'Have a nice day, sir.' Aunt Joyce thought nothing more of the incident, but North and Wayne had recognized each other. And that was the reason Wayne's mood changed. Obviously, the encounter upset him, enough that he snapped at Aunt Joyce when they arrived at their destination, and he was rude and moody for the rest of the day. Aunt Joyce told me Wayne's behavior changed when they entered the church, which led me to believe he saw something or someone in the church that bothered him. But Gloria spoke to him as soon as they got out of the cab, before going inside. He was, she said, barely polite to her, whereas the previous night he'd been charming. He brushed her aside and snapped at Aunt Joyce. I concluded then something must have happened prior to Joyce and Wayne arriving at the church. Something highly significant to Wayne, but so insignificant to everyone else Aunt Joyce hadn't even noticed. He'd seen Detective Kyle North. And from there, I began to speculate that North might be a figure from Wayne's past, someone he didn't want to see."

"I follow you up to a point, Lucy," Watson said. "But lots of people, police and witnesses, were at the jewelry store scene, and then there was the cabby, the salesclerk in the convenience store, people on the street. Why focus on North?"

"Because Detective North didn't extensively interview Aunt Joyce."

"Huh?" Connor said.

"That's what started me down that meandering thought trail in the first place. At dinner Friday night, Aunt Joyce mentioned that North had not questioned her again after we initially found Wayne's body. When I thought about it, I realized how unusual that was. She's the person who knew the dead man best. They'd traveled here together and were rooming together. They'd been seated together at the wedding dinner. But the detective didn't have further questions for her? The only reason I could think of for that would be that he wasn't interested in solving the mystery. Why wasn't he interested in solving the mystery? Because he knew who'd done it. What he was interested in doing was finding someone to pin it on. And that person was Eddie McClanahan. He mustn't have been able to believe his luck when Eddie, who also had a past with Wayne, fled the scene. I believe North was preparing to frame Eddie. You'll find a pen from Blacklock College on North. Eddie left it behind at the police station and North swept it up. He's been carrying it around, looking for a chance to plant it."

"And there I dropped the ball," Watson said. "I should have realized someone wasn't following up with Joyce. I figured North was paying too much attention to Eddie, but I let that go too. North was smart, I'll give him that. He made me think I was too personally involved with your group to be open-minded about the investigation."

"Don't blame yourself," I said. "He was smart. Dangerously smart." Again I saw the madness in Kyle North's eyes, and I dug my fingers into Charles's soft, warm fur. "Once I'd gathered all those facts, it was a simple step to speculating that North must have come to the Ocean Side in the early hours of Sunday morning looking for Wayne. Aunt Joyce, remember, had told him where they were staying. The Ocean Side's a popular place for big events. Easy enough for him to assume wedding guests would be staying at the hotel where the reception was being held. He might have told Wayne he wanted to talk, and the two men went into the hallway together. Coming into the ballroom would have been a big risk; anyone might have seen him. Wayne was a heavy smoker, and North likely smelled the tobacco when he encountered Wayne in the cab. Not many people smoke these days, so if North stayed in the shadows by the door, it's possible he could wait there, hidden, until Wayne came out for a cigarette. I don't know if he convinced Wayne into seeking privacy in that closet or if he forced Wayne inside. Regardless of the details of precisely what happened, he killed Wayne and left the scene, blocking the lock so the body wouldn't be found too soon."

"Why?" Connor asked. "Did Wayne have something on North?"

"I believe he did. Kyle North told me he'd made a mistake. One mistake, he said, to get him out of a financial problem. Somehow Wayne Fortunada knew about this mistake, and according to North, he wouldn't forget. I don't know specifically what he was talking about, but I believe if you search the NYPD police records, you might find that North and Wayne had some involvement with each other. If I had to guess . . ." I looked at Sam Watson.

"Go ahead," he said. "Your guesses often turn out to be on point."

"If I had to guess, I'd guess Wayne had been blackmailing North at one time over this one mistake. That might be the reason North left New York, to get away from his blackmailer. And then who does he see in a cab in Nags Head but the very man. Always remember, *the wicked flee when no man pursueth*."

"I know what that means," Connor asked. "But not in this context."

"Wayne had not come to Nags Head chasing after North, but North's own guilt made him think Wayne had done precisely that. It prevented him from realizing that Wayne Fortunada was in Nags Head for no other reason than to attend a wedding. He didn't kill Wayne for revenge, as I initially speculated might be the reason. Too much reading of Poe, perhaps. He killed because he believed Wayne had followed him to Nags Head with the specific aim of blackmailing him again. It was nothing but happenstance that Wayne's current lady friend had invited him to a wedding in Nags Head."

"And North took it on himself to eliminate the perceived threat," Connor said.

"Yes. He said something to me about it being a mistake not dealing with Wayne at the time, in New York. I assume by 'dealing with,' he meant killing. His own fear of exposure made him see a threat where none existed. I don't believe Wayne had any intention of confronting North again. At the reception, he told Aunt Joyce he wanted to go straight home to New York, not have a brief holiday in the Outer Banks as they'd planned. Wayne spent the evening morose and moody, everyone said. Not gloating or preening as he might have if he thought himself on the verge of making another big score."

"He threatened to bring up Eddie's past," Connor said. "Doesn't that indicate he might have said the same to North?"

"I don't think he did. Threaten Eddie, I mean. I think Eddie, confused and upset, misunderstood. The voice I heard in that hallway, and the man I encountered moments later, was thoughtful, not threatening. *Sad* is the word some people used to describe how he appeared that night. He said something about making more than his share of mistakes in life. I believe he'd come to regret what he'd done, or at least he wanted to do no more of it. He told Eddie that Eddie still owed him, but it sounded more to me like he was saying, *Buy me a beer for old times' sake, and we can forget about it.*" I yawned. "That was my impression, anyway. We'll never know what he was really thinking. And I'm sorry about that."

Watson got to his feet. "Most of this is speculation—everything that happened after Fortunada's arrival at the church, at any rate. Looks like I have a long night ahead of me." His phone buzzed, and he answered. "Be right there." He hung up and turned to us. "Forensics are here. They'll need to check out the kitchen, Lucy. Gather evidence from where you fought with North."

"Where Charles fought with North. All I did was brain him with a frozen lasagna and run away."

"And thank goodness you were able to do that," Connor said.

"Ah, yes," Watson said. "Charles. We'll have to take samples from under his claws."

Charles lifted his head, gave Detective Watson a penetrating stare, and hissed.

"Good luck with that," I said.

Chapter Twenty

Taking evidence from Charles wasn't easy, but I held him on my lap while he twisted and squirmed, spat and hissed, and tried to scratch the unfortunate woman sent to do the deed.

Finally, it was over. Charles curled up and went to sleep while the traumatized humans attempted to recover from the ordeal. The forensic officer left in search of Band-Aids. A lot of Band-Aids.

After the police had finally gone, Connor and I sat quietly, not saying much, just being together, thinking of all that had happened. And lavishing praise on Charles, who took it as nothing more than his due.

But peace and quiet rarely lasts long in my life, and soon the phones started ringing and the doorbell chimed.

"Are we home?" Connor said to me.

"I fear we have to be. Obviously, word has gotten out."

He answered the door. The first arrivals were Aunt Ellen and Uncle Amos, preceded by Gloria and her formidable cane.

"What's this I hear?" the matriarch demanded. "You solved the case. I told you, Lucy, I expected to be consulted."

"Sorry." I suppressed a shudder at the thought of what would have happened had Gloria been involved in the confrontation and the subsequent chase across the dunes. "You were an enormous help. The verbal evidence you gave me proved instrumental in closing the case."

Gloria preened. Aunt Ellen threw her a curious look.

"They're saying Detective North's been arrested and is likely to be charged," Uncle Amos said. "Hard to believe."

"Harumph," Gloria said. "I didn't trust him from the very beginning. Spending time in New York City never did a southern boy any good."

Behind her, Aunt Ellen rolled her eyes.

"I have you to thank as well, Aunt Ellen," I said.

"Me? I didn't do anything."

"You provided the defensive weapon. A frozen lasagna."

She laughed. "I'll be dining out on that for a long time."

" 'Fraid not," Connor said. "It's been taken as evidence."

* * *

About all I did at work on Monday was field questions about what happened to me the night before. Word that Detective North had been arrested for the murder of Wayne Fortunada and the attempted murder of Lucy McNeil had spread up and down the coast at the speed of the incoming tide. Patrons came into the library on the pretext of exchanging books, but in reality they wanted to listen to me relate all the details.

I smiled politely and said the police had instructed me not to talk about it, pending the issue being resolved in court.

The general consensus of everyone who'd had any interaction at all with the new detective seemed to be, "I knew something was off about him."

"You okay, Louise Jane?" I said when I came into the staff break room with my lunch.

She was hunched over a history book, flicking idly through it in a way that showed she wasn't taking any of it in. She started at my voice and slapped an enormous smile onto her face. "Perfectly okay."

"I'm here if you want to talk." I sat down, unwrapped my sandwich, and opened my book.

She said nothing for a long time. I ate and read.

"I did like him, you know," she said at last.

"I know."

"Fortunately, it went nowhere. He didn't seem to return my feelings."

"He had other things on his mind," I said.

"That's true." She pushed her chair back and stood up. "Can't sit here lollygagging around all day. From now on, I intend to pay far more attention to what my senses are telling me."

"What does that mean?"

"When Kyle—Detective North—was here the other night, at book club, something was niggling at me all evening. I had an itch at the back of my neck something awful. You must have noticed me scratching at it, Lucy."

I'd noticed no such thing, but I nodded anyway.

"Yes, they were warning me. And I wasn't paying attention."

"They?" I asked, perhaps foolishly.

"The spirits of the lighthouse, of course." Louise Jane leaned over and peered into my face. "Almost certainly *The Lady* herself. You know how protective she is of the women who live in her room, Lucy."

"I know you believe that." I chose my words carefully. The tale of The Lady, a post–Civil War–era ghost, was one of Louise Jane's favorites, the story she'd used most when I first arrived at the library in an attempt to scare me into fleeing back to Boston, where Louise Jane believed I belonged.

"I'm highly sensitive to otherworldly presences, as you know. The Lady was unable to manifest herself that night, probably due to the number of people in the room and the convivial atmosphere, but she did her best to warn me. Oh yes, Lucy. She got North's number immediately. I disregarded her desperate attempts to warn me. To my peril! And even more, to your peril, Lucy. I hate to think of what might have happened last night if . . ." She leaned toward me and stared at me through dark, intense eyes.

Despite myself, I shuddered.

She straightened up, and the smile returned. "Let's not think about that anymore. All's well that ends well. A lucky escape on my part, yes indeed. Why, when I think about it, you saved me from heartbreak and who knows what else at the hands of Kyle North. I need to call my grandmother and ask what she knows about other instances of the spirits issuing warnings and what happened if the subject ignored those warnings. Good heavens, that might be an entirely new area of research."

She headed for the door.

"Don't you have work to do this afternoon?" I called after her.

She ran back and scooped up her book. "Yes, yes. Some minor bit of research for Denise. I'll get that out of the way and begin my investigations. Who knows where this could lead? It might make my reputation. Lucy, you're a marvel."

"I didn't—" I said as the door slammed behind her.

* * *

When my lunch break was over, I went out front to take over the circulation desk and face a further barrage of questions about my escape from death at the hands of the new detective (allegedly).

As I entered the main room, the front door opened and Tim Snyder came in. "Good afternoon, everyone," he said. "Lucy, I'm glad you're here. I have a surprise for you. For all of you. A gift for the library."

"A gift?"

He glanced toward the magazine nook, where his favorite chair was currently unoccupied. "Mrs. O'Malley not in today?" He sounded surprisingly disappointed.

"Gloria's gone home to New Orleans. She left this morning as planned." I knew that because I'd received a text from Aunt Ellen: ☺

"I'm sure she'll be back."

"Now that she has a great granddaughter to visit, she threatened—I mean, promised—to visit regularly."

"Thus I believe forewarned is forearmed." He swept his arm in the direction of the door as two men came in, carrying a wingback chair, upholstered in an attractive fabric with a design resembling rows of books.

"Put it over there, please, gentlemen." Mr. Snyder pointed to the magazine nook. "Next to that tattered old chair."

They did so, and then they left. Charles approached the new chair cautiously, gave it a good sniff, and then he leapt onto it, circled several times seeking exactly the right spot, and lay down.

"It appears to meet with Charles's approval," I said.

Mr. Snyder smiled at me. "A chair for Mrs. O'Malley. And a chair for me."

* * *

Shortly before closing, Theodore arrived. He hovered around the circulation desk, surrounded by an air of nervous excitement.

He examined the books on the return cart, admired the new chair in the magazine nook, admired Charles enjoying the new chair in the magazine nook, cleared his throat several times. He coughed.

Finally I said, "Theodore, do you have something to ask me?"

"Why yes, Lucy. I do. I'm in need of your assistance."

"That's why I'm here."

"Not library assistance. It's more a . . . personal matter."

"Okay."

"As I told you, Lorraine and I had a such a pleasant time at book club and then we went for coffee after, and I'd . . . I'd like to continue our relationship. You suggested we could go out to dinner together, but I am . . . unsure how to go about accomplishing that."

"Easy," I said. "You ask her."

"Ask her?"

"Yes, you ask her to have dinner with you. You suggest a day. She will either accept, decline with a believable apology, suggesting a better time, or brush you off. And then you'll know."

"What will I know?"

"If she wants to pursue the matter."

He blanched.

"I have an idea," I said. "Safety in numbers and all that. Why don't you invite her to come out for a drink after work one day with Connor and me? A casual get-together with friends. Connor and I will make our excuses and slip away, like people expect a newly married couple to do. Then you can suggest going for dinner. Just the two of you."

He beamed at me. "Lucy, you are a gem among women." He hurried away to make the call. Then he stopped and spun around. "Tonight? Where shall we meet you? Is five o'clock too early?"

"Yes, five's too early, as it's after four now. You don't know if she has plans tonight, and I have to ask Connor. Let's try for tomorrow. Six at the bar at the Ocean Side."

He ran out the door intent on his mission, a happy man.

* * *

Lorraine and Theodore met us the following day as he and I had planned. Earlier that afternoon, Sam Watson called and asked if he could come around to our house that evening, as he had some news. I suggested he meet us for a drink, and he agreed. Then Bertie stopped by my desk to say Eddie was in town for a couple of days, and the after-work cocktail party expanded. It might not be so easy for us to slip away, leaving Theodore free to suggest he and Lorraine go out for dinner, so I phoned him with a whispered warning.

I like Theodore a great deal. He's a loyal patron of the Lighthouse Library. When the library had been in severe financial distress a few years ago, to the point of being in danger of closing, he'd sacrificed a favored first edition to raise money for the needed renovations. He's a genuinely kind man and a good friend to Connor and me. But he can be socially awkward, with his tweed suits and fake accent and esoteric conversation about rare books, and I worried he'd have his heart broken if he wanted his renewed friendship with Lorraine to go further than she did.

Connor and I arrived at the Ocean Side first, and as soon as Theodore and his "date" walked into the hotel lobby, I knew my fears were for naught. Teddy had dressed in a pair of neatly ironed jeans and a casual summer sweater. He'd gone so far as to dispense with the clear-glass spectacles. He spotted us first and said something to Lorraine. The smile she gave him was positively radiant, and she took his arm as they wended their way between chairs in the lobby bar.

I rubbed my hands together. "My work here is done."

Connor gave me a questioning look but didn't ask.

Sam and CeeCee Watson followed them, and then Eddie and Bertie came in. We settled around a low table in a far corner of the bar. It was a Tuesday night and the place was largely empty, so we could talk freely if we kept our voices low.

"What I have to tell you," Watson said, after drinks were ordered and served, along with platters of calamari and bruschetta for sharing, "is confidential. Pending the case going through the courts." He looked at each of us in turn. We all nodded.

"You, Ms. Kittleman," he said to Lorraine, "were blackmailed by Wayne Fortunada at one time, as was Professor McClanahan."

"To my eternal shame," Eddie said.

"And mine," Lorraine said. I glanced down to see her gripping Theodore's hand.

"I see no need for any of that to be discussed in court," Watson said. "It's irrelevant to what happened here."

Eddie smiled at Bertie, and Lorraine let out a sigh of relief.

"That Fortunada was a blackmailer is what eventually got him killed. I've had the NYPD searching for a link between North and Fortunada."

"They found something," I said.

He nodded. "About two years ago, North, newly made detective, answered a call to a private home. The home is a very exclusive Upper East Side apartment. A party had been held at that home, full of important people in the New York art world, and the following morning an important piece of art was discovered to be missing. A small sculpture, small enough to be slipped into a woman's bag or a man's jacket pocket. At home when the police arrived was the homeowner, a divorced woman in her fifties, and her companion."

"Wayne," Connor said.

"The very one."

"Kyle North had a look around the apartment, took the woman's statement and a description of the sculpture, and left. Shortly after that, the lady called once again to say a diamond necklace was also missing. She apologized to the police for not having noticed its disappearance earlier. She assumed whoever had taken the sculpture had taken the necklace as well."

"That's not what happened," I said.

"Apparently not. But at the time, the police believed it had. The woman was known for throwing elaborate parties and had a reputation for not checking her guest list thoroughly. It was not the first time the police had been called either the day after or during one of her parties. The thief was never caught. The sculpture, and the necklace, were never seen again. Prompted by what happened here recently, the NYPD took another look at the case, as well as having a peek into Kyle North's banking records. Shortly after the visit to that apartment, he transferred ten thousand dollars into Wayne Fortunada's account."

"Wayne, always watching people, blackmailed him," I said. "He must have seen North take the necklace, and probably even had a picture of it happening."

"The cad!" Eddie said. "Two cads."

"I'm reasonably confident that's what transpired," Watson said. "There's no record of a sudden increase in funds into North's own accounts, but the man's not a fool. There are ways of laundering money obtained by the sale of ill-gotten goods."

"He said something to me about being in a financial jam," I said.

"A jam of his own making. His banking records show that for a period of about six months before the theft, he was spending far more than had been normal for him. Far more than he was earning. No secret where it was going. It's all there on his credit cards: a fancy new car, an exclusive Caribbean vacation, big bills at high-end women's clothing stores and expensive Manhattan restaurants."

"Why?" I asked.

"He was dating a woman whose name doesn't need to be repeated. This woman spends much of her time among the movers and shakers in the New York money world, and she has expensive tastes. Although, I have been told, she's never been suspected of anything illegal. Or even unethical. The NYPD spoke to her about North, and she admitted she dated him longer than she should have because of the amount of money he was spending on her. The fancy holiday, business-class airfare, shopping money, the lot. They eventually broke up, and North found himself in severe financial straits indeed. The fancy car was sold, the credit card bills paid off, slowly and steadily, not causing any concern at his bank. We're now assuming the money came from the sale of the necklace, minus Fortunada's cut."

We sat in silence for a few minutes.

"Wayne might have done Detective North a favor," I said. "North told me he'd made one mistake trying to get himself out of his financial jam and he wouldn't have done anything like that again. I don't believe it. If he'd gotten clean away, he would have tried it the next time the possibility of a quick snatch presented itself. And then the next. Instead, Wayne scared him out of a life of crime."

"It's all very sad," Lorraine said. "How one man's greed can ruin so many other people's lives."

"And eventually lead to his own demise," Bertie said. "When he came across the wrong person."

"Speaking of art theft," CeeCee said, "Bertie, I've been roped into helping with the details of that American Impressionist tour that's coming to town over the summer."

"I hope you're not planning on something being stolen from that," Watson said.

She grinned at him. "I might have wanted to pursue a life of crime, but then I met you. And now I wouldn't dare, not with the formidable Lucy around."

"I'm formidable?" I asked.

"You are, Lucy," Watson said. "In the annals of crime fighting, you are."

Connor groaned. "Perish the thought."

CeeCee turned back to Bertie. "I'm hoping the library can do something to help promote the show."

"We'd love to," Bertie said.

"We have plenty of art books," I said. "Let us know what artists are going to be featured, and we can see about arranging a display. Maybe we could do something about the history of impressionism in general."

And the conversation carried on.

Sam and CeeCee were the first to leave. He said he was expecting another long day tomorrow as the case against Kyle North continued taking shape. Then Bertie and Eddie got to their feet. "I've been thinking, my dear," Eddie said.

"What about?" Bertie asked.

"I have scoured memories of my past thoroughly, and I have to confess that I can find nothing else I need worry about being uncovered."

"That," Bertie said, taking his hand. "I'm pleased to hear."

"Time we were going too," I said to Connor.

"Are you sure? I didn't have much of that calamari, and I'm thinking the restaurant's right here, and—"

"I'm so tired all of a sudden. Dreadfully tired. Will you look at the time? After eight already. My bed's calling to me." I swept up my bag. "Come along now."

"Uh . . . okay," he said.

Lorraine reached to pick up her own purse. While her head was bent, I caught Theodore's eye, pointed to Lorraine, and mouthed, "Dinner!"

He blinked.

Connor saw us, and comprehension dawned. "Oh, I get it. Right. Teddy, no need for you two to leave just because we are.

I'm feeling pretty tired too. Looks like there are lots of empty tables in the restaurant."

He grabbed my hand, and we practically bolted out of the bar.

"Playing matchmaker now, are you?" he said.

"Why not? I'm happy. You're happy. I hope you're happy. Are you?"

He said nothing, just gave me that look that contained all the joy in the world.

"And talking about making people happy," I said as we crossed the hotel lobby hand in hand. "I might give Aunt Joyce a call. Find out how things went in Florida with Wayne's family. I'd like to think he'd changed his ways, at the end. He could have taken advantage of running into Eddie and Kyle North, both of whom had started new lives they wouldn't have been happy to have him interfering with. Instead, he wanted to go straight back to New York. Maybe he'd seen the error of his ways. I hope so."

Connor lifted my hand and touched it to his lips. "Not only are you a formidable presence in the annals of crime but a woman with a good heart."

"I'm not so sure about the formidable part. But I know where my heart belongs."

We walked out of the hotel together.

"You're not really planning on going to bed when we get home, are you?" Connor said.

"No. That was a clever ruse to get us out of being third wheels on Teddy's date."

"Maybe not so clever. Lorraine knew what you were up to."

"Doesn't matter, not if it worked. I'm thinking an evening on the couch surrounded by guidebooks to Paris might be a good idea. It's time you and I did some serious planning about the next adventure in our life together."

"An evening on the couch," Connor said. "Sounds mighty good to me. Why don't we order a pizza?"

I squeezed his hand, and he returned the gesture as we walked down the steps into the warm, soft dusk. We'd have many more pizza evenings on the couch together, and I couldn't think of anything I'd like more.

Author's Note

The Bodie Island Lighthouse is a real historic lighthouse, located in the Cape Hatteras National Seashore on the Outer Banks of North Carolina. It is still a working lighthouse, protecting ships from the Graveyard of the Atlantic, and the public is invited to tour it and climb the 214 steps to the top. The view from up there is well worth the trip. But the lighthouse does not contain a library, nor is it large enough to house a collection of books, offices, staff rooms, two staircases, and even an apartment.

Within these books, the interior of the lighthouse is the product of my imagination. I like to think of it as my version of the TARDIS, from the TV show *Doctor Who*, or Hermione Granger's beaded handbag: far larger inside than it appears from the outside.

I hope it is large enough for your imagination also.

Read an excerpt from

THE STRANGER IN THE LIBRARY

the next

LIGHTHOUSE LIBRARY MYSTERY

by EVA GATES

available soon in hardcover from
Crooked Lane Books

Chapter One

As the saying goes, "I don't know much about art, but I know what I like."

Although that's not entirely true, not anymore. Connor and I had the most fabulous honeymoon in France and Italy and, between enjoying great meals, exploring old neighborhoods and historic buildings, watching daily life go past over Aperol Spritz and pizza, café au lait and croissants, and simply reveling in each other's company and our newly married state, we saw a lot of art.

So much art, at times I was almost overcome by how magnificent and truly awe-inspiring it all was. I loved the Renaissance and Baroque art of Italy, and the Impressionists of France most of all.

I took thousands of pictures, so many that when I got home and made a screensaver slide show of them, I couldn't always remember what painting was by what artist or where we'd seen it.

I considered telling Connor we needed to go back for our next vacation, so I could make better notes, when, in one of those coincidences that make life so interesting, great art came to me.

Not Renaissance or Baroque, but Impressionism, American as well as French.

CeeCee Watson, loyal patron of the Bodie Island Lighthouse Library and member of our classic novel book club, was heavily involved in bringing a traveling expedition of nineteenth-century American Impressionism to the Outer Banks. The paintings were original and valuable, and had come with a great deal of security concerns, not to mention all the hard work of finalizing the arrangements.

We couldn't hang any of those invaluable works at the library but, as an addendum to the main exhibition, CeeCee convinced library director Bertie James to host an ancillary exhibit from whatever we could scrounge in the way of reproductions or imitations, as well as books on art history. Bertie eagerly leaped into organizing it. Meaning she'd assigned me, the assistant director, to set it up.

Eager to show off my newly acquired art knowledge, I'd taken on the task willingly. Giant tomes on art history were borrowed from other collections or dragged out of dusty storage cabinets; smaller books about individual artists taken off the biography shelves; patrons begged for a loan of prints of famous works they might have. I'd originally planned to arrange the display in the alcove we regularly use for special features, but, powered largely by my own enthusiasm, the display grew and grew . . . and grew . . . until it filled most of the admittedly limited space of the Bodie Island Lighthouse Library.

"I think I see a spot," CeeCee Watson said. "On that shelf there. You might be able to squeeze a pamphlet in. Sideways."

"Couple of empty inches on the walls," Denise Robarts, our academic librarian, said. Denise had been instrumental in gathering much of the needed material for me. "A postcard should fit."

"If it's a small one," Louise Jane McKaughnan said.

I was stung to the core. I expected praise, not criticism after all my hard work. "You think I went too far?"

"I think, Lucy," CeeCee said, "it's absolutely perfect. Your enthusiasm for the subject is so obvious." Normally an undemonstrative person, she gathered me into a giant hug. Denise joined in. Louise Jane sort of patted my back.

"If you're all finished congratulating each other, I could use a hand here," my cousin Josie Greenblatt called.

We might have filled the library to the brim with art books and prints and reproduction paintings, but we can always find room for the food.

The circulation desk by the front door had been cleared off and turned into the bar. A framed print of *Girl with a Pearl Earring* by Vermeer hung over the desk. The canapés were overlooked by Mary Cassatt, and the desserts, fittingly, had been placed under a half-sized version of Renoir's *The Boating Party*.

Our own party was intended to be a small, low-key affair to show our exhibit to the movers and shakers behind the real exhibition, as well as library donors and select patrons. As always at a library function, the guest list took on a life of its own, and I worried we wouldn't fit everyone in. Fortunately, it was a lovely, warm summer's night, so people could take their drinks, snacks, and conversation outside if they wanted. The real party, for the real art exhibition, was scheduled for tomorrow night. CeeCee had wrangled me an invitation in thanks for my work in setting up the library display.

Louise Jane and Denise hurried to help Josie, hired to cater the party. Ronald Burkowski, our children's librarian, was already setting up the bar, laying out rented glasses and opening the cash box for drink donations. Tonight he wore a tie splashed with *Sunflowers* by Van Gogh.

"Almost showtime." Bertie came into the main room. "You've done a marvelous job, Lucy, everyone. I'm truly excited about this initiative. In particular the lineup of children's programs Ronald's created around it. Young people today spend far too much time on their phones, playing games, gossiping with friends, or discovering things they shouldn't be discovering. Exposure to great art will go a long way toward opening young minds." She laughed. "Okay, I'm preaching to the choir. I hear a car arriving. Lucy, will you do the honors?"

"Happy to," I said. I ran to greet the first of our guests.

Who just happened to be the mayor of Nags Head, my own husband, Connor McNeil. "I'm unfashionably early," he said, giving me a quick kiss. "My meeting ended on time, wonder of wonders, so I came straight here."

"Tub of ice is in the break room," Ronald called. "As Your Honor's first official act of the night you can bring it out and then get the beers out of the fridge and into the ice."

Connor might be unfashionably early, but so were many of our guests. I peered out into the gathering twilight to see a line of cars wending its way down the long laneway on the other side of the row of tall red pines. I wiped my hands on the hips of my nice dress, although I knew I had nothing to be worried about. I'd achieved exactly what I wanted in arranging this exhibit, and most of the attendees were sure to be book and art lovers. Those who came mainly (or only) for Josie's catering would have no criticism. As long as the food held out.

Before long the library was filling up. Hugs and air kisses were exchanged, (fake) art admired and books examined, gossip spread, and everyone eagerly tucked into the provisions. The final, and most important member of the library team, Charles, did the rounds, greeting those he knew with an air of cool distain, and greeting those he did not know with over-the-top enthusiasm that wasn't always appreciated. All the while keeping one sharp blue eye focused on the tray of crab cakes, in hopes of one of the catering staff momentarily looking away.

Like Charles, I knew most of the people who came. Longtime library patrons, volunteers, board members. A handful of town councillors, always eager to show up for what might be considered a happy occasion, as long as catering from Josie's Cozy Bakery was provided. Assorted relatives of library staff. My aunt Ellen and uncle Amos had come, and they both swept me into hugs.

"We haven't seen you since you and Connor got home from Europe," Ellen scolded. "For once that is not entirely my fault."

"Sorry," I said, meaning it. "The moment I put my foot through the door on my first day back at work, I've been consumed by this project."

"I want to hear all about your trip, every last detail," Ellen said.

"I might have a couple of pictures to show you. Unfortunately, no pockets in this dress, so no phone on me. On the other hand, that's probably a good thing. It will take all night to show you my favorite photos."

Uncle Amos wandered away to say hi to his daughter, Josie. And, not incidentally, grab a couple of mini shrimp skewers. The Bodie Island Lighthouse Library isn't big, but somehow it seems to be able to stretch at the seams when needed. The main room was filling up as guests poured in, and the noise was building as everyone greeted friends and relatives, not to mention frenemies, asked for drinks, and helped themselves to canapés or desserts (sometimes canapés *and* desserts). Charles continued doing the rounds of the room, greeting guests and begging for snacks, all while trying to avoid having his tail stepped on.

"When Bertie told me the extent to which this project was growing, I had my doubts, Lucy," Aunt Ellen said. "I thought you were being overly ambitious. But I should have known that if anyone could pull this off, you could."

"Thanks for the vote of confidence, but it truly wasn't difficult. It took a lot of time and coordination, yes, but we're not handling multimillion-dollar, or even priceless, works of art here. Everything on the walls is reproduction, poached from public buildings as well as people's homes; even framed prints of someone's vacation pictures. We have most of Denise's collection of art-themed fridge magnets collected from her travels on the notice board. None of the books we're featuring are rare or valuable. The security at Granger House where they have the real things, must be impressive."

"CeeCee can tell you some stories about the trouble they've gone to in order ensure the safety of the works on display there. I'll let you get on with it," Ellen said. "Lovely dress, by the way. Did you get it in Europe?"

"Yes. In Paris." I twirled around to display it. The dress was a deep, rich scarlet, with an off-the-shoulder neckline, tight across the bodice with a cinched waist, and a skirt of multilayered flaring tule. Tonight I'd paired it with the small ruby earrings and matching necklace I'd inherited from my paternal grandmother. "It cost a mind-boggling amount, but Connor insisted. His mother gave him some money with specific instructions to treat me."

"I'm glad. You deserve a treat now and again." Aunt Ellen slipped away, leaving me momentarily alone. Connor was in mayor mode, smiling and pressing the flesh. Josie's team circulated with platters of canapés, refilled supplies on the tables, or whisked away abandoned plates and napkins. Ronald served as bartender while the other library staffers were busy chatting to our guests.

I asked Ronald for a sparkling water and sipped it while I wandered through the crowd.

"One of the greatest artists of all time, certainly of the nineteenth century," Mrs. Peterson was explaining to two of her daughters, Charity and Primrose. The girls couldn't have looked more bored if they tried. And, I guessed, they were trying. Mrs. Peterson had a tendency to force what she considered culture on her daughters. The oldest, Charity, in particular would rather be on the field playing ball. "Claude Monet is known for the graceful lines of his ballet works." She was showing the girls a Degas. I didn't bother to correct her. If Mrs. Peterson thought a Degas was a Monet, then it was a Monet.

"Not many people know Robert O'Callaghan was a direct ancestor of mine," Louise Jane was telling CeeCee Watson when I joined them.

"I didn't know that," CeeCee said. "It's truly lovely."

"Our family's sole claim to fame," the elderly lady with them said.

The three women were admiring a painting of a sailing ship in distress in a storm. I joined them and was soon lost in the drama taking place in front of me. A wooden ship heaved as it crested angry waves, time and sea-worn boards creaking under the strain. The sails were torn to shreds, the mainmast close to collapse. Tiny panicked figures huddled against the gunwales as they helplessly awaited their doom. I'd printed out cards for each picture we hung, giving the name of the painting it represented, the original artist, and his or her dates. This was *Stormy Seas*, by Robert O'Callaghan. The picture, a framed reproduction behind glass, had hung in pride of place in the home of Louise Jane's maternal grandmother, and Louise Jane had persuaded that lady to lend it to us. In return, Mrs. Sawyer had been invited to tonight's reception.

"What's truly marvelous about Impressionism as an art form," CeeCee said, "is how they were able to create so much drama and meaning with the barest of strokes."

"Thus," Louise Jane said, "creating an impression rather than an outright reproduction of the scene."

Robert O'Callaghan was one of the best-known American impressionist painters, active in the last decades of the nineteenth century. He was born and raised in Nags Head, so it was entirely possible he was an ancestor of Louise Jane, although how direct might be in question. Outer Banks family lines twisted all over themselves. Louise Jane had not yet found a connection between the McNeils and the McKaughnan family, but I knew she was looking. And, knowing Louise Jane, if she didn't find the evidence she needed, she'd make it up.

"How is Mr. O'Callaghan related to you, Mrs. Sawyer?" CeeCee asked politely.

"My mother's great-grandmother was Robert O'Callaghan's eldest daughter, Marie Joan. He had three daughters, no sons, as is the norm for my family. We have a severe lack of boys, always have. So much the better, I always say. Robert had only one brother, George. George was the elder. He never married, which according to my grandmother is something to be thankful for."

"I didn't know that," Louise Jane said, "What's the story there?"

"We were a wealthy family, by the standards of those days and this place. George O'Callaghan managed the family's canning plant, and was hated by his workers and anyone who did business with him. Bankers have long memories, but after George's death his sisters sold the factory, and that particular memory died along with him. Both the brothers passed when they were comparatively young, and after their deaths the O'Callaghan name died out in these parts. But I can assure you, the line did not, as I am evidence."

"Me too, Grandma," Louise Jane said.

"This picture," Mrs. Sawyer said, "is an imitation of our illustrious ancestor's best-known work. It was painted by the aforementioned George, in homage to his brother. It has been in my family since it hung in Marie Joan's parlor after the death of her uncle. My own mother gave it to me when she moved into her retirement residence. She said she didn't trust it around some of her light-fingered fellow residents."

I was trying to wrap my head around the family lineage, guess why George would reproduce his brother's work rather than paint something of his own, and what Louise Jane's great-grandmother might have been implying about the habits of the other occupants of her nursing home when Louise Jane said, "I was thrilled when CeeCee told me this painting, the original I mean, was on loan from the Frick for the touring exhibition. I can't wait to see it in real life. Are you okay, Grandma? Would you like me to find you a seat, or refresh your glass? Mr. Snyder has captured the best chair, as usual, but I can kick him out of that."

Mrs. Sawyer snorted. "The day Tim Snyder makes room for me, it will be in his grave."

I didn't quite get the point of that comment, and judging by the puzzled look on her face, Louise Jane didn't either. "O'Callaghan has a couple of pages in one of the books in the alcove, Grandma. Would you like to see it?"

"Where's Sam tonight?" I asked CeeCee once they'd moved on. "Not an art lover?"

"Not an art lover in the least," she said with a smile. "He texted me a few minutes ago to say he was delayed. Something at work."

Sam Watson was the lead detective with the Nags Head PD. He was often "delayed" at work, but after almost thirty years of marriage to a cop, CeeCee was used to having her plans change and making her own way home. She looked over my shoulder and broke into a grin. "Here they are now. Our special guests. I was getting worried they were lost. Come on, Lucy, let me introduce you."

CeeCee bustled me across the room. Four people stood in the doorway, checking out their surroundings. I guessed, by how excited CeeCee was, these were the people from the art world.

"Welcome," she said. "I'm so glad you made it. You had no trouble finding the place, I hope?"

"Considering you can see the light from miles away and there's only one road off this stretch of the highway," one of the new arrivals said, "we had no trouble at all."

"May I introduce you to Lucy McNeil? Lucy's responsible for everything you see here tonight."

"Not everything," I said. "I had a lot of help."

A man in his late forties smiled and held out his hand. "Mark Farrago. I'm the chief organizer and head bottle washer of *American Expressionism: A Comprehensive Retrospective.*" Mark was a good-looking man, not tall at about five feet seven, but lean, with a mane of dark hair only slightly touched with gray, strong cheekbones and jaw, and large eyes under glasses with thick black frames. He wore pressed slacks, a blue and red checked shirt under a blue linen jacket, and brown loafers. His handshake was firm and his smile steady.

The other man was a few years younger. Tall, thin, twitchy. "Ethan Livingston. Mark's assistant at Farrago Events." His handshake was weak and damp, his smile tight. He blinked rapidly at me. He looked as though he'd woken up from a nap and not had time to change, in rumpled khakis, a white shirt that appeared to have never felt the touch of a hot iron, and sneakers with tattered laces dragging on the ground.

The woman introduced herself next. She was older than the two men, in her fifties. She was short, about my five foot three, so thin her collarbones protruded from the top of her sleek, scoop-necked navy dress. Her hair was dyed blond with darker highlights cut sharply at her chin, and her makeup was subtle and perfect. Tiny diamonds sparkled in her ears and a diamond tennis bracelet caught the lights as she held out a flawlessly manicured hand. I was in my brand-new French dress that cost way more than I'd ordinarily ever spend, but next to her I felt positively dowdy. She had applied a generous amount of good perfume, but it mingled with the strong of tobacco clinging to her good clothes. "Lisa McMahon," she said. "I have the honor of being one of the sponsors of the show."

The younger woman next to her rolled her eyes.

"And this," Lisa said, "is my daughter. Francesca."

"Hi there," the younger woman said. "My mother calls me Francesca, a perfectly hideous name. Everyone else calls me Franny." I guessed she was in her mid-twenties, taller than her mom but not by a lot, slim without being scrawny. Her hair was dyed jet black, shaved to the scalp on one side of her head and about four inches long on the other. A row of silver rings ran up her right ear. She wore a knee-length black and red checked dress over black leggings and clunky black boots. "I have the honor of not being interested in the sort of art you get at fancy shows like this in the least. But when Mom said she was going to the Outer Banks, I grabbed my bag and ran out the door after her. Barely caught her as the car pulled away, right, Mom?"

"An exaggeration, as always," Lisa said. "CeeCee, dear, may we have the tour?"

CeeCee grinned broadly. "I'd be delighted. Would you like something from the bar first?"

"Never say no to a free bar." Franny peeled away from the group and headed toward Ronald and the drinks. Although I could have told her the drinks were not free, but by donation. We are a public library, after all.

CeeCee signaled to Bertie to join them, and I slipped away, as she repeated the introductions.

The door opened once again, and a man I didn't know came in. He stood in the entrance, looking around, an expression on his face I could only describe as bemused. He was of average height, slightly built, in his early forties, and strikingly handsome, with intense dark eyes under thick lashes, olive complexion, sharp cheekbones, two days worth of stubble on a strong square jaw, thick black hair curling around the back of his neck and across his forehead. He was dressed in a heavily worn black leather bomber jacket over a blue shirt and faded jeans.

"Good evening," I said politely.

His eyes turned to me, and a spark of interest flared behind them. I smiled, slightly uncomfortable under the strength of his stare. Then he held out his hand. His eyes didn't move from my face, and he gave me a grin full of good white teeth. "Tom Reilly. Pleased to meet you."

"Lucy Ri . . . McNeil. I'm the assistant director of the library. Welcome."

"You hesitated over your name." He gave me a wink. "Newly married or newly divorced?"

I blushed so hard I could almost feel my toes changing color. "The former."

"I should have guessed. You have that newly married glow." Before I could blush any more, he turned his attention from my face and looked over my shoulder to study the gathering behind me. "Looks like quite a show. Either you've got the world's greatest art gallery secretly hidden in your little local library, or that's fake." He indicated the framed print of Caravaggio's *The Calling of St. Matthew*, which Mrs. Fitzgerald, our library board chair, had brought home from a trip to Europe.

"I wouldn't even say it's fake. Nothing we have here is attempting to be taken as an original. All mass-produced tourist stuff or from art gallery gift shops. We even have some not very good photographs of paintings. We're a library, so our purpose is to introduce patrons to art and to start the conversation about what makes great art great. All the good stuff is at the show at Granger House in Nags Head. Are you interested in art?"

"In a way," he said.

"Tom." Mark Farrago had spotted the new arrival. "I'm surprised to see you. I didn't know you were in town. What brings you here?"

"I heard there's a party." Tom's eyes danced with amusement. "Always love a party. Two parties. I'll pop into yours tomorrow."

"That event is invitation only."

"I'd better wrangle myself an invitation then. I see Lisa now. Talk to you later, Mark. Nice to meet you, Mrs. McNeil." Tom headed for the bar. Lisa McMahon saw him, and the look she gave him before she turned sharply away was not friendly.

I glanced at Mark. He was not smiling as he watched Tom.

"Everything okay?" I asked.

Mark blinked and focused on me. "Yeah. All okay. I'm wondering what he's doing here, that's all. Nice party." He wandered away.

Sam Watson had arrived, and he and Connor were chatting quietly in a corner. I joined them, and Connor slipped his arm around my shoulders. "I'm tantalizing Sam with details of all the meals we ate in Italy."

"Oh yeah." I smiled at the memories. "Fortunately, we walked so much every day we worked it all off."

"The night seems to be going well," Connor said.

"It does. The usual library supporters are here, plus people from the arts community. We're always glad of an opportunity to introduce people to our library."

"I don't see Theodore Kowalski. Not like him to miss a library event. Particularly not one with people from out of town. He's always looking for a chance to talk old books with someone new."

"He was disappointed, but he had to take his mother to some family reunion in Raleigh. Speaking of library fixtures, have you seen Charles?"

"Not for a while. I suspect he escaped to seek some privacy. Can't say I blame him," Sam said.

I smiled at him. Art may not be Sam Watson's thing, but he always supports CeeCee's endeavors whenever he can.

"Did I hear someone mention Italian food?" Bruce Greenblatt said. "I hear a new Italian place has opened in Manteo. We should try it some day." He held a beer in one giant paw. The tiny woman with him laughed. "When it comes to food, Butch has hearing like a bat. I swear he heard the magic words from the other side of the room and his head just about did a one eighty to see where it was coming from."

"Thanks for being here." I gave Stephanie Stanton, one of my closest friends, a hug. Stephanie was my uncle Amos's law partner and also the girlfriend of Officer Butch Greenblatt, he of the bat-like hearing.

She drew me away and left the men to chat about whatever men talk about when women aren't around. Food, most likely. "Never mind what you ate, I want to hear about the clothes and the shoes and the shopping. That is the most gorgeous dress. I bet you got it on the Champs-Elysees, right?"

"Not quite, but close."

"What," a voice boomed across the room, "is great art anyway? Is it great because it's good? Or is it great because people like you say it's great?"

Steph and I turned to see who was talking. He was of average height, large-bellied, with a prominent nose lined with rosacea, an unkempt black and gray beard, and matching bushy eyebrows. I'd never seen him before. He was talking to Mark Farrago. Although talking "to" wasn't quite the right word. More like talking "at." He stabbed his index finger against the glass protecting the O'Callaghan painting. Traces of paint, red and yellow mostly, were trapped in the deep lines on his hand and under his fingernails.

"Great art," Mark said, "has universal appeal. The original of this work, for example, was painted more than a hundred and thirty years ago. Yet here we are, gathering to admire it today. Some of the other art represented in this room is five, six hundred or more years old. It still speaks to us. To twenty-first-century people living and working on the western shores of the Atlantic Ocean. Because it's great."

"What absolute rubbish. People like you, like her"—the pointing finger moved to Lisa McMahon—"declare something great, and to you that means valuable, because you can. Why is he"—the finger moved back to the painting, the man's voice grew louder—"considered better than any other Outer Banks artist? Why is—"

Conversation around the room gradually died as people turned to see what the commotion was about. Tom Reilly, glass of wine in hand, wandered closer to listen. His eyes brimmed with amusement.

Mark was speaking in a low voice, Lisa not saying anything at all. But the big-bearded man's voice was rising with every word; blood flooded into his face. I saw Butch hand Steph his beer, ready to intervene if necessary. Sam Watson moved away from Connor.

CeeCee stepped between Mark and the bearded man, her smile firmly in place. "Ivan, so nice to see you here this evening. If I may say, you've made your point many times before."

"Not to these folks here."

"This is not the time nor the place."

"What better time? What better place?" His accent was pure Outer Banks.

Bertie joined forces with CeeCee. "Ivan. It's been a while."

Some of the anger drained out of his face as he studied my boss. Tonight she wore a calf-length multicolored dress that swirled dramatically when she walked. A string of beads each the size of baseballs hung around her neck. Her brown hair, heavily streaked with gray, was gathered behind her head in a sparkly clip.

"Bertie James," he said in a low voice. "A long time indeed."

Out of the corner of my eye I saw Butch relax. Fractionally.

"Have you seen the books we have on display in the alcove, Ivan? Some of them are on loan to us, and many haven't been on the shelves in this library for years. Space issues, as always. The focus of the show at Granger House is, of course, American Impressionism, but we at the library decided to go much broader afield. Lucy went to some considerable trouble to try to represent not only Western European and North American art, but that of other countries and continents as well. If memory serves, at one time you had an interest in Chinese scrolls."

"That I did. Okay, Bertie. For you, I'll take a look at your books. As for you two"—a glance at Mark and Lisa. "You can be sure I'll drop into your little art show, check out the great and the good."

"Is that meant to sound like a threat?" Mark asked. "Because it does."

"No threats. I'm sure you've got lots of security for all your million-dollar paintings. Some of which probably aren't much better than the stuff hanging in a kindergarten classroom. I'm interested in seeing what you've decided's worth the big bucks. And, of course, what isn't."

"We haven't decided anything," Lisa said. "The American art world—"

Ivan snorted. He turned his back on her and walked away. Bertie followed him and a grinning Franny followed them.

"I'm so sorry," I said to Mark and Lisa. "I don't even know who that man is. Or who invited him."

"I did." CeeCee said. "Although inadvertently. Ivan Novak is a local artist. As such he's a member of the arts co-op. Some of the co-op members have volunteered to help at the show, and I invited them tonight as thanks. I can only assume Ivan thought the invitation included him. Which it most definitely did not. Even among his fellow artists, Ivan has a reputation of being rude and difficult."

"We were introduced to him," Lisa said, "and straight away he started lecturing us on corruption in the art world."

Tom chuckled. Mark threw him an angry look, but Tom merely smiled in return before following Ivan and Franny to the alcove.

"Ivan has a mighty big chip on his shoulder," CeeCee explained. "His work is good, and I'm happy to admit it. But," she lowered her voice, although the man under discussion was not in hearing range, "it's nothing at all exceptional. We have a great many genuinely talented artists in the Outer Banks. Ivan is of the opinion that he isn't shown in the best art museums or sold in the best galleries because he doesn't play the game, as he calls it. Meaning flatter the people who decide what's worth showing. I'm afraid he's getting more resentful, and more obnoxious about it, as he gets older and the recognition he so desperately wants is increasingly out of his grasp."

"He picked the wrong people to argue with tonight," Lisa said. "None of the artists being exhibited in our show are alive today or have been for decades. I'm not that old, so I can assure you not one of them flattered me. Speaking of uninvited guests, did you invite Tom Reilly, or whatever name he's using now, Mark?"

"No. He told me you had."

"As if. I don't know what brought him here, but I'd advise you to step up security around our show. Are you ready to leave? If not, I can grab a cab. Where did my daughter get to?"

"We're ten miles out of town, remember," I said. "No cruising cabs pass here. I can call for one if you like."

"You go ahead, Lisa," Mark said. "I'm enjoying myself. I never mind sparring with unappreciated artists. If Franny isn't ready to leave, she can come back with me. Because Ethan's driving tonight, I'm going to have another drink. And some more of those crab cakes. Might be the best I've ever had." He walked away, intent on his mission.

I glanced around the room. Ronald's wife Nan had taken over at the bar as he'd been cornered by Mrs. Peterson. Who was almost certainly instructing him on the programs in art history she wanted him to conduct for her five daughters. Louise Jane was telling everyone who was interested, and many who weren't, about her familial relationship to Robert O'Callaghan. Louise Jane's grandmother had taken control of the wingback chair in the magazine nook, leaving Mr. Snyder to perch uncomfortably on an office chair at the computer table next to Mrs. Fitzpatrick.

Butch and Steph were chatting to Josie, who, now the party was in full swing, had left most of the work to her staff and could relax while keeping an eye on everything. Sam Watson stood alone, next to the cooking and gardening books. Charles perched on the top of the shelf above him, tail slowly twitching. The expression on their faces and the look in their eyes were almost identical, always watching out for trouble. Connor was talking to Uncle Amos, and Aunt Ellen was laughing in a circle of library volunteers. Denise was showing Ivan, closely watched by Bertie, the art books, while Tom Reilly listened. Franny, Lisa's daughter, had joined them. Her mother came up behind her and spoke to her. Franny waved her away without bothering to turn her head. Lisa's red lips twisted in disapproval before she pulled herself together and attempted to look interested in what Denise was saying.

I walked through the room, in search of a phone. "American Impressionism," Mark said to an eager group who'd gathered around him, "owes a great deal to the Europeans, of course, but—"

"So sorry to interrupt," I said to Ronald. "I need your help with something."

Pure relief crossed his face. "Sure, Lucy. Sorry, Mrs. Peterson, looks like I'm needed."

"But I haven't told you about—"

"Gotta run." He grabbed my arm and pulled me away.

"I have to make a call and don't have my own phone on me," I said. "I could have used the phone in the break room, but you looked like you needed rescuing."

"Which I did. When that woman gets an idea in her head—"

"One of our honored guests is ready to leave and wants a taxi."

"Sure. I'll make the call. I heard what sounded like the beginning of an argument a few moments ago. All okay?"

"A minor disagreement about who decides what makes great art. And, more to the point, who decides what isn't great art."

Ronald went outside to make the call, and when came back he held up all his fingers, indicating to me the cab would be about ten minutes. I went to locate Lisa to let her know.

I found her chatting to a guest I didn't know.

"Cab will be ten minutes," I said.

"Thank you. Lucy, have you met Jessie?" She indicated the other woman.

"No, I haven't."

Jessie smiled at me and held out her hand. "I'm on vacation in your lovely town, and when I heard about what you've done here, I called your library director and begged an invitation. I'm a librarian at the National Archives in Washington, and American art is one of my personal passions."

"The National Archives. Wow. That must be an amazing place to work. You're more than welcome to our humble little library."

"Little perhaps, but hardly humble. Every library is a monument to knowledge. I love what you've done here," Jessie said as Lisa slipped away to catch her ride. "Educational, informative, as it should be. But most of all you've obviously had a great deal of fun with it, and that's what draws people in and encourages them to learn more."

"That's our intention."

"Now, if you'll excuse me, my husband's waving at me from the other side of the room and pointing at his watch."

"I hope you enjoy your time in the Outer Banks," I said.

When I passed the O'Callaghan picture, the crowd had dispersed, leaving only Louise Jane and Tom Reilly admiring it.

Tom stood in front of the painting, not close, but not too far away either. He studied it intently as Louise Jane said, "A legend in Outer Banks art. As it happens, Robert O'Callaghan is a direct ancestor of mine. On my mother's side."

"Is that so?" He turned to her and gave her that slow, lazy smile. "This one is a reproduction. And not a very good one, to be honest."

Louise Jane looked startled and then she peered closer. "I like it."

"Only in comparison to the original, I mean. Which is truly an outstanding piece. If memory serves, Robert's brother George wanted to be an artist as well. He never got over his jealously of his successful brother."

"Goodness," Louise Jane said, "you know an awful lot."

"Most great artists have fascinating biographies. I'm a minor collector myself, and I'm always interested in American art. I don't suppose your grandmother has any original O'Callaghans hanging around the house? Tucked away in the attic, long forgotten maybe?"

Louise Jane tittered in a very unLouise Jane like way. "Wouldn't that be something? No, sorry. Nothing I know of, although, come to think of it, I've never actually searched Grandma's attic. When my great-grandfather died and Great-Grandma moved into a retirement home, my mom and grandmother threw a lot of their things away. Wouldn't it be awful if they had thrown out an original painting?"

"Happens more than you might think," Tom said. "Which is why a collector and dealer such as myself needs to be always on the lookout. People often don't recognize treasures when they see them. Sometimes we get lucky and can track a piece down from the slimmest bit of evidence. Then again, more often than not the trail turns into a dead end. My name's Tom, by the way. Can I get you a drink?"

* * *

Finally, the last of our guests staggered out into the night. The party had been a huge success and our special exhibit was positively received by both the library and arts communities. Ivan Novak attempted to corner Mark once more, but he was deftly maneuvered out the door by Bertie, who in her many years of working in public libraries had learned how to both deftly and forcefully maneuver patrons who'd overstayed their welcome.

Before leaving, CeeCee came to say good night and offer me her thanks. "It was totally my pleasure," I said. "I'm excited about talking to patrons about the art exhibition and the art world in general. I think we'll get a lot of mileage out of all this. Everything ready for tomorrow?"

"It is. This is the biggest project I've ever been involved in, and I'm loving it. Best of all, at this level everything's so well organized, we volunteers scarcely had to do anything except make suggestions and recommend local contacts. Mark's company are the chief organizers, and they have a lot of experience in arranging big money art shows."

"Does Lisa work for him?"

"No. She's just a lowly volunteer. Like me. Although considerably more well-heeled than me. She's active in the arts world in Manhattan, or so I was told. As for tomorrow night's reception, Josie's catering, of course. I can't imagine how she manages to do that two nights in a row, plus run the bakery, and with a baby to boot."

"Lots of help and a great husband," I said. "Plus a supernatural lack of the need for sleep such as we ordinary mortals have, and restless energy that thrives on constant activity."

"That sounds like Josie. See you tomorrow. Oh, I'm loving the book club selection. It's a much-needed change from some of the more classic tomes we've been reading lately. Although I have to say, Sam doesn't approve."

"He doesn't approve of the criminal as the protagonist? I wonder why?"

This month the Bodie Island Classic Novel Reading Club had chosen *Ripley Under Ground* by Patricia Highsmith, the follow-up to her best-known book, *The Talented Mr. Ripley*. As CeeCee said, some of our group members were starting to tire of the genuine classics we'd been reading, and when Theodore suggested Highsmith as a classic of the mystery genre, everyone eagerly agreed.

CeeCee and Sam Watson were the last guests to leave, in the company of Mark, Ethan, and Franny. Franny, I hadn't been able to help but notice, had been a regular visitor to the bar. But as long as she wasn't driving and didn't get obnoxious or bothersome, I let it go. Once her mother left, she'd spent most of her time in the alcove, flipping through the art books. In front of her mother she'd said she had no interest in art, but the attention she paid to the books told me something else. Typical teenage contrariness. Except Franny was well into her twenties. Rather late for that sort of behavior.

All of which was absolutely none of my business.

I'd happened to overhear Tom Reilly saying his good nights to Louise Jane and mentioning he hoped they'd run into each other again. Louise Jane had sucked in a breath and agreed with an excess of enthusiasm. She mentioned that she worked here, at the library, and told him he was welcome to come back any time.

"I might just do that," he'd said. "Good night."

Josie and her staff packed up all their supplies (there were no leftovers) and departed. I told Bertie to go home, and she did so without arguing while Denise, Louise Jane, Ronald, and I, with help from Nan and Connor, and no help from Charles, quickly put the library back to rights. Finally we stepped out into the warm night.

Our library is a good distance out of town, set well back from the highway, surrounded by the marsh. The night was full of the calls of frogs and insects, the movement of creatures who love the dark, and the distant sound of ocean waves rushing to shore. It was late enough that almost no traffic sounds came from the highway running between Nags Head and points farther south. High above us the first order Fresnel lens flashed its comforting, constant rhythm of 2.5 seconds on, 2.5 seconds off, 2.5 seconds on, and 22.5 seconds off as it would throughout the night.

Louise Jane lives in a small apartment on the fourth floor of the lighthouse, which I'd occupied until recently. I called the little apartment my Lighthouse Aerie, and I'd loved everything about living there. Not least the commute to work. But when Connor and I became a couple, the studio apartment with access only through the public rooms of the library was hardly a home for two people, and I'd moved out.

She shouted good night after us, and I heard the twist of the lock in the door as we walked up the path to our cars.

"Another successful evening," Connor said. "No high drama. No one murdered. That's always a relief."